PRAISE FOR *DEFYING FUT1*

'This uncommon and engaging ca
"what ifs" and "if onlys" that are
situations. The stories spotlight the heroism of the creative
maverick in averting or fixing disaster situations: In this, it
suggests the actions of even one independent thinker could
prove to be the saviour from a multitude of possible crisis
consequences.'

- Gerry McCusker, author of *Public Relations Disasters*, Managing Director of The Drill Crisis Simulator

'Using an interesting mix of well-known and less infamous
disasters from recent history, *Defying Futility* works as a series
of thrilling short stories, as thought-provoking speculative
fiction, and as a much needed, positive reminder that it's not
too late to take action against the climate crisis.'

- Stewart McKay, author of *The Ballad of Billy Lopez*

'When is a disaster story not a disaster story? When it's
reimagined by the glorious Grace Chan – aka Steve Willis and
Jan Lee. These are stories of real disasters, reimagined with
happy endings. By showing us how taking a different path can
lead to a different, better outcome we can feel empowered to do
the same. This is especially important when the problem looks
as big and overwhelming as climate change. I loved the
characters in the book, who are warm, sensible human beings
like us. I found myself trying to solve the puzzle they are facing,
and being stunned by the clever solutions dreamed up by the
protagonists, If you fancy a feel-good, optimistic collection of

stories that gives us all hope for the future, then I highly recommend *Defying Futility*.'

- Marina Pacheco, author of the *Medieval Life of Galen* series

'Stop watching "Black Mirror" and instead read *Defying Futility* – it's a "Green Mirror" alternative to climate doomerism'

- Catherine Cole, Sustainable Growth Catalyst, B Corp

PRAISE FOR *FAIRHAVEN*

'We can't navigate our way to a better future fed on a diet of nothing but doom and gloom. We need stories to challenge, provoke and inspire to help us dare to imagine and act with hope - Fairhaven does just that!'

- Nigel Topping, UN High Level Climate Action Champion, COP26

It's wonderful to see more solutions-focused climate fiction being published by people with the expertise to see a future that's really possible. Fairhaven fills me with hope.'

- Lauren James, founder of the Climate Fiction Writers League

'Best climate fiction book on the planet. When we look back 50 years from now at how we tackled climate change, this book will be seen as a trendsetter, a break with the dystopian climate narratives that did very little other than depress and polarise people, and a book that showed how climate storytelling should be done instead.'

- Kris de Meyer, Director, University College London Climate Action Unit

'In a time when the narrative matters more than we can possibly imagine, the need for storytelling that lets us reflect on who we are, who we're becoming, and the world we wish to create is incredibly important. This book is that story. It will open up a door to your imagination while serving as a bridge to the place of yourself that remembers our strengths and why we're here. It's beautiful and engaging and a true testament to our times. Here's to even more optimistic and inspiring climate fiction!'

- Anne Therese Gennari, Climate Optimist, Author & Speaker

DEFYING FUTILITY

The Fairhaven Stories
Grace Chan

By Steve Willis and Jan Lee

Habitat Press

ISBN 978-1-7390889-5-8

https://www.greenstories.org.uk/fairhaven/

To all those who suffer from disasters that don't have to happen

CONTENTS

Prologue: Anxiety

Excerpt from the novel Fairhaven – A Novel of Climate Optimism

Once again, Grace Chan sat alone on her balcony, looking at the extraordinary view.

On paper, her life was perfect. She was doing meaningful work, well-paid. She lived in a beautiful penthouse apartment, with people whose company she enjoyed. But none of it could stop the dread.

'You'll fix it,' her young cousin Clara had told her. But in reality, nothing could be done. Fairhaven itself, the largest climate adaptation project in the world, couldn't stop the world from boiling as she watched. There on the thirty-eighth floor, she could enjoy a breeze at night, but thousands, millions, billions of people were once again facing violent floods and typhoons. Winter in the northern hemisphere brought wildfires to the south.

And nobody was coming to save them.

It was spiritual vertigo: invisible from the outside, until the moment the victim reeled from its effects. Among others, she could hold it off, but there, alone on her balcony, she too often felt the 'call of the void' – a wild impulse to scream at the top of her lungs, smash her fist right through the sliding glass doors, or hurl herself headlong over the edge.

It's all pointless, she thought.

Auntie Janis recommended she keep a diary, that she quit her job, or that she at least make herself a soft boiled egg.

Later. She'd already been keeping a diary for ages, where she wrote stories and vignettes to make herself feel better. In another hour she would wipe away the tears. But in the moment, all she could do was to sit on the plastic outdoor furniture, staring at the skyline.

She'd given up the idea of asking her parents for sympathy or advice long ago. Her resources must come from within.

7.00 pm, Friday, March 19, 2027
George Town, Penang – India House

Sixteen chairs were arranged in a circle, with fourteen occupied. As Grace entered the room in the shadow of her Auntie Janis, the meeting was just getting started. Preoccupied with the thought that they might be interrupting, it took Grace several minutes to realise that the large figure in the far seat was her colleague, Hans de Jong.

'Sorry we're late,' trilled Janis, oblivious, wrapping herself in a voluminous shawl against the air conditioning. 'Grace, sit, sit, sit!' In that instant, Grace once again felt twelve years old, but managed to give a surreptitious nod to Hans, evoking a sheepish half-wave in return. She scampered over to the empty seat nearest the door. To her surprise, she recognised two other people from work. Auntie Janis, satisfied, plopped herself down next to the meeting's leader and offered a broad smile to the room. 'Don't mind us!'

The leader pressed his lips together, but seemed more amused than disturbed. 'Okay, now that we're all here, as I was saying, I'm Wen Xin. Who'd like to go first?'

He waited a beat before nodding at a thin woman in her forties. Only then did Grace notice that the woman's hand was half-raised.

'Go ahead. The floor is yours.'

She stood. 'My name is Yong. And I'm terrified that we're the last generation of people to live on this planet.'

Everyone in the room gave a polite smile, and clapped.

An hour and a half later, Auntie Janis left, Yong and Wen Xin drifted away somewhere, and Grace and Hans were the last to remain in the room.

'Wanna go get curry *mee*?'

'After that ordeal? Absolutely.'

Two bowls of noodles plonked down on the melamine surface of the table, followed by two bottles of Tiger beer, condensation pearling on the surface. Chilli oil floated on the surface of the noodles.

'Careful,' warned Grace. 'The curry *mee* here is spicy.'

'I can take it.'

'We'll see.'

'So did you cry?'

Hans slurped a large spoonful of the broth. Before he could answer, tears began to stream down his face.

Grace laughed. 'I didn't mean that kind of crying!'

'Very funny. Strong men don't cry.'

'Zygmunt said that the exception is when their team concedes a goal. He also said it's wrong to say football is a matter of life and death – because it's much more important.'

'Yeah, our boss is a big football fan. And I know people in Holland who think like that. But I'm not one of them. I don't even like football.'

'You make a pretty good show to the contrary! I hear you and Ivan going on about it all the time.'

'There's nothing else men are allowed to bond over, so I make it a point to learn enough to have an intelligent discussion. But it's not my passion.'

'That's a relief. I was bracing myself.'

Hans laughed and offered his bottle, and they clinked. Grace found, once again, that something about his smile released a fragment of the constant tension that had tied ever-tighter inside her over the past years.

'So if football isn't your passion, what is?'

'Flower pressing! Penang is great for flowers. And I bake a good sourdough loaf. During the pandemic I was teaching everyone else, because I'd already been doing it for years.'

'Flower pressing? Bread? You're not winding me up?'

'My mother and grandmother did those things, so I took them up, too.'

Grace shook her head in disbelief. 'Did you have one of those big bread ovens when you were growing up?'

'Yes, when I was small. We lived on a farm on Vlieland. That's a Frisian island outside the main dykes. The 2017 flood here wasn't the first one I'd seen. A big one hit when I was eight –

Cyclone Anatol. We all got out, but we had to go live in Rotterdam after that. You could say we were climate refugees, of sorts. They raised and reinforced the dykes, but we never went back.'

'I had no idea.'

'We used to keep a big, yellow axe in the attic on the farm. Maybe you've heard about that practice among the Dutch; my grandmother was strict about it — like she was about a lot of things. Her parents chopped their way out through the roof during the great flood of 1953. And she was prepared for it to happen again.'

'Wow. How old is she?' Grace asked.

'She's eighty-eight. I'd love to introduce you to her some day. You know, she used to read to me all the time. She's the real reason I was able to get an education. I didn't like school much, but she made it interesting for me.'

'I'd love to meet her.'

Hans took a smaller slurp of his noodles, his eyes crinkling. 'My family's very close. I miss them.'

'But you did a good job of ignoring my question,' Grace pressed.

'You noticed.'

'And?'

'The answer is no, I didn't cry. At least, I didn't let anyone see it.'

'Have you been going to these meetings for a long time?' she asked.

'This was my second one. Are you going to come back?'

5

Grace, her mouth too full of curry *mee* to speak, her eyes watering from the chillies, nodded her head in confirmation. When she swallowed, she continued, 'So what did your grandmother read with you?'

'All sorts of stuff. Lots of it was ancient. Jack London, HG Wells, Asimov, Tolkien, Wyndham. Thea Beckman.'

'I loved all those, too. I was a real bookworm. But I had to read it to myself. My parents were never around.'

'It's what I do instead of crying,' Hans explained. 'I disappear into a good book, or into a film. That's not to say I don't sometimes cry as well. Sometimes there's nothing else you can do.'

'It's worse now than it's ever been.'

Hans nodded as he took another swig from the bottle of Tiger.

Grace continued, 'You know, I've always known it was coming. In primary school, we learned about it just as a normal part of science class. But it was this huge, distant thing, like that massive cliff in Yosemite Valley. In my mind's eye, that's what it was like: big, but far away. Now, thinking about it at work every day has brought me to the foot of the cliff. It fills my whole view. There is nothing else.

'And now we're on the cliff, a hundred metres up. My nose is pressed against the rock and my knees are trembling. Meanwhile, you and the rest of the team always look so confident; I always thought I was alone.'

'Obviously not, given the company tonight.'

'But I'm still terrified. For all of us. I'm convinced we won't make it. We'll fail in a valiant effort and all get picked off one by one. We can't fix it.'

'By the way, you're pretty good with extended metaphors. Have you ever tried writing it down?'

'I do. My auntie gave me a journal.'

'I'm not much of a writer,' Hans mused. 'Typical engineer. Good with a calculator, bad with a pen.'

'I don't just stick to diary-writing. In fact,' she confessed, after a long pull from the bottle, 'I've been writing short stories. Alternative histories of the past. They're all about disasters. Real disasters, I mean – but I've written each story as if the disaster had been prevented. It's something that can give me hope, where problems are solved, and we can look forward to what's ahead. What I really want is to get these stories in front of people, so they can see how disasters can be averted, or at least made less devastating.'

'It's possible. If you do it right.'

'In the stories I can say what I want. But in real life I can be impatient, and blunt.'

'Too blunt – are you sure you're not Dutch?'

Grace laughed and shook her head. 'Given my family background, it's possible! We're just about everything you can think of – Chinese, Malay, Indian, Portuguese, and who knows what else. Maybe Dutch. One of my other aunties tried to assemble the family tree a couple of years ago and had to give up.'

'So are you going to come back to the next Climate Anxiety session?' Hans asked.

'I have to. Auntie Janis made me go because she found me crying after family dinner last week.' Grace didn't add that part of the reason for her tears was the harangue from her Auntie Annie, who told her that at twenty-eight, she was risking being 'left on the shelf', that she herself was already married with three children by that age, and that Grace was getting old and ugly. She was once again grateful that she could go home to the casual, anonymous commune of 8 Gurney Drive.

'Maybe you should bring along something you've written.'

'I'll think about it.'

'Do. I want to read it.'

'It's personal. But I might make an exception for you.'

Hans had finished his noodles but remained still in his seat. 'Grace, speaking of personal things ... do you want to ... come over to my place tonight?'

She laughed and took his hand. 'I live there, after all. But yes. I would very much like that. I've been waiting for an invitation. Later, I can show you some of the stuff I've been writing. I've been working on a piece about the *Titanic*.'

Defying Futility

A story by Grace Chan

The sinking of the Titanic *is one of the most horrifying calamities of modern history. More than 1,500 people lost their lives on that January night in 1912. For more than a century, we have been asking: could they have been saved?*

In April 1912, the global temperature was 0.1°C above the pre-industrial average. As we approach a modern calamity on a planetary scale, we must ask ourselves the same question. Can we act now to avert a climate disaster, or at least mitigate its impact?

This is us: it is too late for us to change the past. But we still have a chance to change the future.

The *Titanic*, still moored at the Southampton dockside on that chilly April morning, was like nothing anyone had ever seen. Two ladylike Patrols of Girl Guides, fourteen girls in all, were murmuring to each other, but they fell into awed silence as they piled out of the hansom cabs and retrieved their haversacks. Several of them stopped in their tracks, congesting the growing crowd for a moment.

'Come along, Guides! We've got to get going,' said Lady Agnes Baden Powell, in a measured contralto.

One of the older girls gathered the rest of the Company. 'The 1st Pinkeys Green Girls should be prompt and considerate of others!' she admonished. The sound of their own Company's name was enough to set them moving again, breaking the spell of the enormous vessel before them. Even the prospect of their arrival in the United States of America, one week hence, was not as daunting as the idea of climbing on board – but as Girl Guides, they were ready for any opportunities to build their character. Their motto was the same as the one the Boy Scouts adhered to: be prepared.

In that spirit, they spent the first day of the voyage, a Wednesday, exploring the ship. Lady Agnes had written to White Star Line, who arranged that the sixth officer, Sub Lieutenant James Moody, would be their liaison.

James greeted Lady Agnes with unexpected politeness for a rough-and-ready sailor. 'Good morning, Miss Baden-Powell, and a warm welcome to all of you. I am to be your liaison officer while you are aboard, and I am at your service.'

'How do you do, Lieutenant Moody? Girls, Mr Moody will answer your questions in due course, but you must not disturb him from the proper operation of the vessel.' The Guides murmured their assent. 'The girls are so interested in how the ship has prepared itself for any eventuality.'

As the day and their explorations progressed, some Guides tittered behind their hands when any of their number admitted to feeling the motion of the vessel. But another would rush to the aid of their stricken comrade, bearing a knob of ginger, or a box of black horehound lozenges. Those who could manage it cast aside all thought of seasickness, and marched to the bridge, where they found Captain Smith, a commanding gentleman with a trim naval beard, bewildered by the sight of a gaggle of schoolgirls. They saw the engine room, the kitchens, and the Marconi room. They visited the crow's nest, the bow, and the coal store.

'Lieutenant Moody is so much fun,' wrote Constance that evening, who had sworn to send a postcard to her parents every single day they were away. 'He let us address him by his Christian name, which is James! He let us clamber around the lifeboat, as long as everything was put back in place neat and tidy. My friend Dorothy knows everything about ships and asked a thousand questions.'

At breakfast on the following morning, Dorothy approached Lady Agnes.

'Miss,' she asked, with a curtsey, 'Why is there space for 1,178 when there are 2,208 passengers and crew?'

'What on earth do you mean, Dorothy? There is accommodation for every one of the passengers and crew, each in staterooms that meet their accustomed style of lodgings.'

'I mean the lifeboats, Miss. I asked James – I mean Lieutenant Moody – and he said there were lifeboats enough for 1,178 people.'

'That leaves 1,030!' piped up Ivy, who had a good head for figures.

Lady Agnes sipped her coffee. 'Surely not everyone in the ship would need a lifeboat at the same time.'

'Excuse me, Miss, but on the contrary, there is one singular case in which the lifeboats would be necessary, and in that case, surely everyone would need them.'

'You raise an interesting point, Dorothy. It is not anything we need to concern ourselves with, since the ship is said to be unsinkable. But you may use this occasion to exercise your mind. If you believe there is a shortage of lifeboats, then I encourage you to think about it and come up with a solution. Do not forget our motto: be prepared!'

'Yes, Miss. We'll do so, just as you say!' Dorothy curtseyed again and, hand in hand with Ivy, ran back to a group of chattering girls.

Within two days, the navy-blue uniforms of the 1st Pinkeys Green Girls were known throughout the ship. To some passengers and crew, they were a perpetual annoyance; others found their enthusiasm refreshing. Young Mary Chater possessed an endless repertoire of tunes, and could get them all singing along at a moment's notice. 'Listen to this one!' she would cry; and in short order, both men and women would be whooping out the words to the chorus.

On the fifth evening of the voyage, Captain Smith was smiling to himself as he stood at the bridge of the ship and peered through a pair of binoculars. The girls were doing a marvellous job of raising the spirits of a group of rich, elderly passengers. Those tended to be the crankiest and most demanding, and the girls distracted them all through the long, cold afternoon. The view over the North Atlantic, with its wine-dark waters and distant icebergs, was mesmerising to someone in love with the sea, but less so to jaded socialites. The young folks helped even the crotchety millionaires John and Marian Thayer appreciate the gorgeous vista.

The Captain lowered the binoculars and passed them to Second Officer Lightoller, who had the watch. 'Have an eye out for those bergs. Twenty-two knots is well enough for the open sea, but we don't want to give our First-Class passengers any bumps to complain about.'

'Aye-aye, Sir!'

Late that evening, well after the Guides turned in – since it was well known that going to bed early, and rising with the sun, was both healthful and built strong moral fibre – a heavy, grinding thud and a tearing screech jolted the lighter sleepers awake. 'What is it?' asked Constance, one of the youngest Guides. 'Why have the engines stopped?'

Having shed their nightclothes and donned their uniforms, the Guides emerged by twos and fours from their berths. Helen, the eldest, sent a pair of scouts down the passageway to assess the situation. It took no more than a few minutes for them to return with the news.

'We've struck an iceberg,' Edna reported, steadfast despite her shivers. 'The purser told us we shouldn't concern ourselves, but I caught a glimpse of James – I mean Mr Moody – and he'd quite the grim look in his eye.'

'Did you speak with him? Lieutenant Moody, I mean.'

'No. But my assessment is that the situation is serious.'

Ivy, who had been huddled with Dorothy for the previous day, working on a mysterious project, was the first to state out loud what they all knew – the 'exercise for the mind' they had been discussing for the past two days. 'There are not enough lifeboats.'

Space for 1,178, when there were 2,208 passengers and crew.

'We've been working on this, you know,' Dorothy addressed Helen, and then the entire company. 'Do you remember last year at Windermere?'

'Where we built the canoe tent?' Helen asked. 'Modelled on the Polynesian double-hulled canoes? Those ocean-going canoes?

'Yes,' replied Ivy. 'Each of them could carry hundreds of people.'

The girls nodded. Yes. They remembered.

'I've got my notebook ready,' Ivy offered. 'With our sketches. Shall we show Lady Agnes?'

'I'll wake her,' Helen nodded. It was not a task to be taken on lightly, but as the eldest, she was ready to don the mantle, and the risks, of command.

To their surprise, Lady Agnes was already awake and dressed. They found her on the deck, wrapped in a heavy rug, agitated, speaking with James.

'Miss Baden-Powell?' Helen asked. 'Please excuse us. It's important.'

'What is it, Helen?'

'Dorothy's got a plan.'

Lady Agnes examined the beautiful pencil drawing, doubtful at first, but with increasing interest as the girls explained the details.

'We can make one,' said Dorothy. 'I'm sure of it. A single lifeboat can only hold sixty-five. But with two lifeboats of this size, each pontoon can hold several hundred people. It will be more than enough for everyone.'

'Your plan has merit. And given that we are already feeling a slight list to the vessel, I am inclined to put it into practice.'

Lady Agnes called James over and explained the plan, showing him the sketch.

'Thank you, but there's not much time, Miss Baden-Powell. I've been ordered to launch these boats and get the women and children on board. You'll all be safe, as I'll make sure you're on the first boat.'

'No, Mr Moody. I believe we can do better than that. Allow us to launch the two boats together, and build the pontoon to show it can be done. And in the meantime, I shall convince the Captain to do the same for the others.'

For the past five days, the Lieutenant had been plagued during every waking hour by the questions and proposals of fourteen clever girls. He wanted to cut them off several times. But with persistence as maddening as the girls themselves, their questions stayed in his head. He was realising that they had converted him to their side.

'It goes against the Captain's direct orders. But he's a reasonable man, and this isn't a situation we anticipated. You there! Petty Officer Green! Stop what you're doing and follow the instructions of Miss Hollingsworth. Here's a sketch for you to refer to.'

Dorothy smiled and curtseyed, despite her shivers.

James continued, 'I shall return before long, Green, and I expect to see the design carried out.' Only the Petty Officer's long years of training kept him from challenging the orders of someone with a superior rating, and could not prevent him from casting a sceptical glare at the younger man. 'Meanwhile, Lady Agnes, we shall go together to Captain Smith.'

After a brief, intense discussion with Dorothy and Ivy, Petty Officer Green supervised the descent of the first boat, with four of the Guides aboard. Surrounded by twenty passengers and two crew, the girls were struck with a sudden fit of shyness. Violet, one of the newer guides, bounded across the boat and sat next to Ivy and Dorothy. Helen was still on board, rounding up the rest of the Guides.

Dorothy whispered, 'Violent – I'm sorry, I shouldn't call you by your nickname in such a situation – do you think our plan will work? How will we get these seamen and passengers to do what is needed?'

'Never mind the name. I know I've got a reputation for playing hard at hockey. In fact, I rather like being known as Violent. I've been watching you and Ivy these past few days, and I think you've got the right idea. You're just getting the jitters, like I do before a big match. You've got to learn to love the anticipation. But if you're not feeling up to it, you tell me what you want everyone to do, and I'll get it done.'

Dorothy agreed, grateful. Soon, she and Ivy were providing quiet descriptions to Violet, who bellowed orders to Green, who then relayed them to the passengers. An older woman in furs attempted to shush the brash young woman. 'I say! Sit down, young lady, and be quiet! We need to get to safety!'

Green, without missing a beat, replied, 'I've got my orders, Ma'am, and I'm starting to see what they're about. These girls have got a plan and you'll do well to stay out of the way.'

'I say! I shall have you reported!' the woman replied, as she harrumphed back onto the uncomfortable bench.

Violet was bawling at the passengers, 'Everyone! Yes, you! Form up into pairs! Who's got a knife? Cut that rope into twelve-foot lengths. We'll need you to lash the oars together. Like this.'

The seamen manoeuvred their boat alongside Lifeboat Five, despite the interference of the passengers. They were soon bridging the gap between the two boats with a frame made from the masts, gaffs, and oars that came with each lifeboat, and covering the frame with the sail. By this time, Green and the two sailors on the other lifeboat understood the plan, and were pitching in with gusto. Violet stood at the centre of the scrum. 'Lay the mast across the central rollocks!' she cried. 'And the same on the other boat! What next, Dorothy?' The sailors' laughter at the young ladies' use of nautical jargon created plumes of vapour in the icy night.

It took ten minutes to get all the cross-pieces in place. To the surprise of both the sailors and the Guides, the woman in furs was tying quick, elegant knots. 'I've spent enough of my life around horses to know a clove hitch from a bowline,' she said with a sniff.

Installing the first sail, however, presented more of a struggle: too many hands were trying to help, becoming frantic, and fumbling in the semi-darkness. Just when Violet's shouting capability was threatening to devolve into hoarse whispers, she heard the calm, clear voice of young Mary Chater coming from Lifeboat Five like a beacon, singing one of the sea shanties that she had already taught many of the First Class passengers. Grinning with recognition and joining in on the chorus, the passengers relaxed into the work. The second sail was much smoother, as most of the eager hands were still tightening and securing the knots of the first sail. Two of the other guides on Lifeboat Six moved with cool confidence among the frightened women and children, teaching or reteaching them how to tie reef knots and do lashings, retying granny knots, and providing general organisation.

Lady Agnes, followed by James, ran down the starboard side of the ship, each minute growing more unsteady as the deck dipped towards the sea, searching for the Captain. She had, of course, understood that the *Titanic* was among the largest ships ever to sail, but its enormity never struck her with such dreadful awe as when it prevented her from finding the man who could save more than a thousand lives.

It was a full twenty minutes before they found him, on the port side of the bridge wing, in heated discussion with a man she recognised as Thomas Andrews, the *Titanic's* builder.

'Captain!' she shouted, before James could speak a word. 'I need your help.

He turned his attention away from the builder with a look of frustration. 'You should be at a boat, Miss Baden-Powell. Indeed, if you go now, you might still get on one – it's women and children first.'

'Captain – we can still save everyone – but we need your orders.'

'I wish it were the case, Miss Baden-Powell. But it can't be done. There's not enough space. Mr Moody, please conduct Miss Baden-Powell to one of the remaining boats.'

James spoke up. 'Captain Smith – Sir – please listen to Miss Baden-Powell. She's got a scheme which may save all of us.'

'Captain, I must insist,' Lady Agnes shrilled. 'Come with me to the starboard side. I'll show you it can be done!'

'Madam —'

'Do you want to go down with your ship,' she thundered, 'or do you want to go down in history?'

Helpless against her tirade, the Captain relented, and pulled out his binoculars. 'Where? Be quick about it.'

He paused when the deck creaked in a way that none of the three had heard before. Its starboard list was, ominously, correcting itself. Andrews spoke up. 'Captain, it's my estimate that we have less than two hours before she goes down.'

The Captain remained silent, squinting into the binoculars, searching the moonless night. 'Here,' Lady Agnes replied with impatience, reaching into a voluminous carpet bag. 'Our astronomical spyglass is more powerful, I believe. We were planning to do planet spotting on the top deck, you know. There – there! Look at that pair of boats.'

Captain took the telescope and peered into the darkness, focusing. 'What the blazes are they doing?'

'They are making a pontoon, Captain. A catamaran. Like the Polynesian canoes that Captain Cook recorded with the *Endeavour*. And that's what will save us.'

As they watched, the girls on the pontoon waved at the ship, while the crew loaded more passengers on board. An empty boat was already heading back.

'Well, I never!'

'If we can get all the other lifeboats set up like this, we can still save everyone.'

At that moment, the Captain made his decision. From a subdued, fateful determination, he roared to life. 'Mr Moody! Get me First Officer Murdoch! We've got a way out, by God, and we're going to take it!'

He turned to another officer, standing by. 'Boxhall. Work your way down the starboard side. I'll take the port side. Tell every boat crew that my new orders are to make every boat already on the water part of a pontoon, like that one, and to shuttle everyone out to these rafts with the remaining boats.

'Miss Baden-Powell, go with him, and take this whistle – it will help attract their attention around the boat davits.'

'Yes, Captain.' She rushed with Boxhall towards the milling crowds, desperation replaced, at last, by determination and hope.

The flurry of action did little to calm the desperate passengers, however. Within an hour, the tentative list to starboard was first replaced by a slight list to port, and then by a subtle but unmistakable descent of the bow, with the inexorable flood of water from one compartment to the next. The Guides returned again and again to the ship, to help with the lashings on the next pontoons. The first pontoon, now as laden as it would ever be, rode dangerously low in the water, but on a calm sea, it held steady.

The smallest boat, with the Second Officer on board, along with eight strong oarsmen, volunteers from third class, raced between the pontoons. He shouted through a megaphone, passing orders from the Captain and organising the shuttling of passengers.

Three burly cooks gathered dogs from the kennels. Ivy took a moment to calculate the total fares collected from the canine passengers, who were each brought aboard for the price of a First-Class child, and shook her head with wonder at the frivolities of wealthy Americans. Within 90 minutes, seven pontoons were carrying over 2,000 people. One of the smaller collapsible boats was used for the dogs, which had to be muzzled and bound or put in sacks. 'I do believe the same treatment should be accorded to certain First-Class children,' Ivy commented, as they worked away at the knots.

As the ship's bow grew ever lower, the Captain, Agnes and James found themselves on the last boat, a collapsible. Murdoch, with his eight oarsmen, drew alongside. 'The men are doing the final count, sir, but we believe we have all of them. We've determined that each of the pontoons can bear more than 300 people, as long as they don't shuffle around much.'

'Very good. I've had word from the Marconi operators that the *Carpathia* is not far away, and has been apprised of our situation. For now, we've got to keep these people warm! Let's think how: it's no use telling them to do callisthenics if the pontoons won't bear it, so we'll have to gather them in groups – men with men, women with women – and use the heat of their own mortal forms to keep up their temperature.'

'Sir,' piped up James, we've checked that all the pontoons are now a safe distance away from the ship. Two had to be rowed further out, but everything should be in order now.'

'Very good, Mr Moody. Mr Murdoch, take note.'

From across the flat, shining water came the explosions of the dying ship. But they were no more than an arrhythmic percussion behind a clear, treble voice from one of the pontoons, issuing forth a soaring hymn. A tentative violin from the ship's band joined in, and then played with confidence. Soon, knots of passengers, huddled together, covered with a motley collection of furs, rugs, and coats, were singing along.

'We're lucky, Captain,' commented James. 'The night is mirror calm. The pontoons would have been harder to build on a rough sea.'

'We're lucky in more ways than one,' he replied. 'Miss Baden-Powell, we're not out of this yet, but by the Lord God and the Devil himself, I beg your pardon, Miss, we'll have a story to tell when we get to New York.'

Shock

A story by Grace Chan

At lunch hour on January 15, 1919, a huge storage tank of molasses, owned by Boston's Purity Distilling company, burst. It unleashed a deadly tsunami of molasses that travelled at thirty-five miles (fifty-six kilometres) per hour, engulfing and suffocating twenty-one people and injuring 150 as it congealed in the winter air. The streets of the city smelled of molasses for decades afterwards.

This tragedy – later named 'The Great Molasses Flood' – didn't have to happen. Many specialists, especially those who shared information across informal networks, knew early on that something was wrong with the tank and had identified the risk long before the disaster occurred. However, they lacked the agency and authority to take action. Could anything have been done to prevent it?

This is us. In 1919, the global average temperature was still just 0.1°C above pre-industrial levels, and few people understood the risks of greenhouse gas emissions. But we know the risks today. Will we listen to specialists and empower them to speak, take advantage of informal networks, and take decisive action?

Mary Margaret O'Halloran loved the smell of molasses, no matter how much her co-workers complained.

To her, it evoked more than a Boston distillery. It brought her dreams of Jamaica, where there was no dirty, coal-strewn winter, and no forbidding brick factories that blocked out the wash-water sun. She imagined field workers, their dark skin shining, singing as they chopped the cane for its journey to the refinery.

She wrapped her scarf tighter around her neck. Peg Ridge had knitted it for her as a Christmas gift, and she'd cried when she unwrapped the brown paper and jute string. If she arranged her scarf and her thick, curly hair just right, she could cover both her ears and her nose against the biting wind.

The bitter, pre-dawn wind was blowing directly towards her as she walked past the Common, driving tears from her eyes that streaked back towards her hairline. She wore all three of her petticoats, and her woollen stockings along with them, but that didn't prevent the snow from sneaking into the tops of her boots, melting at first, but later caking in icy clumps around her shins.

Her toes were no longer just cold; they ached.

If only the snow would remain as white as the day it had fallen! But the coal smoke would not allow it. White became slate by nightfall.

The one saving grace of it was that the darker snow melted faster. Peg said it had something to do with dark colours absorbing the heat of the sun. Peg had had an education, which was why she acted as secretary to the foreman, while Mary Margaret was still working in the factory canteen, cooking from before the sun rose and serving up meals to the working men from eleven in the morning until two in the afternoon.

The men joked with Mary Margaret, asking her to dish up a larger portion. She dared not. The factory boss claimed he ran his plant on modern principles that included the provision of meals to the workers, but the reality was that mid-day dinner was a 'modern' way to keep the men working longer and at a lower overall expenditure. 'How dare you come to me with your greedy demands!' Mr Whitman roared whenever a worker mentioned a pay rise. 'Don't I already offer you free meals daily? Didn't I give poor Tim a job, when no one else would hire him on account of his shell shock? There are a hundred other men back from the war who would give anything they had for a job this good.' In the kitchen, every ounce of flour and mutton was carefully recorded, and her pay would be docked if she went over by a grain.

Still, every once in a while, Mary Margaret would slip an extra spoonful of stew to Frankie Robertson, a coloured worker with skin so dark he looked as if he must be covered in coal dust himself. She did it because his smile made her think of the sunshine and fruit trees in the West Indies, even as she shivered in the Boston chill.

Some men, she'd heard, snuck bottles into the plant and syphoned off portions of the finished product. It was a dangerous game: the alcohol produced from their molasses was meant for industrial munitions, not for human consumption, and it could be deadly. The men who were already silly, giggling at eleven o'clock in the morning, flirting with Mary Margaret, were the ones it wouldn't pay to get too attached to.

Frankie Robertson came up after he'd finished eating, scanned the room to see if anyone was watching, and spoke to her in a low voice. 'Thank you. I know you're not supposed to give me any extra. You're a good woman, Miss O'Halloran.'

She felt the heat rise from her chest, and within a moment it appeared on her face. 'It was nothing – but you'll keep it quiet, won't you?' Frankie Robertson smiled and looked into her eyes as he assured her he would.

'You know my name, then?' she added, before he could go back to the boiler room below, where he spent six days of every week.

'Why, every fellow in the plant knows your name and face,' he laughed. 'The Irish Rose, who's always blooming no matter how cold it is outside.'

Suddenly curious, she blurted out, 'Tell me, Mr Robertson, are your people warmer? When the sun shines on you, I mean. Do you absorb the heat?'

He did a surprising thing: he grasped her pale hand and brought it to his cheek. 'No, Miss O'Halloran,' he smiled, 'we're just the same temperature as everyone else.'

Flustered, she snatched her hand away and hastened to explain her question. 'You see, I'd heard that when the sun shines on something dark, it heats up – it expands.'

He nodded his head. 'Heat is a curious thing. When you apply it to metal, it expands, and when it's cold, it shrinks. I've heard the rivets popping at the big tank by the dock when the molasses gets to fermenting in the sun. But when you heat up ice and melt it, why, it takes up less space than it did before.'

She stood, pensive, her hands automatically stacking the dishes and scraping whatever meagre scraps remained for Mr Whitman's hogs. 'So how do they keep the tank together, in summer when the sun shines on it and in winter when it's shrunk? Don't the molasses leak out?'

'Well, it – Miss O'Halloran, I've got to get back to the boiler room. I can already see the foreman looking my way. Will you come out this Saturday evening? There's a dance they hold weekly at Jack Johnson's new club, Café de Champion in the West End. We can speak at our leisure there.'

The warmth of his cheek still tingling on her fingers, Mary Margaret found herself giving him the address of the boarding house near the Charles Street Jail, where she and Peg had been staying for more than a year. Was she imagining it, or did he, too, smell of sugar and vanilla, and citrus? Once, when she was a little girl, her mother had got an orange at Christmastime and divided it into eight pieces, one for each of the children. Mary Margaret could still remember the smell, her memory even stronger than the sulphurous smell of the coal smoke.

The Saturday dance at Café de Champion was in a basement, and if Frankie Robertson had expected to talk, he would be disappointed. A band was playing a wild, careening type of music that Mary Margaret had never heard before. Couples were dancing to its immense noise, showing off moves so athletic she feared she'd never be able to imitate them. To her surprise, a handful of Irish girls were present.

Mary Margaret gaped at the dancers, wondering if she could bring herself to attempt their gymnastic feats. Before she could dwell on it at any length, Frankie drew her into the throng, guiding her with a sure hand placed at her lower back.

Suddenly, she was copying his steps, responding as if they were a single, electric unit and not two exhausted workers who had spent their day in toil. She whooped in exhilaration and was rewarded with a brilliant smile from Frankie, who lifted her up by her waist, spun her around, and then swung her between his legs along the slick, tiled floor. When he brought her up again, she couldn't erase the grin from her face.

Later, not wanting to be left alone in the dark, pulsing basement, she joined him in the alleyway. A group of men were smoking, the smoke mingling with the vapour of their breath. They took swigs from small glass bottles. She wondered if any of the contents had come from their distillery.

'Oh, I thought it was all over for us that day,' mused a tall, older man with a thin moustache and short, tightly curled hair. 'The boiler was straining and gonna blow. They had the safety valves screwed down. But by the Lord Jesus she held up and we walked out of there alive.' His cigarette, a twist of brown paper, gave off a smell closer to cloves than tobacco, and she wondered what it was. She thought of her grandfather's pipe. It had been her privilege to knock out the spent ash and return it to him as he sat on his big, wooden bench.

Frankie explained that the attendees of the dance were the boiler men of Boston, the coloured ones, who had first met in the barbershop to share their jokes and sorrows, and later rented this basement to expend the pent-up energy from the frustrations of their week.

'I spend my whole life in basements! Maybe my skin's the same temperature as yours,' Frankie joked, 'because it never gets the chance to absorb any sun in the first place.' Mary Margaret blushed and held her tongue. 'At least on Tuesday and Wednesday I've got a shift up at the dock. It'll be cold, but it'll be out in the open. They say there's fermentation in the tank again, and we've gotta try and get that frozen top vent open and clean up the surrounding area.'

The men were discussing the gruesome accidents they'd seen or heard about. Curious, Mary Margaret pressed them with questions. The older man, a bottle in one hand and his queer cigarette in the other, explained. 'The thing to remember with any kind of container isn't just the overall pressure, it's how strong the weakest joint is. A tank with strong seams can hold much longer than you'd imagine, even enormous pressure. But when you take a tank with weak joints, then you'd better think twice before you let the pressure build up inside. It'll crack if you're not careful.'

Mary Margaret nodded her head. 'It's like when the men make their home brew down at the plant. Emily found all their bottles in the closet, where the men had been making up something to get them through the wintry afternoons. But when she touched one of the bottles it shattered in her very hand from the pressure inside. The noise was so loud that the men who were back from the army thought they were on the battlefield once more! And no matter the frost outside, inside the bottles there was a surprising amount of heat.' With these last words, she found herself looking up at Frankie, but continued, 'Poor Emily got docked two days' pay for that and cut her hand beside, and dunked it straight into the hot wash water. And then she had to throw it all out, for we sure didn't want to be washing the dishes in bloody water. But the hot water she threw went straight onto the newspaper boy, and wasn't he steamed!'

The men laughed at her unintended pun, and she laughed with them. The older man threw the butt of his cigarette to the ground, crushed it beneath his boot, and offered Mary Margaret a swig from his little glass bottle. She shook her head.

'Man, the fellows upstairs could learn a thing or two from us,' Frankie mused, as he smoked his own cigarette. 'When the molasses delivery came in, they had to heat it up, to make it pour easier into that tank by the dock. And when the weather's cold it might be all right, but when it's warm it ferments and the pressure builds up inside. Not to mention the tank is only four years old, but the men think it was never built right to begin with. It already leaks; the children bring cups to collect the molasses that oozes out. It's only a matter of time before the thing cracks and the stuff starts leaking out in earnest. Could be any day now. The children would have their fun, then!'

A younger man, with his sleeves rolled up and the muscles of his forearms showing, piped up, 'How much that tank hold? It look like it fifty feet tall.' Mary Margaret had been wondering the same thing.

Frankie shook his head. 'A hell of a lot, excuse me, Miss O'Halloran, a whole hell of a lot. More than two million gallons. But I don't know why we're talking about sweet molasses when I've got a sweet Irish girl on my arm. Let's get out of this funk and get back to the music. We ain't bring those boys out from Chicago to play ragtime – let's boogie-woogie!' He grinned, grabbed Mary Margaret's hands, and pulled her towards him. The older man opened the door and they descended the little staircase, back into the darkness and noise below.

For the next several days, Mary Margaret's head was swimming with the experience. Thank goodness Peg let her in! It wouldn't be the first time one of the girls had stayed out late, but there would have been a scene with Mrs Martin if she hadn't been ready for church in the morning, her head well covered and her face clean. She wondered if the scent of cigarettes and sweat still lingered in her thick hair as she listened to the Psalm. The Gospel reading was about how Jesus had overturned the moneychangers' tables in the temple, and Father Daniel's homily expanded on the topic. It was the only story that remained consistent in all the Gospels, he said, and therefore it was something the Lord wanted His children to remember. Sometimes, Father Daniel mused, a man had to break things in order to do the Lord's work.

Mary Margaret had to admit that Father Daniel had often exceeded his responsibilities as a priest, and had himself broken more than his fair share of moneychangers' tables. Some of the older folks were suspicious of his close friendship with Martin Lomasney, the politician and ward boss of the West End, the one called The Mahatma.

Sunday dinner was subdued and contemplative. There were few comments at dinner, and those only about the homily. But as Mary Margeret struggled out of bed in the dark on Monday morning, it was Frankie Robertson's brilliant smile that she couldn't get out of her head. There was porridge for breakfast, and coffee, and on the strength of these warming stores she tackled the frozen morning.

The January air was frigid. A thermometer in a shop window, almost obscured by icicles, read two degrees Fahrenheit, and her toes ached even more than they had before. In another ten minutes she would arrive at the plant and begin her backbreaking work, and at least there it would be warm.

In another week it would be St. Sebastian's Day, the feast day she'd always celebrated with her youngest brother. She hadn't had a letter from Sebastian in months, but she treasured the one she had, and folded its creases over and over again. She couldn't read it, but Peg did that for her, and she imagined his pudgy fingers tracing out the sentences by gaslight. Sebastian said that her mother was thinking of sending their next-oldest sister out. Annie was not yet fourteen, but was a hard worker, knew how to figure, and was good with children.

The telltale smell of hot molasses drew her thoughts back to the present. Frankie had told her a big shipment was due in the next few days. As she approached the gate, she heard a voice. 'Why, it's the Irish Rose herself!' It was Tim, the guard, who'd come back from the war with shell shock. It didn't affect him much during the day; men with shell shock always said the nights were the worst. She saw nothing but a cheerful greeting on his face today. 'And where's Miss Ridge this morning?'

'She'll be in later on.' Tim was carrying a torch for Peg, and anyone could see it. 'Big delivery last Friday?' she asked.

'The biggest! Half a million gallons, straight from Puerto Rico. They heated it up to make it flow, for it was solid as coal tar in this weather.' Tim's information was ready and copious, but never quite reliable. Mary Margaret glanced at the big distillation column, beginning to sparkle in the first rays of dawn. The January sun rose late; as yet, it was only a glow on the horizon.

The thought of the big tank wrenched Mary Margaret away from the casual morning banter. The image of the broken dishes and bloody wash water sprang unbidden to her mind. Springing a leak would be one thing. Bursting open would be quite another: far more dangerous than an annoying leak.

Would the tank hold?

She brooded throughout the day. Mid-morning on the next day, once Peg arrived – her shift began only when the foreman needed her – Mary Margaret stole a minute away from the sweltering kitchens to pose an odd question to her friend. 'Peg, have you learned arithmetic and such when you did your schooling?'

'Didn't I just! Why, I was the top of sister Angeline's class before I came away.'

'And could you,' she clutched Peg's arm with sudden intensity, 'could you make a calculation? I want to know how far the molasses would flow. I mean if the big tank by the dock were to fail.'

Laughing, Peg replied, 'I don't know what's happened to you, Mary Margaret! First you sneak out on a Saturday night with Frankie Robertson and you're only back at cock's crow, and then you're listening to Father Daniel's homily like he was the Lord Jesus himself, and now you come to me worried about a tank breaking up.'

'But can you do it? Can ye tell with your pen and paper, how far it would go?'

Still smiling, Peg got out a scrap of paper from the wastebasket and began scribbling. She furrowed her pretty brow, paused, and asked, 'Do you mean now, when it's full? Or when it's only at half capacity?'

'When it's full.'

Peg continued her scribbling, and her face grew grave. She retrieved a second scrap of paper from the basket and covered it with calculations. At last she raised her carroty head and said, 'It wouldn't go well for them, to be sure. Even at half capacity, anyone within half a mile would drown. If it were full, the kinetic energy would be –'

'What's kinetic energy? No, never mind. Tell me.'

'It would rush out of there at more than thirty miles per hour, Mary Margaret. Faster than a horse at full gallop. No one could survive it.'

The two women sat in silence, imagining the disaster.

Mary Margaret was the first to speak. 'We have to stop it.'

'There's nothing a woman could do,' Peg replied. 'They won't listen to the likes of us.'

'Can you not show your arithmetic to the foreman?'

'Mary Margaret, don't you know how lucky I am to have this place? He's already been hinting that there are men home from the war, now, and they're the ones who should be doing my work. It's only because he's too lazy to change anything that I'm still here.'

Mary Margaret nodded her head, glanced at the clock, and grasped Peg's hand for a moment before running back to the kitchens below. Her head was filled with images of Frankie Robertson, spinning her around, his hands on her waist, Frankie grinning down at her, Frankie happy to be working out in the open on the river, his head covered with a fuzzy woollen cap, asphyxiating in sudden terror as a wave of molasses engulfed him.

Upon entering, she gave an excuse to the cook, blaming her brief absence on her female issues. The cook acknowledged her with a curt, 'Get on with it, then.'

Get on with it. If she couldn't stop it, she decided, at least she could delay it. The Lord Jesus had known what he had to do, and he had overturned those moneychangers' tables without a second thought. She couldn't let anything happen to Frankie Robertson, who was the kindest, most intelligent man she'd ever met.

She rummaged around the medicine box in the back, passing up the boric acid and tinctures of camphor – recognisable by their distinctive bottles – and retrieved a large bottle of Syrup of Ipecac.

It would have to be the mutton stew. It was the only thing all the men ate.

She waited until the cook's back was turned, and poured the entire bottle into the giant iron pot.

The effect was more immediate than she imagined. Before the last men in the line were served, the first men were already excusing themselves to rush out of doors and vomit. But those first men in line were also the hardest drinkers, and it was not uncommon for some to be suffering from the effects of the previous night's binge on Monday morning. However, by the time the next shift came in, some men were starting to wonder.

Frankie came to get his dinner, and Mary Margaret forced herself to look him in the eye as she dished out the stew, same as the others. *I'm doing this to save him,* she reminded herself. Half an hour later, she saw him reeling to the door, his face ashen. *But he's alive,* she muttered under her breath.

Two o'clock came at last, and the plant was in chaos. Hardly a man was back at his station, and the workers who were supposed to have been sent out to the dock were scattered along the streets, finding gutters and alleyways to profane with their puking. The foreman, who'd had his lunch sent in, raged around the plant in impotent despair. 'What has become of these men? Call an ambulance! Has the Spanish flu returned?'

Mary Margaret herself rushed out of the kitchen, pretending to suffer along with the others although she hadn't had a bite since breakfast. Her belly certainly ached, but it was from hunger. Still, if she were the only one unaffected, it would be suspicious. The cook, who always was the last one to eat after the final worker's dinner was served, was not sickened by the meal, but was in tears. 'We'll all be on the street tomorrow, and myself first! What could have happened?'

Mary Margaret tried to comfort her. 'There was nothing we could've done. It must have been a bad cut of mutton. How long was it in the store?'

'Tweren't that. It were frozen solid. And you girls keep the cooking pots clean as a whistle. What is to be done? What is to be done?' She collapsed into the corner, wiping her eyes with the corner of her apron. 'And me with a family to feed.'

Mary Margaret began to understand the import of the crime she'd committed. The courage of her dawn convictions was fading in the hard, bright sunshine of mid-day. Would anyone connect her with the illness the men faced? If they found her, she could be put away for attempted murder. They would call her an Anarchist. But even if they couldn't pin it on a single person, the cook was right: the entire kitchen crew would be sacked, and they would all suffer.

Shock

The one saving grace was that not a single man was working out at the tank today. They were in no immediate danger. Frankie Robertson, Tim the guard, and every man on the distillery floor – they were all weak, retching until they could bring up no more. One or two of them tried to calm their stomachs with the pure alcohol they kept on hand, but it only made the retching worse. It would be at least a week before they could assemble a crew to work. The stench was awful, despite the chill. Mary Margaret shook her head, imagining what it would be like in putrid, steaming July.

She gathered her things and glanced at the other kitchen girls, who were all nursing their aching bellies and weeping. Taking advantage of their distraction, she snuck out the back door, walking at an ordinary pace until she exited the factory premises, then quickening for the next block.

By the time she passed the Common, she was running.

'Father Daniel!' she cried, bursting into the rectory, almost blind with tears herself. 'Will you absolve me? For I've done a terrible thing.'

He looked up from his desk and saw the terror in her eyes. 'My child, only the Lord can absolve us. But if you have need of the holy sacrament, then come to the confessional.' He put away his pen and paper, and stood, extending a hand.

'Bless me, Father, for I have sinned,' she began, and told him what she'd done.

At first he followed the form of the sacrament, asking her, 'And are you repentant before the Lord?'

'I surely am, Father! But what can I do now?'

Father Daniel opened the grate. 'I think you'd better come back to my office, Miss O'Halloran.'

There, she explained the entire situation from beginning to end. He raised his eyebrows when he heard about her attendance at the underground boogie-woogie dance, but said nothing until she finished.

'Are you sure this tank is ready to collapse?'

'Why, that's what all the boiler men said, and who would know better than the ones working on tanks all day?'

Father Daniel sat back in his leather chair, his hands together as if in prayer. Mary Margaret waited. Then, he asked something curious. 'This Frankie Robertson. Is he a Catholic?'

'Frankie? Why, I never asked. But he's no infidel.'

'And you say he has connections with all the Negro boiler men?'

'All over the West End. And then some.'

Father Daniel leaned forward. 'I may be able to help. The way I see it, there are two issues at hand. First, you've come here for sanctuary, and it's something the Church has delivered to those in need since the Middle Ages. We'll provide it now. And the second one is how to save those poor men before that tank fails. It sounds as if you've averted disaster for the men of the plant, but it's only a stopgap measure and there are others at the dock that need our help.'

'Praise the Lord,' Mary Margaret sighed. 'What must I do?'

'Put me in contact with this Frankie Robertson, and with Miss Ridge, too, while I'm thinking of it. And in the meantime, go home and gather your things.' He shouted for an assistant, even as he was scribbling a note, blotting the ink, and folding it.

'All my things?'

'Everything you want to keep in your new life. Do you speak German?'

'German? No, just English. And the Gaeilge we used at home.'

'Never mind. The family you'll be working for won't expect it. And they're desperate for a new nursemaid.'

Six months later, Mary Margaret was wiping the face of three-year-old Otto, when Gloria, the charwoman, handed her a letter. Mary Margaret thanked her, even as she shouted, 'Heinrich! Stop taunting your brother. Five years old is big enough to know better. Go outside and play with Carl-Wilhelm! It's stifling here inside in the summer heat, so I sure as sugar don't know why you're bothering him.'

After a short negotiation, Heinrich agreed to go outside and play with the bigger boys while Otto wandered around the kitchen, and Mary Margaret had time to piece together the meaning of the letter. It was hard work, but her employer, Mrs Schubert, was a good teacher and insisted that all the household staff learn to read and write. Mary Margaret had made tremendous progress in a short time.

Dear Mary Margaret, she read, *I received your letter from the hands of Father Daniel. All of us at Mrs Martin's are glad to know you're safe. There's a rumour that you've gone to New York, though Father Daniel won't say a word. I'm happy to hear that your sister Annie will be joining you in your new position. You'll be glad enough for the company, I suppose, though there is little scope for advancement for a girl in service.*

You will be wanting to know what happened at the plant.

Father Daniel was as good as his word, but like our Lord, he works in mysterious ways. He brought Frankie Robertson over to the rectory to have what he called a 'little chat'. And who should be there but Martin Lomasney, the ward boss, the one they call the 'Mahatma' himself! They tell me it's a Hindoo word, though I'm sure I don't know why he would go in for heathen customs. He's been out of office this past year, and now he's wanting to take the Fifth Suffolk District. But he said he couldn't do it without the Negro vote. So if Frankie and his boiler men promised to undertake to deliver it, then in return The Mahatma would use his political influence to get the tank condemned that very day.

Frankie agreed to the deal, and by evening Mr Whitman had decided, 'of his own accord', that the distillery was to be shut down. He said it was inevitable given the end of the war and the ratification of Prohibition. The same night they all had their talk, there were big signs pasted on the tank saying it wasn't to be used. The next morning, they found workers somewhere, outside ones, who put out sandbags and drained the molasses right onto the frozen ground! Though it were no longer frozen, with the temperature outside already at forty degrees. Our workers were all put out on the street, but most of them have found new positions by now. None of the places offer dinner, however.

What is most important is that they are alive and well. If those boiler men hadn't shared their stories, if you hadn't done what you did, it might have gone much worse for them. The men dismantled the tank the next week, and while they were doing it, they found the steel itself was more brittle than it ought to have been – it may have been lacking manganese, someone said – and its rivets were flawed. So it was much weaker than anyone had suspected. Mr Whitman is bringing a lawsuit against the manufacturer.

I hope you are well. The coppers came looking for you at first, when you disappeared, but when they said you'd fled the city they gave up quickly enough, saying that it was likely the female hysteria that made you do it.

But I've got to tell you one more thing: I've got a new place myself. I shall become a bride!

Oh, she's accepted Tim at last! Mary Margaret thought happily. Or has the foreman finally been roused to action, and spoken for her?

You'll be surprised to hear that in November I'm to become Mrs Frankie Robertson. It's a pity you won't be able to come to the wedding, but all the girls at the boarding house think of you and wish you well – wherever you are.

Your dear friend,

Peg Ridge

Mary Margaret had only a moment to take in the news before Otto came over, wailing, having scorched his finger on the hot kitchen stove.

'Oh dear,' she said, 'let's take a look.' She examined the tender hand, kissed it, and comforted the sniffing boy.

'Don't be shocked by the sight of a little burn,' she told him. 'It could have been much worse.'

R101

A story by Grace Chan

The tragedy of R101, a British rigid airship, is less-known than that of the Hindenburg. *Yet its maiden voyage was even more deadly: it crashed in France on October 5, 1930, killing forty-eight of the fifty-four passengers and crew. Its victims included the Air Minister responsible for the programme, as well as a team of government officials and the dirigible's designers.*

The risks of hydrogen and of large-scale airships were already known at the time of the crash. In particular, the expertise developed during the First World War was proving invaluable to engineers around the world. But a fundamental question was never asked: is what we are doing safe?

This is us. In 1929, the global average temperature was 0.2°C below pre-industrial levels. Will we have the courage today to take stock and ask the same question of ourselves?

'We'll have to drop the piano,' said Albert Price, handing the offending sheaf of papers back to his colleague, as if the contents would be more acceptable at a distance. 'It's not just me. Any engineer would tell you the same.' He turned up the collar of his raincoat against the damp, and shoved his hands into his pockets as they walked. He did not notice that he had created a momentary tableau of pathos: a sorrowful supplicant before the great cathedrals that were the R101 airship construction hangars. Each of the extraordinary buildings was as tall as St Paul's, and twice as broad. His boots crunched on the gravel path.

'What!' bristled the bewhiskered promoter, Toby Collins, hurrying to catch up. 'Why, it's a signature piece, and a crucial part of my poster campaign. No family of any standing would want to travel without a piano. You're making a mockery of the entire Royal Airship Works.' He tucked the papers under his arm before he, too, shoved his hands into his pockets with finality. They were heading toward   the scraping sheds, which stood downwind of the project office. In the distance, the setting sun did its best to penetrate the fog. Beside them, however, the two enormous hangars blocked whatever warmth the pale orange disk could provide at this late hour. The majestic doors towered over them, their tops almost obscured in the fog, but the men, absorbed in the task at hand, failed to appreciate the grandeur of the scene they were passing.

'My good man, something's got to go,' Albert retorted. 'The computing team have gone over the weight of all the components in all the categories. If we keep that piano, we'll hardly be able to get the craft to clear the next hedgerow, let alone fly to India.'

They were now close to the scraping sheds, and Toby wrinkled his nose: nearing the end of the day's work, the sheds reeked even more than they had at dawn. Several stout, grim women were clearing out for the day, untying their bloody aprons and hanging up their tools. Their hands were grimy with months of disgusting labour. Yet its purpose sanctified their filth, for it was at the heart of the technology that allowed an airship to fly: its gas bags. A quarter-mile from the lofty hangars, their chapel was a miserable barn full of rotting offal, where they prepared sections of a cow's digestive tract to fashion the bags.

'What about those – what was it – access ladders?' asked Toby, averting his eyes from the unfortunate women. 'What're they for?'

'To fly the airship, you ninny!' snapped the engineer. 'This isn't a toy boat on the round pond in Kensington gardens. It's one of the largest manmade structures ever built.'

They were still arguing as they entered the project office. 'We need the ladders and walkways to allow the crew to reach the ballast to release it,' Albert pointed out. 'It's vital that the trim of the ship is managed carefully, or the poor girl could end up standing on her nose. We don't want to end up like the ZR-3!'

The others, already in the conference room, chuckled at the reference. Toby's puzzled expression as he approached the wooden table prompted a languorous voice from the corner to explain. It was Sir James Marshall, the young project lead, handsome and cheerful, relaxing in an upholstered armchair. 'The ZR-3 – what a dreadful business that was. The blessed thing was tethered at the Lakehurst high mast in Los Angeles, in America,' he recalled. He ran his fingers through his fair, fluffy hair, leaving it even messier than before, as if blown awry by a gale. 'A gust of wind caught her tail and lifted it up so far that the crew were scrambling to climb aft along the keel as if it were a ruddy fir tree, trying to put the weights in the right place.' He paused. 'In the event, it didn't help,' he mentioned to the man sitting next to him. The latter, a tense, middle-aged man with a trim moustache, made a note in a small book, the scratch of his pen audible to everyone in the room.

Toby was still on his feet. 'You're telling me that managing the trim – vital to keeping the craft stable, according to what you just said – is controlled by a bloke running along a ladder and untying a knot to drop a bag of sand?' He gave a sarcastic snort. 'Indeed, the Golden Age of Technology hath come unto England at last!'

Albert shrugged. 'That's how it's done. It worked perfectly when the Montgolfier brothers did it in 1783, and it works just as well today in 1929.'

'Why can't you do it through mechanical means, as they do in the railways?'

'That sort of suggestion was made early on,' countered Albert, 'and it was rejected as unproven. In any case, my opinion, sir, is that you should stick to your posters and keep your nose out of my designs!'

Albert and Toby continued in the same vein until Sir James's patient drawl defused the argument. The little man next to him remained silent. 'Mr Price,' said Sir James, 'we're grateful for your opinion, dreadfully so. I suggest you and your men have a peep into any other areas at all where weight can be saved, so that Mr Collins can keep his pianoforte. We can go over the weight calculations again when we meet on Monday. In the meantime, Mr Collins, I suggest all the same that you consider other options, anticipating the unhappy circumstance that your instrument cannot be accommodated. Now, we must move to other topics. What does the latest financial report show?'

Grumbling, Albert gathered his papers and glared at Toby. They remained subdued while the other department heads delivered their updates but revived their discussion in low grumbles when the meeting ended. The other men rolled their eyes, shrugged on their coats and nodded to Sir James as they filed out into the foggy dusk.

Only the dark man with the precise moustache remained in the room, his face half hidden in the shadow cast by the dim electric bulb.

Sir James flashed a white-toothed grin and addressed him. 'This is what we are facing, I'm afraid, Mr Clay. Terribly boring. Always scratching for a few ounces here and there.'

Fithian Clay spoke for the first time. 'Saving ounces and pounds – and a few pounds sterling while you're at it, eh, my lad?' He rummaged in his jacket and brought out a pipe and matches.

'While we are, naturally, only too aware of the financial constraints placed by His Majesty's treasury on the Imperial Airship Scheme in the present circumstances, our principal aim is to develop a model – two models, really – that can lay the groundwork for the future of civil airships. If we should meet with success, they will be capable of service on long-distance routes connecting the whole of the British Empire.' He again ran his fingers through his unruly golden hair.

'Good. And I hope for your sake the project does what it says it will. But we want to keep things straight, smart, and above all, safe. The Royal Society have put me in charge of this inspection because they know I know what I'm about, and I intend to give them their money's worth.' He took a vigorous puff of his pipe, and the smoke wafted up towards the electric bulb.

Sir James cleared his throat. His cousin Georgie at the Royal Society had warned him about Fithian Clay. Fithian was in the employ of the Royal Society for a joint project with the Factory Inspectorate, in preparation for the centenary of the latter – apparently King William IV had appointed the first Factory Inspectors back in 1833 – and the fellow was terribly serious about his job. As an inspector, he had worked on railways, mine shafts, and spinning mills. Now, he was to prepare a report about the safe development of new technologies, and the Imperial Airship Scheme was his subject.

Georgie had asked Sir James, 'Would you mind ever so much having a "fly on the wall" there, to understand how you go about things and such?' It was only after Sir James had already agreed that Georgie introduced his 'fly': the precise man with the little moustache.

While Fithian Clay had no true power over the project, his report might damn or praise them – and, as such, either propel them upwards or halt them before they got off the ground.

'Mr Clay,' Sir James began, 'we naturally are of one mind. You are welcome to watch our little teatime debates for as many days as you please, if you believe it might be of any use. In the meantime, I'll assign an apprentice to show you this and that. Now, it's Friday evening, and the hour has arrived where I myself must be toddling back to my little flat in Chelsea, lest the wrath of my golden angel turn unfairly towards her faithful suitor – as the revue said, "There's life in the old girl yet." Shall I have my man drop you in ....' he trailed off without finishing the sentence.

'No need for that. I'll see you here tomorrow.' The little man clamped on his hat and strode from the room.

Three days later, Toby and Albert were at it again.

'What have you got?' asked the former.

'The answer is another gas bag,' declared the latter, as he unrolled a large blueprint onto the table. 'More gas means more lift. I've added another large one, right in the middle. You can keep your piano, and thank me for it later.'

'Gas bags! I knew it – he's determined to spend more time with the shed girls,' quipped an apprentice from the back, eliciting a general guffaw. Albert spun around with a scowl, but could not identify the wag.

Sir James had always wondered what it was about a cow's gut that made it impermeable to hydrogen. Whatever the reason, it was the best material available for the job.

The scratching sound of Fithian Clay's pen in his little book emerged during a lull in the laughter, and the merriment subsided. His presence, despite Sir James's welcome, cast a pall on the entire operation; his probing questions unsettled the younger designers and frustrated the more experienced ones. He made constant references to the *Titanic*, since he had been on the team investigating that tragedy seventeen years earlier.

'If I may interrupt, *gentlemen*,' he said, putting emphasis on the final word as he rose to his feet, 'This would mean a total of sixteen gas bags of different sizes on the R101.'

'That's right,' said Albert, narrowing his eyes.

'I can't help comparing this with the *Titanic*, with its fifteen bulkheads.' Someone in the back groaned, but the little man continued. 'As I understand it – please correct me if I'm wrong – the loss of one of the ten larger bags would mean that the ship can no longer float – or fly, whichever is the correct term.'

Toby, sensing a new threat to his beloved piano, jumped in to defend Albert. 'Well, an aeroplane only has two wings and it needs both of them to fly. For that matter, an ox cart has two wheels and it needs both of them.'

'Indeed,' Fithian Clay admitted. 'We should recall that flight is an inherently challenging environment. If you lose a single significant element, the only way is down. In this case, all sixteen bags need to hold up for the entire journey – or the journey will end unexpectedly. Are leaks common?' he asked, turning back to Albert.

'Why, of course,' replied Albert. 'Hydrogen's a tricky sort of gas. It leaks out of anything you try to hold it in. And you can't keep the bags from rubbing on the structure. But the crew do conduct inspections, and they can repair the bags in-flight. The boys've got a devilishly clever method to monitor things, you know – they give a whistle to hear if the pitch of the note changes, and if it does, why it means they're in a cloud of hydrogen. They use themselves as canaries, you might say.'

Fithian Clay nodded his head. 'And as I understand it, the bags are single skinned. If there is a hole, the gas will flow out – not under great pressure, but steadily and relentlessly. You compared it to the wings of an aeroplane, sir,' he said, addressing Toby. 'But in this case we have sixteen points of failure instead of two, known to experience regular leaks, and the entire enterprise will fail if just one of them ceases to operate as required.'

Toby shifted in his seat. 'Mr Price, you've got a plan for that, I suppose? That doesn't sound like a piece of information I want to include in my publicity campaign.'

Albert shook his head. 'We can't make the bags double layered, if that's what you're suggesting. It would just increase the weight, and then we'd need more bags, and so on. Not to mention, your "points of failure" have doubled as well.'

'Not to mention the cost increase,' came Sir James's lazy voice from the corner. 'We must be aware of His Majesty's budget following the recent setbacks in the world of – ahem – trade. Nevertheless, we don't want our R101 falling out of the sky. Gentlemen, I suggest you consider Mr Clay's points and see what might be done. We shall reconvene on Friday.'

Once again, the men filed out and Fithian Clay stayed behind with Sir James. This time, however, he adopted an almost apologetic air. 'I know my ships and trains, sir, but I'm at sea when it comes to aeronautical manoeuvres.'

'Quite all right, I assure you,' Sir James chuckled.

'If it wouldn't be too much trouble, sir,' Fithian asked, 'I'd like to bring an associate along with me. One who's been helping me out here and there, as I rummage through all these designs.'

Sir James had trouble imagining what an associate of the little man might be like but answered with an affable smile. 'Why not? What's the fellow's name?'

'It's my daughter, sir, Gladys. She did some work with the Royal Air Force during the war and has a keen eye for the figures.'

Sir James gaped. 'Of course, Miss Clay is welcome to observe,' he said hastily, 'but I'm sure a young lady has far more interesting occupations to pursue than listening to a bunch of men arguing about gas bags.' He made a quick calculation, and realised that the woman would hardly be young; she must be nearing thirty, if she'd been employed during the war a decade earlier.

'Oh, she'll find it interesting, all right,' Fithian replied. He shoved his hat onto his oiled head and headed to the door before the astonished Sir James had the opportunity to say anything further.

The apprentices were the most amusing ones to watch, thought Sir James four days later. When they saw Gladys Clay, neat and elegant, sitting beside her father in the corner of the conference room, one made a visible attempt to thrust out his chest. Another fiddled with his watch chain. None of them dared to meet her eye. Despite their awkwardness and distraction, however, Sir James appreciated the rise in tone that the presence of a lady created. There were no more ribald comments about the shed girls, and Toby had corrected himself three times just prior to issuing oaths and insults about the laziness of the rendering artists, the uncertainty of the project planners, and the paucity of the budget.

Fithian approached the table, where Albert was scribbling figures onto the blueprint with a wax pencil. 'May I?' he asked. He peered at the document through a pair of cloudy pince-nez. He gestured for his daughter, and Gladys joined him in his inspection.

A moment later, she spoke. 'Excuse me, Mr – Price, is it? – I would like to clarify something. Putting aside weight for a moment, would it be possible to structure the gas bags in two layers, with the inner bag acting as a honeycomb structure?'

'That's a big thing to put aside, Miss Clay, for the weight's what matters. But yes, in theory you could do it. To what end?'

'Hydrogen gas has a tendency to permeate through membranes. An inner honeycomb of cell balloons could confine the gas within the outer skin, and any leakage could then be pumped back into the inner honeycomb to reduce gas loss. And if a projectile were to pass through the honeycomb,' she mused, as her eyes gained a faraway look, 'only a small selection of the buoyancy chambers would be lost – assuming that the penetration doesn't cause a fire, of course.'

'Fire is another notable concern,' asserted her father.

'If you're thinking of changing to a different gas,' Albert said, 'you can forget it. Hydrogen is the best lift gas, the lowest density, easy to replace. Helium couldn't lift this structure even without the weight of the extra bags.'

'Not to mention the cost,' pointed out Sir James, affably.

'If you could get any helium at all!' added Albert. 'It's rarer than hen's teeth. Gentlemen – and – I say, gentlemen, we're moving backwards. Last week I was worried about getting Mr Collins's piano off the ground, but with all these new demands we'll be lucky if we can get the craft itself to rise.'

Fithian Clay poked the blueprint with a tobacco-stained finger. 'A highly flammable gas,' he said, 'sixteen flimsy bags, and if any   of them leaks, the ship sinks.' He punctuated each point with an additional prod at the paper.

'Flying is a risky business,' mused Sir James.

'Sir, are you a sailor?' asked Gladys.

'Not me,' he laughed. 'I can hardly cross a bridge without getting a bit green.'

'My father and I have been sailing many times on boats with no motors, and we've got a sailor's dread of a lee shore. The last thing a sailor wants is to get caught with the wind pressing him onto a rocky beach, and no room left for manoeuvre. Your beautiful airship, with its enormous windage, is not unlike a huge sailing ship. But there is a key difference: it isn't possible to drop the sails.'

'We need no sails; we've got five engines.'

'And therein lies another challenge. The airship depends fully on its fuel and engines. When they are not available, no adjustments can be made. But the only safe harbours are at either end of the trip. A sailing ship without an engine can still float, and an aeroplane can put down into a field and come to a stop, however lumpy – many pilots in my squadron can attest to the latter. But even earlier, smaller zeppelins required up to 500 people to manhandle them into their shed. Unlike a ship, it can't throw down an anchor to ride out a storm or conduct repairs. Halfway to India, what will happen?'

The men glanced at each other uneasily.

'Not to say that the project is ill-conceived. I've done my own calculations,' Gladys continued, bringing out her own sheaf of papers, 'and I believe it could be made to work. But perhaps not with the technology available today.'

'Miss Clay,' Sir James intervened, one hand on his wayward blond locks, 'Our men have been at this task for some time and have raised no issues such as the ones you now wish us to address. Is it not, perhaps, your most commendable feminine timidity that leads you to look for risks over opportunities?'

'Individual timidity, feminine or otherwise, is not a factor here. Indeed, as Miss Earhart in America has shown us, a woman can now fly solo across the North American continent and back in an aeroplane just as a man can. No, I speak of public risk: you wish this to become the basis for a new programme, supported by our government, serving the great and the lowly of our society. But if you want to succeed, you need at least five things that are at present not in your arsenal.'

Toby harrumphed. 'And what would those be?'

She turned to the chalkboard at the end of the room and paused. A blushing apprentice scrambled to hand her a piece of chalk. For the next minute, there was no sound other than the clacking of the chalk and the steady thrum of rain outside, as she listed the items. She finished and turned. On the board was written:

Problems
- Unpredictable weather, high wind – manoeuvrability
- Gas leaks
- Ground damage from crash (H_2 – fire; He – drag)

Solutions
- Chambered gas bags – multiple perforations
- Lightweight engines (fuel?)
- Anchor (~100 tonnes)
- Low level bollard network
- Improved weather forecasting

The men gaped at the blackboard. 'An anchor of 100 tonnes!' cried Albert. 'And what's going to lift that? We haven't got capacity for Mr Collins's piano as it is!'

'Who let her in here, anyway?' grumbled Toby, to nobody in particular. 'Get back to your ironing!'

'Might as well end the project straightaway,' harumphed Albert, standing at Toby's side.

Sir James stood, but remained silent, reading the points Gladys had written. Ladies had such elegant handwriting. 'What do you mean here, Miss Clay? A low-level bollard network?'

As she dusted the chalk from her hands, Sir James handed her a handkerchief. 'The damage from an airship if it goes down is better imagined than seen,' she warned. 'If it is hydrogen, it may combust, while a damaged helium ship may be dragged across the countryside. An airship of this size would need to do the equivalent of a ship's anchor, at a place of its choice. A hard point, which could take a 100-tonne bollard pull to hold it in a stiff wind. Low level bollards could be set in the ground all along the planned route. At a push, a heavy steam locomotive could be used, although there would be a significant chance of derailment.'

Sir James nodded and glanced at Fithian Clay. What was the inscrutable expression behind the man's dark moustache, he wondered? Could it be pride? He tilted his blond head in thought, picked up a piece of chalk, and circled the word 'anchor'. 'So the anchors would be along the ground, not with the ship in the air.'

'A transportable anchor travelling with the airship would have to be 100 tonnes or more, and winchable up and down. It could be the cargo container.'

'I fail to see how it would be possible,' wondered Sir James. 'Anything heavy enough to hold the ship would be too heavy to lift.'

'More gas bags,' winked an apprentice.

Gladys took the chalk, brushing Sir James's fingertips. 'Indeed, the greater question is that of the gas bags. The airship is vulnerable to loss of a single one. Yet the technology does not exist today to construct a honeycomb chamber with an over layer, not as long as our only viable material comes from that scraping shed.' Sir James raised an eyebrow. Had her father told her about that?

He ran his hand through his hair three times before speaking, dulling it with chalk dust. 'Gentlemen, let me take some time to consider the matter. In the meantime, the hour grows late, Lady Marshall is, no doubt, awaiting my return, and I must not disappoint her. All the same – Mr Clay – Miss Clay – will you remain for a moment?'

Gladys nodded one by one to each of the engineers, quantity surveyors, promotion men, managers, apprentices, and shorthand minute-takers as they marched past her, into the dying light of late afternoon. The scene resembled mourners leaving a funeral service, though no final benediction had been uttered.

Mr Clay's final report would be submitted at the end of the month, but Sir James could already guess the contents.

'You mustn't be disappointed, Sir James,' Gladys said, placing a chalky hand on his sleeve. 'It may be a delay – perhaps a few years, perhaps more – but your R101 will rise.'

Sir James managed a smile. 'Mustn't grumble. Indeed, it's just as well. That tedious maiden voyage, with Lord Thomson, the Air Minister, and all those boring senior government officials, was bound to be a dismal pilgrimage.'

Chloe Marshall squinted for a moment at the brilliant sunset reflected through her double-glazed window from the side of The Shard. She pressed an inconspicuous button at the side of her gleaming melamine desk, and on the other side of the room, the blinds began their silent descent. 'So they shut down the entire project before they attempted a single long-distance trial?'

'Exactly,' replied Brandon Williams. 'And they were proved right, just a few years later, when the Hindenburg succumbed to exactly the problems they predicted.'

'I'd have liked to meet that Gladys Clay. She sounds like quite a woman. Born the same year as my great-great-grandmother, from what it says here.'

'Your great-great-grandmother, Lady Marshall, was equally skilled in her way. It was only through her sound financial management that her husband, Sir James, was prevented from frittering away the family fortune during those difficult years. The investments she made then formed the basis for Marshall Industries, the enterprise that exists today.'

'You don't need to tell me my family history!' she laughed. 'I get enough of that from our family office – from my brother in particular. But I want to know more about the project that's on the table now. What're we looking at?'

On the transparent display beside her, Brandon brought up the image of an old typewritten document. 'As you saw from the meeting minutes taken that day, one thing Gladys Clay said was, "I believe it could be made to work, but perhaps not with the technology available today." She even gave us a handy list of specifications: to be a viable form of long-distance transportation, an airship would need to withstand penetration, avoid gas leaks, reduce the fire hazard, manage awkward landings in remote locations, and be able to stay up indefinitely if bad weather chased you off your destination.'

'And?'

'It's been a century since anyone has taken a serious look at hydrogen airships. But many of the technologies she said were needed have, in the meantime, been developed. Strong, gas-impermeable, lightweight materials. Enormously efficient engines that can be powered in part through onboard solar films and wind turbines. Weather prediction whose accuracy would stun our ancestors.'

Chloe tapped her perfect fingernails on the desktop. 'Even if it could be done, I doubt anyone I know would want to travel to St Tropez by zeppelin.'

Brandon nodded. 'When most people think of air flight, their first thought is passenger travel, or perhaps cargo. But there are other duties, ones ideal for an airship and not for a plane, or a helicopter, or even a drone. Getting big equipment lifted into remote places. Landing the heads of wind turbines atop their spires. Fighting peat fires in Siberia or in Indonesia. Trailing behind a ship for cloud brightening.'

'Fine. Let's go over your projections. And you know I'm going to challenge every one; my sisters and my brother don't appreciate get-rich-quick schemes.'

Brandon muttered a subtle phrase, and a row of figures appeared on the display. 'Take a look. But before I go into detail, there's something I haven't included.'

'Oh?'

'You've seen what the EU is doing,' Brandon said. 'Emissions regulations are getting stricter by the day, but the supply of sustainable aviation fuel is so tight we'll be battling for it in cage fights. What it means is that sooner or later, conventional flight will become even less profitable than it is now. It may be abandoned altogether.'

Chloe had a faraway look in her eye.

'By the time that happens, we need this technology up and running,' Brandon continued.

'I'll keep it in mind,' Chloe replied.

'And once that happens – once it becomes an option – people will start thinking of more uses for it. We don't yet know what those uses will be, but we know they're out there.'

'Go ahead and speculate,' Chloe said, looking at the thin sunbeam shining from the edge of the blind onto the polished, marble floor, and listening to the quiet hum of the air conditioning. 'We've got time. It's damn hot today, and I'm not going outside any time soon.

The Mother of Erbil

A story by Grace Chan

In one of the worst cases of mass poisoning ever recorded, at least 459 people (and possibly ten times that number) suffered an agonising death when they consumed seed grain treated with methylmercury to prevent fungus growth. The grain, provided by the government to farmers, was labelled in English and Spanish as not fit for consumption. But literacy rates and knowledge of foreign languages were still low in the affected provinces of Nineveh, Kirkut, and Erbil.

What could have prevented people from consuming the treated grain, even though it was mistakenly delivered after the main planting season? How could it have gone differently?

This is us. In 1931, the global average temperature was 0.2°C below pre-industrial levels, and even in 1971 it was still only 0.14°C above pre-industrial levels. Will we educate our citizens and allow them to make the right choices about our future?

Samer and Zahra spent a bittersweet day with family members in Baghdad before their journey to the North in the spring of 1931. As newlyweds, they were brimming over with the emotion and excitement of new possibilities. As citizens of a new country, they were alive with the zeal of nation-building. But as a dutiful son and a loving daughter, they shed many tears bidding good-bye to the homes they had known since childhood.

'What will you do once you've taught the entire province of Erbil to read?' asked Zahra's mother.

Zahra did not reply, but embraced her. Her mother was still young, with sparkling eyes and smooth, unworn skin. By the time she was Zahra's current age, twenty-one, she had already borne four children. But it was a new era. The Kingdom of Al-'Iraq would be different.

'Keep your wife away from the Kurds,' advised Samer's father. 'They are not to be trusted, and their women indulge in witchcraft.'

Samer laughed. 'I refuse to abide by those old superstitions and tribal rivalries, Father! We didn't win our freedom from both the Ottoman and the British Empires just to fall back into barbarism. It's a time of peace, now; a time to bring learning to all the people of Al-'Iraq, no matter what their tribe might be.'

His father harrumphed at the new name of the country. It was created through artifice and back-room deals, constructed from lands and peoples who had been rivals for a thousand years. 'Idealism is a luxury, you know,' he told his son. 'You have an education, which I never had. Let it guide you in what is necessary to survive.'

They took a bus to Kirkuk, where they would stay for a night before proceeding to Erbil. Through its dusty windows, Samer and Zahra watched the endless processions of pale green fields, rumpled mountains, and blue skies. They grabbed each other's arms in excitement when they passed an oil well just being constructed. Oil! It would put their new nation of Al-'Iraq on an equal footing with the other countries in the League of Nations. 'Imagine, Zahra,' said Samer, his eyes fixed on a point beyond the horizon, 'and end to all war – all the peoples of the earth, collaborating as one!' His smile was ecstatic.

Although at thirty-one, her new husband was ten years her senior, Zahra couldn't resist chiding him. 'We have joined the League of Nations, it's true. But it's neither your role nor mine to stop all wars. We're teachers: we must educate the people, so that they can fulfil their civic duties, and their duties to their families.' She turned her gaze from the beauty of the landscape to the narrow, sand-strewn road, full of potholes and treacherous stretches. Within the crowded bus, old men and hungry children on their mothers' laps returned her regard with hollow eyes. 'Our path will not be an easy one.'

'The people need us, and it's our duty to serve,' he replied. 'No matter what we face, together we will do God's will.' His warm, brown eyes gave her confidence, and she smiled.

They had been operating their little school in a village outside Erbil for almost two years, when a new student arrived in the early days of 1933. Barefoot, furious, as tiny as the nursery students, Nadia claimed she was already ten years old, and that her father had fought with the famous Englishman, El Aurens. Zahra, amused, wondered if this time the claim might even be true; there was something fierce in the girl's eyes. Although Nadia knew what books were, she had never held one in her hands. Oh, her hands! They were well-formed and delicate, but they struggled to hold a pen and write letters, no matter how many times the other girls showed her how. Zahra scolded her when she gave in to frustration and howled like a jinn.

But within a short time, Zahra herself was also ready to howl at Nadia's incessant questions. 'The other girls listen and do as they are told,' Zahra told her husband one evening, 'but Nadia pays no attention to how the others act. "Where does the sun go in the evening? How do we know when it's time to plant the fields? Who were the Ottomans? Do the spirits live among us?"'

Samer laughed out loud to hear his wife's uncanny imitation of the demanding girl. 'Oh, I wish we could exchange places for a day! Some of my boys this year are active, others dutiful, but I have none like your little Nadia!'

'Be careful what you wish for!' Zahra chuckled. 'Perhaps one day we will have a daughter and she will be the one to pester you with questions.'

Samer held her hands tenderly and smiled. 'I will never resent a single question that she asks.'

By the time Nadia had been coming to the little school for three years, she had mastered the art of handwriting at last, and far surpassed the older girls. In early 1936 she began her studies of English and other languages, and Zahra despaired of her own ability to stay far enough ahead to teach the girl. Samer reminded his beloved wife to stay alert to the larger context. 'Nadia may grow up to be a teacher herself, or she may raise her own children. But as important as her progress is to you, she is not your only student. Even in these past five years, we have taught hundreds of boys and girls to read. Who knows what fate may bring them?'

Zahra leaned against her husband's shoulder. She was surprised to see that just above his cheek, a single grey hair had appeared at his temple. 'What's this?' she asked, touching it.

'You noticed it, too.'

'It is the badge of your honour. You have taught not just hundreds, but thousands of boys to read. You have taught many of them to understand English. Thus have you earned the sorrow of a single, grey hair.'

They both knew that the grey hair had nothing to do with the stress of teaching; the profession was as much a joy to them now as it had been the day they began. Their sorrow was of another kind, secret and shameful. Five years was too long to wait.

'We're still young and healthy,' Samer said, knowing what was in his wife's mind. 'Maybe it's this diet that they follow here in the North. A teacher's salary cannot pay for more, though I would feed you all the sweetmeats in the world, to make you strong and bring you what you desire.'

Nadia was ten years out of school when she came back to visit. 'How I longed to see my first teacher!' she cried, embracing Zahra. 'I thought you would've stopped teaching long ago.'

'I have no duties beyond this and my husband,' was Zahra's simple reply.

Nadia's voice had mellowed from its childish shrill to a deeper, woman's tone. She used erudite words that Zahra didn't recognise, and carried herself like the daughter of a Shah. 'During the war, as late as 1945,' Nadia said, 'I feared the worst – but you came through it all.'

'I read your stories in the *Erbil News*,' Zahra said. 'You interviewed the rebel, Mustafa Barzani, and we learned what was in his heart.'

'You never could stop me from asking questions,' Nadia laughed, 'and now it is my profession! And they say there will be war again. I will find out.'

'No one could stop you,' her old teacher advised her. 'But don't go so far away; there are many questions to ask right here in Erbil.'

Nadia was not the only student to return, as the years passed. By 1955 some had moved to Baghdad or other cities; many of the boys in Samer's classes went as men to work on the oil wells. Others stayed in the region to plant crops, as their parents and grandparents had done for centuries. Still others moved to the provinces of Nineveh and Kirkut, and started their own schools. Once every few years, a student of exceptional ability would come along, whether a waif wandering in from the mountains as Nadia had, or a rich child from the town, made bratty by lack of challenges. Samer and Zahra taught them all.

Samer died in his wife's arms in winter of 1959. In the last hour, his eyes were clouded with pain, but the fire of learning still burned bright behind them. He spoke with revolutionary zeal of the new Republic of Iraq, and the change it would bring to the nation. Zahra smiled through her own tears. 'My darling, my strength! You're not yet sixty years old. You're far too young. I wish I could have brought you what we both desired. But you have taught so many children; you have accomplished more in your years of life than other men have, even those who lived for 100 years!' He held her hand, and she leaned her head against his shoulder, as she had in the old days.

'You yourself are the mother of all those children,' he replied, in a whisper, and spoke no more. When the time had passed, she willed herself to reach over and close his eyes.

She continued to teach for another decade. The pleasure was still there, to see a child able to decipher, for the first time, a few words or a sentence. There were never enough books in the Republic of Iraq, but she asked the children to scour the land for any scrap of written material, especially anything in English: labels of canned food, many in foreign scripts, newspapers, T-shirts imported from the West with strange slogans. They made a game of it. Using the same principles of literacy they had learned from their teacher, the children treated foreign languages like codes, and flocked to the tiny shelf of books in her classroom to look up the mysterious words.

Yet she no longer had a fraction of the energy she had shared with Samer when they were young. Her body ached every morning and it took her twice as long to get out of bed as it had in the past. Was it something she ate, or didn't eat? She remembered meals of *masgouf* and flatbreads that her mother had prepared. But times had changed, and her parents were long dead. The League of Nations was gone, replaced by the United Nations. Empires had fallen and new ones had arisen. Every day, more and more foreign items were finding their way into Iraq: clothes, tools, food and people were changing their habits. Did the people of Baghdad even eat *masgouf* nowadays?

One morning in 1970, she found she did not have the strength to arise at all.

67

A year after she died, three of her former students gathered at the village souk to shop, eat and gossip. A new kind of barley was on sale. They welcomed its appearance; the drought of the past several years meant that there was not much grain in the stores, and although the latest season's planting was over, the harvest was still far away. The three ladies inspected the sacks and challenged the vendor to give them a good price. As one of them haggled, another peered at the writing on the side of the sack.

'Huda, my sister,' said Yasmin, 'do you remember when we played the game with our teacher, looking up the foreign words?'

'I do!' replied Huda. 'I was the undisputed champion of our class. Give me a piece of writing and I will tell you the meaning, no matter whether it is in Arabic or in English!' she boasted.

'Here – look at this sack.'

Huda looked.

Amal, joining them at the grain stall, snuck a glance over the shoulders of her two friends. 'NO USARLA PARA ALIMENTO,' she said, sounding out the letters. She shook her head. 'I can read well enough in Arabic and Kurdish, but it was always Huda who was best at English. She was always the favourite of our old teacher, may she rest in peace.'

Huda was frowning. 'I think this writing is not in English. It looks as if this grain comes from Mexico.' The three knew very well where Mexico was, for they had seen it on the great map that their teacher hung on the wall; Zahra had to redraw the map's borders many times over the years, as countries grew and shrank, and governments rose and fell. 'But over there, look, the vendor has another sack, with wheat in it,' added Huda. 'The writing on that one is clear: NOT FOR USE AS FOOD.'

Yasmin addressed the surprised vendor. 'Hey there, are you trying to sell us some kind of bad grain? Where did you even get this?' She turned to the other two. 'I'm sure this grain should not be for sale in the first place; no doubt he stole it from the government's donation to farmers. He has torn it from the bleeding hands of the starving poor!'

The vendor defended himself, outraged. 'Oh, look who's so clever, that she can tell everything about the wheat just from looking at a sack!'

'We will not be fooled by your tricks!' shouted Amal. 'We're no simple farmers, you know – we're educated by the great teacher Zahra Hussain Khalil!'

'As who is not, in our region?' whined the vendor. 'You farming women read everything now, thanks to that teacher, but you cause me nothing but headaches when you do. It all comes of giving girls an education,' he grumbled. 'Of course, yes, this is the wheat that the government gave to farmers for seed. But the planting season is already over, so a few of those who had enough stores of their own offered it for sale. What could be more natural?'

'That may be, but we will not put a single grain of it onto our husbands' plates,' Amal cried. Their argument grew heated, attracting the attention of other market-goers, including an elegant woman in her fifties, holding a notebook.

'Hello,' she said to the vendor. 'My name is Nadia Barzani. I am a reporter with *Erbil Farming News*. Where did you get this grain? Is it safe to eat? What does the label say?' She bent down to look. 'Why, the ladies are correct! It's treated grain, meant to be planted, not eaten. You say you got this from the farmers who already had enough to eat? Many others may already be eating it. You cannot sell this as food! See – it says so, here.' Other vendors and customers, curious, gathered to observe the action. Nadia asked each of them for a statement. 'Have you bought a bag of this grain? Did the one who sold it to you claim it was safe to eat? Who is the middleman? When did the product appear on the market? Yesterday?'

The evening edition of *Erbil Farming News* was full of the story, warning farmers not to eat the treated grain, and householders not to buy it. Thanks to the unusually high literacy rate in the province, the rural newspaper was a thriving concern, with both morning and evening editions. Farmers and townspeople alike pored over it, passed it from hand to hand, and discussed its contents over glasses of tea.

By the following morning, newspapers around the country had picked up the story and spread it throughout the provinces of Nineveh, Kirkuk and Erbil. Housewives and farmers tried to determine whether their rice was safe to eat. Nadia questioned agronomists, experts and academics, and each gave their advice: wheat and barley with a pink or reddish-orange hue, with the words NO USARLA PARA ALIMENTO on the sack, should be saved for the next planting season, and neither consumed nor dumped in the water. Livestock who had eaten the grain should not be used for meat. Readers were also reminded that the colour might wash off, but the poison would remain. In a long interview, much discussed in rural areas, Nadia grilled the department head of the Erbil Agricultural

College on how the same grain could be considered safe to plant but not dangerous to eat. The interview was cut out of *Erbil Farming News* and stuck onto boards at the entrances of markets and trading posts throughout the province. A government investigation was launched.

By spring, the scandal had almost died down, but a terrifying echo sent shivers down the spines of those who heard about it.

At an isolated household in Nineveh, a goat was fed on the red-hued grain when its other feed ran out. A week later, it began to stagger as if drunk, and shortly thereafter died in apparent agony.

The same afternoon, Nadia rushed to the farm to cover the news. There, she found a small, barefoot girl, weeping, her arms around the dead animal. The child's mother was attempting to comfort her, telling her to be thankful that it was only the goat who had died.

Nadia remembered that first day, decades ago, when she had marched into Zahra's classroom, barefoot and angry. She felt a sudden shudder of her own.

'It could have been me,' she said to herself. 'It could have been any of us.'

Regicide

A story by Grace Chan

Over the course of the entire twentieth century, around 100 million people died prematurely from smoking. Even today, the WHO estimates that more than eight million people die prematurely yearly from tobacco use. Tobacco has killed more people than the two world wars combined.

Unlike the consumption of alcohol and fermented fruit, however, which has been attested as a core human and animal behaviour at every stage of history, large-scale global tobacco addiction was a deliberate, man-made calamity. Yet throughout its worst excesses, scarcely any leaders spoke out against it. What might have changed if any had?

This is us. In 1952, the global average temperature was 0.1°C above pre-industrial levels. Will our leaders do what is necessary?

Three men met in a small room where every piece of furniture had a pedigree. The ancient fireplace was unlit.

'I have killed one king,' said Harry Atkins, 'and another is dying.'

Across the room, Lord Francis Hollingsworth pressed his thin lips together. 'I hope you understand what you are suggesting.' He removed his immaculate pince-nez, polished them with an immaculate linen handkerchief, and replaced them on his immaculate face.

Harry clasped his hands in his lap, and looked up at Lord Hollingsworth and the Honourable Thomas Fosterleigh. 'I understand. This is why,' he said, with a small cough, 'I believe it would be in our best interest to bring it to the public.'

Lord Hollingsworth turned to the Honourable Thomas, who sat at his side. Their twin armchairs matched their twin suits: traditional, spotless, but worn; the war had affected even the men sitting in this dark, velvet-bedizened room.

'I'm terribly sorry,' the Honourable Thomas replied, 'but that might cause several tiny problems.'

'Yes,' Harry replied, with stubborn sorrow. 'But I will not stay silent. My guilt is too profound. It has been years –' he stood abruptly and walked to the window.

'Come now,' said Lord Hollingsworth, 'don't flatter yourself. If anything – and I'm still not convinced His Majesty is in as bad shape as some are saying – he's done it to himself.'

'Are you so sure?' Harry replied from the window. 'Imagine yourself in his world. Every moment of his life is scheduled, from when he arises to his last cigarette before retiring. He hears what his advisors want him to hear and he knows only what they want to tell him. My position –'

'Is that your official title?' asked Lord Hollingsworth. 'Keeper of the King's Tobacco?'

'Not really. But it is what the rest of the staff call me. "Keeper" has a long history, after all: Keeper of the King's Swans, his Seal, even his Stool. They have all been real titles in the past, while mine is an unofficial one. I give His Majesty his first pipe in the morning and his cigarette after he dines. I did so for his father as well.' He turned back to the other two men. 'I could go to the press. If it's my only option, I will. But it's not my aim to create any embarrassment or difficulty for His Majesty or any member of the Royal Family.'

At his mention of the press, Lord Hollingsworth raised a narrow eyebrow. 'What makes you think the press would listen to you?'

'Don't be daft, Biffy,' the Honourable Thomas told him. 'Of course they'll listen. Those ravening jackals will take any bit of offal a member of His Majesty's staff lets fall from the Palace gutter. Can you imagine if this fellow offers them a full-length interview – a "confession", however trumped-up, of regicide, of all things! Of double regicide, should His Majesty's prognosis prove overly optimistic.'

'That's why the people must know,' Harry said from the window. 'This scourge affects not only His Majesty's subjects at home, but those throughout the Empire. Don't you remember, when His Majesty's elder brother took his North American tour, how the people fawned over him, how they imitated that gilded cigarette case he used to affect? Sales of tobacco must have tripled within the week. Not to mention the ladies who were led into vice by the example of –'

'Yes, yes, by that woman.' Lord Hollingsworth could never be brought to speak aloud the name of the American who had caused the downfall of the Duke of Windsor, as he was now known. 'We all know what havoc she wrought.'

Harry remembered the last days of King George V, the father of the current monarch. To the last day, they told him he would regain his health, even after they had to drain his lung, and his once cultivated voice was reduced to a whisper. Harry looked through the window again; a dusting of snow gave the Palace grounds a veneer of superficial prettiness that masked the greys and browns of early English winter. How many more there would be! Harry thought. And that poor girl, the Princess who would soon be Queen. He'd held her when she was a toddler. As a girl, she filched a cigarette holder from him so that she and Princess Margaret could play-act as the American President and his wife. These days, Princess Margaret, that scamp, was smoking as many cigarettes as she could find. Where would it end?

For years, he had kept a ledger and stock book, noting down the health of his Sovereign every day. The Royal family had lived a privileged life even during the World Wars. They had good food and warm homes with attentive doctors and never suffered from overwork. When young, they were avid horse riders, enjoying the outdoors. Throughout the Kingdom, families prayed for their health every day.

They should all have lived to a ripe old age.

'As children, you know, they don't smoke,' Harry said, as if addressing the empty lawn outside. 'But as adults, they became furious enthusiasts. And then they become dependent: forty, sixty or even 100 a day, even between courses at meals. Their complexions go grey. They wheeze and cough. They suffer recurring bronchitis and pneumonia. And then cancer. When you stand there all day, every day, watching attentively, you see the changes.'

'What is your aim?' asked Lord Hollingsworth. 'Do you wish to deprive the common man of his one comfort after a day of hard work in the mines? The soldier in the trenches of the only thing that will warm him?'

'Not to mention,' injected the Honourable Thomas, 'the conviviality of cigars after dinner. The gentlemen might as well skip their port while they're at it, and go immediately to join the ladies for coffee.'

Harry spun to face them. 'If it must be, then yes! I would have the working man live long enough to know his grandchildren, to enjoy the last years of his life in the bosom of his family, not gasping for breath as his daughters are just on the threshold of adulthood.'

'Biffy,' said the Honourable Thomas, 'let us consider the matter in practical terms.' He stood, tapped his cigarette in the ashtray, and joined Harry at the window. 'If we don't at least make a wee bit of an attempt to appease him, the fellow is going to cause considerable grief to the entire household, not least His Majesty and their Royal Highnesses.'

'Appeasement!' snorted Lord Hollingsworth. 'Look where that got us a decade ago.'

'As His Majesty's private secretary, you can bring the proposition to him, and help him understand the situation. Should he decide not to speak, to say nothing to his subjects about the matter, and then this fellow empties that bowel of a mouth into the waiting maw of the press, at least you and I will have done our duty.'

'I don't need to remind you that he is part of your staff, not mine,' replied Lord Hollingsworth, 'while you expect me to head the forces and storm into the fray. Bloody typical. That's how it has been ever since we were in third form together. But yes, as you say, that is the only *practical* thing to do.'

The Honourable Thomas beamed. 'Splendid! I shall look forward to His Majesty's decision about the matter in due course.'

Harry's expression was not one of triumph, but of profound regret. He sank back into the armchair facing the fireplace.

Lord Hollingsworth addressed him. 'Tell me – have you given up the habit yourself, being as it is that you're such a proponent of preaching its evils to others?'

Harry continued to stare into the ashy fireplace. 'May God help me,' he said, 'I smoke three packs a day. I can't stop.'

His Majesty's voice had become familiar to his subjects during the darkest hours of the war through his radio broadcasts: a slow voice, but steady and pure. Its lack of bombast, its refinement without glamour, was what made it so reassuring. Since the war's end the urgency had lessened. But the authenticity, the tenderness of his words in his new address to his subjects was like nothing they had experienced even when the armies of Fascism were closing in on their islands with relentless force.

Their King spoke with the deepest respect of the death of the former monarch, his father. His reserve and delicacy in approaching such a topic could be faulted by no one. Unlike the Americans, who bared every emotion to the world in an outpouring of grief, or the hot-headed people of southern climes, this was the way of the true Englishman: letting the silences between his words speak more than the words themselves.

He made an oblique reference to his elder brother, now sulking in France, a reference so indirect that it could have been missed had there not been ten million pairs of ears straining to hear any such mention. Those who analysed each word, later, agreed that His Majesty's manner of expressing himself had been perfectly correct.

When he at last returned to his own condition, and revealed what would follow as sure as winter followed autumn, many people swore that they could hear the gasps of their neighbors up and down the street. One weatherman claimed that the barometric pressure all over London had dropped a fraction of an inch due to their collective intake of breath.

He said not a single word that could have been interpreted as political; nor did he expose any lurid personal details other than those which were his duty to reveal. Yet everyone who heard him swore he had created violent emotions in their own hearts. Some were stricken with immediate grief, and wept themselves blind for an evening. Some were relieved to know that their personal struggle was shared with the greatest of the land. Many were enraged; the Thames was polluted for days with cartons of discarded cigarettes and cigars.

A hundred thousand men turned off their radios at the end of the broadcast and reached for a smoke to calm their nerves. Some got as far as lighting it and taking the first puff before cursing and tossing it into the coal stove.

The following day, the great machine of the British press printed the first of many volumes of news and essays on what they dubbed The Great Renunciation. Over the weeks that followed, the topic fed upon itself like a brush fire, producing headline after headline. Some were factual, others quirky. The owner of a building company volunteered to collect every porcelain ashtray in the Kingdom, and grind it up into concrete aggregate for the construction of New Towns. Ladies' societies in every village held tobacco dunking fêtes. These sometimes descended into riots, as cigarettes, cigars and pipe tobacco were plunged into sewers, to the cheers of ragged boys and rowdy men.

The Princesses returned to their father, Princess Elizabeth abandoning her African safari to be at his bedside. Princess Margaret, in particular, was observed by an enterprising delivery man at the Palace, who informed one of the lesser papers, 'Her Royal Highness was as white as a wax candle.'

A day passed when the Renunciation made no headlines, but it was the calm before the tempest. For the following day, page editors across the nation had the opportunity of a career: to set the headline proclaiming the death of their monarch.

And the stories continued.

Some time later, on the other side of the Atlantic Ocean, four men met in a carpeted office on Madison Avenue.

Lloyd Johnson and Tom Miller stood before an easel, explaining the new campaign. 'The old series we were running, the one about "nine out of ten doctors", ended up creating quite a lot of bad blood for the industry. You know, after the British thing. So we've looked for a way to regain the customer's trust.'

'All right,' said Wilmer Reynolds, seated in the office chair that faced him. 'Let's have it.'

Johnson turned over a leaf on the easel, revealing a drawing of a man standing alone on a ranch. The man wore a ten-gallon hat and was gazing into a sunset. 'I would like to introduce a new icon for your brand. A rugged individualist. A true American. He represents freedom, courage, the life every man wants to live. The Marl–' he looked at his clients' scowls, and stopped, confused.

'A cowboy? That's what you've brought us?' said Reynolds.

'Look, son,' said Jefferson Chauncey, hooking his thumbs into the vest of his three-piece suit. "Down in North Carolina, we've got a saying. If the hog is sickening in the pen, it ain't the time to be heatin' up the pan for pork chops.'

Miller spoke up. 'With this campaign, we believe –'

'I don't care one way or another what you believe, boys, because what we've got here is a hog that's already put two front feet in the grave, while his back feet are diggin' in deeper! This British thing, as you call it, didn't just give us a little tiny paper cut. It dealt us a death blow. Did you see those headlines? Miss Marilyn Monroe told *The Hollywood Reporter* that she gave up smoking after she met the Queen of England. In Hollywood, all the leading men are forming renunciation societies. Even right here in New York city, for Chrissake, the damn beatniks have banned cigarettes from their coffee houses! No,' he concluded, 'what we need now is a way to keep our asses from getting sued out of business prematurely, before we can close up shop on our own terms. So what have you got for us, Mr Johnson, that can do that?'

Johnson stared, and then turned the top sheet of the easel back over to obscure the offending cowboy. 'Well, Mr Chauncey, that's not the brief we were prepared for, but let's "brain-storm" for a moment.' He exchanged a glance with Miller.

Chauncey snorted at the young man's use of corporate jargon, but remained in his seat.

'What if, and I'm just thinking out loud here,' Johnson said, 'what if we start up our own renunciation society? We wouldn't call it that, of course. But we could create a nationwide club. Sell the outdoor, rugged individualist, but instead of cigarettes, he symbolises clean living. You'll help people give up smoking and embrace the great outdoors.'

'It would help keep us out of trouble with the Justice Department,' Reynolds mused. 'They've been breathing down my neck ever since the Los Angeles Renunciation Society complained we'd addicted them on purpose.'

'We did addict them on purpose!' fumed Chauncey. 'That's the whole point of selling tobacco. But what's the future of this idea you're proposing? We get everyone to stop smoking, and then what?'

'If you're going to be out of the tobacco business in a few years anyway, the farmers are going to need to find a new source of income,' Johnson replied. 'Let them sell "clean food". Addict your customers to nature. Sell them tours of the Smoky Mountains, led by real mountain men. Sell boots and cowboy hats. Flannel shirts.'

'Have you ever met any of our actual mountain men?' Chauncey chuckled. 'Still, you might have an idea there. God damn it, we need to do something. Might as well try this.'

The bead of sweat that had formed on Johnson's forehead as Chauncey spoke dripped down the side of his head, and disappeared into his collar. He scratched at it in relief. 'Great! Tom, let's get a few of the men to put together a new plan.'

'Fine, fine. Now, son, I wouldn't say no to a little drink if you've got any whiskey on that bar cart of yours. In North Carolina we don't mind having a little something in the mornings to keep up our strength.'

Johnson rushed to fill three glasses with ice and Kentucky bourbon. He smiled and proposed a toast: 'To clean living, gentlemen – and our future!' They clinked.

'I would offer you a cigarette, sir,' said Miller, 'but I'm afraid it wouldn't sit right with the Clean Living brand.'

'Don't you worry yourself about that, son,' Chauncey replied. 'I gave it up years ago. I want to meet my grandchildren, after all.'

Over the next decade, 'Clean Living' became as much a part of the American psyche as GI Joe and a slice of pie to go with your coffee. In particular, the Clean Living Clubs were a hit with the State Department. The government seized on them not only to create jobs for out-of-work tobacco farmers, but to shore up patriotism among young Americans in the face of increasing threats from the Reds. Strong soldiers might be needed for the next war, after all. They pumped funds into the campaign behind the scenes, and within a decade and a half, the 'filthy habit' was only found in out-of-the-way hovels and back alley slums.

Thus it was that by 1972, when five men held an historic meeting on the opposite side of the Pacific Ocean, an awkward moment occurred.

The Chairman, concerned, leaned over to his interpreter. 'Is he seriously ill? Offer him some tea. Was it the crowds?'

The President, green in the face and asphyxiated with coughing, waved away their offers of assistance. 'No, thank you!' he gasped to his own interpreter. 'Tell them I'm – I'm just not much of a smoker.'

'The President accepted your offer of a cigarette at this first, private meeting in the spirit of friendship,' the Chairman's interpreter explained, 'and as a symbol of his readiness to compromise in their negotiations towards our eventual establishment of formal diplomatic relations. But he had never attempted to smoke before, and did not know how. The Americans gave up the custom,' he admitted, 'some years ago.'

'Is it true? He has never tried a cigarette?' the Chairman asked, astonished. He smiled broadly, stood, and strode across the room to pat the President on the shoulder. 'Tell him I appreciate his gesture of friendship, but that it is not necessary.'

'We have a great deal to learn from each other,' replied the President when he had regained his composure, 'and to learn about ourselves through our mutual interest. Although this, our first official meeting, has been primarily symbolic, I hope we can make plans to share our mutual endeavors with the rest of the world in due course. Should I be re-elected this year, our friendship will form the backbone of the relationship between our two great nations.'

'I should add, by the way, that we have every reason to believe that the President will be re-elected without any difficulty,' said a bespectacled, curly-haired man from the corner, the architect of the event.

'Indeed!' the Chairman replied. 'Now, let us discuss some of those matters of mutual interest.'

Long after their meetings ended, the Chairman could be seen taking up a cigarette, opening his lighter, and then replacing both on the table beside him. His advisors wondered what was going through his mind, but did not interrupt him. At one point the Chairman stifled a cough and glanced around with suspicion to see who might have heard.

Over breakfast, he called his Minister of Industry to him. 'The health of the Chinese worker is crucial to our continued pathway towards a thriving domestic industrial base!' the Chairman declared, as if to a cheering audience.

The Minister, puzzled, agreed.

'What is the total output — I mean our national tobacco production?' asked the Chairman.

The Minister riffled through a sheaf of papers that never left his side, and asked, 'The reported figure or the estimated actual figure?'

'The what —? Oh, never mind. It is of no importance. You are to dismantle all our tobacco factories within this month, and redeploy the workers towards duties that will bring prosperity to our nation in line with the fundamental principles of Marxism-Leninism.'

'All of them, Comrade?' asked the Minister, blanching.

'Yes. We are at last reclaiming our proper role as a leading nation. We are a people of great inventions, ancient and celebrated literature, and distinguished philosophy. No foreign addictions will stand in our way! Comrade, please inform the proper people and let me know once the appropriate steps have been taken.'

The Minister took his leave, and the Chairman relaxed, content with his decision. The workers – the workers above all! This would be part of his legacy.

He made a note in the small book he kept at his side, and smiled.

The Shepherd

A story by Grace Chan

On a Sunday in April at the Basilica of St. Teresa in Caracas, Venezuela, an elderly worshipper brushed a veil against a candle, causing a small flame to take hold. The church was packed with more than six thousand people, and an alarmed member of the congregation screamed 'Fire!' In the ensuing stampede, fifty-three people were trampled to death and at least a hundred more were injured.

At important inflection points, rapid action can make the difference between a temporary annoyance and a disaster. In 1952, the global temperature was 0.05°C above the pre-industrial average. Will we listen to those who have the expertise during the crucial decision moment that faces us today, and have the bravery to stand against a crowd?

'Chiquilín, away to me! Bruno, come by!' Before Alberto had finished shouting, the two dogs were already speeding past the sheep.

Alberto stood at the fence and watched them hurtle through the April morning. They'd separated a ewe from the flock for him with expert precision. Chiquilín, tall, energetic and sleek, was the leader; Bruno, smaller, wily and loyal, held back a hair and took in the entire scene even as he streaked around the edge of the flock. They were smart dogs, black and white border collies bred to the job since the time of the Romans, and

Alberto would rather have them looking after his stock than any human shepherd.

Alberto was a llanera stockman whose flock was half again the size of his nearest neighbour. He sold the ram lambs for meat and sheared the ewes for wool. In the semi-arid Lara plains 300 kilometres west of Caracas, it made more sense than trying to keep cattle.

He examined the young ewe and satisfied himself that it was still healthy; its odd gait was more likely the result of a bruised hock than anything serious, and he let it rejoin the others. His next objective was to move the sheep towards fresh grazing grounds through a gap in the long fence that separated them from the lush grass on the other side. Through long years as a stockman, Alberto had discovered that it was healthier for both the sheep and the land to graze in one area until the grass was cropped down to the shoots, even the varieties the animals didn't care for, and then move them all to another area where the sweeter types of grass enticed them while the previous field re-grew. Although the gate was still closed, some of the younger sheep were already attempting to poke their noses through to chomp at the longer blades.

Alberto's younger brother, José, was at the back of the flock on a squat, powerful cow pony, picking up stragglers. Big and slow, José was happy to work hard and let Alberto do the thinking.

There was a lot to think about these days. Since the end of the war half a dozen years before, the country had been through booms and busts, a period of democratic rule and a coup d'état. Each time there was a change of government, the demand for lamb, mutton, and wool would rise or fall, making it impossible for Alberto to plan more than one season ahead. José trusted him to take care of the ranch and of the family, but some things were beyond his control. Politics was one of them: three parties would compete for dominance in the November elections, but rumours were going around that no matter what the outcome, Jiménez would still seize power.

Alberto didn't like the direction things were going. Oil was at the heart of it. It made people greedy, thoughtless. When they heard the very word, they became as stupid as a flock of sheep rushing towards sweet grass, paying no heed to their surroundings. He'd been thinking it was time for the two brothers to pack up and move to the city, where they could find steadier employment.

He whistled, and the dogs tore back toward him, pure exhilaration winging them across the field. When they arrived he praised them, pummeling their shoulders and ruffling their fur until their tails flew back and forth with joy.

The next step would be tricky. It was time to move the herd. He approached the fence, unhooked the gate, and let it swing outwards toward the new field. 'Chiquilín! Away to me!' The collie raced to the back and found his position beside José.

The enormous flock of sheep, following the promptings of the larger dog and big José on horseback, began their lumbering movement toward the gate. Alberto knew the beasts would get caught up in the narrow opening if they all attempted to enter at once. To avoid this, he and the smaller dog stayed steady in front of two placid ewes, holding them in place, while the rest of the sheep streamed around them on either side. Although some snorted and stumbled on their way through, they remained calm. The sound of their plaintive bleating echoed across the plain, followed by grunts of pleasure as they tucked into the grass on the other side of the fence.

Several minutes later, the flock was through. Alberto closed the gate and praised the dogs again, embracing them with rough affection before sending them home to the barn.

José climbed down from his cow pony and asked, 'You still think we should go up to the city this week?'

Alberto nodded. 'Just to get a feeling for things. Nobody knows what's going to happen these days, but I like to take my time, learn what's going on, and get to know the situation. If I'm forced to make a quick decision later on, at least it will be based on experience.'

'Who's going to look after the flock?'

'I've already asked Luis to take care of things here for a few days; his son will look after their place. It'll be a good opportunity for the boy to handle things on his own. Anyway, let's go in and start packing. The bus comes at around seven o'clock in the morning the day after tomorrow.'

José nodded, content. His brother always knew what to do.

A few days later, however, even Alberto was concerned, for the capital city of Caracas was a jubilant mess. Pickpockets, vendors, and honking cars competed for space in the streets, while the air was thick with the odours of food, exhaust, and dust. José, taller, found it easier to see over the mass of pedestrians thronging the plaza in front of the Basilica of St. Teresa but he hesitated, not knowing which way to go.

'It's Sunday,' Alberto declared. 'At home or abroad, we go to Mass.' He led the way through the crowd toward the four lofty columns that marked the entrance to the church.

The Shepherd

Shining white in the hot April sun, not as tall as the great cathedrals of Europe, the Basilica boasted a great dome at its centre, a series of small domes along each side, and two domes at its rear. The walls of grey stone along each side gave visitors the feeling that the roof and its domes were floating above the main structure. Two square towers greeted visitors above the entrance, and two pairs of columns flanked the anterior door.

Ducking into the cool, dim interior, Alberto felt a sense of relief despite the press of the crowd. The pews were full. Old women, mothers and children, and serious-faced men numbered among the pious. The women's veils ranged from a full skirt of black lace that covered the entire head to a careless pocket handkerchief pinned on in haste. Wealthy church-goers dressed in their finest, and poor men at the back came in the only shoes they had – their own bare feet. Alberto and José crossed to the opposite side of the church, taking a moment to genuflect, and stood to the left of the great double doors.

'There must be a thousand people here!' José whispered in awe.

'More like five thousand, if I know how to count sheep,' replied Alberto, making a quick estimate. A thin woman brushed past him, and his hand flew to the pocket where he kept his wad of bills and his papers. To his relief, everything was still there. What he had to steal was little enough, but it was all they had, and Alberto had heard stories. One of the double doors was shut for that very reason – to make it that much more difficult for a fleeing thief to escape.

The Mass was about to begin. The resonance of the last bell died away, and the shuffles and sighs of the congregation were soon replaced by the swell of the choir from the upper gallery.

When the processional hymn ended, the familiar cadence of the Latin mass began: In nomine Patris et Filii et Spiritus Sancti. The brothers crossed themselves.

Half an hour later, the priest completed the Agnus Dei and Alberto heard the hymnals of the choir rustling as they prepared to sing again. The Mass concelebrants gathered at the head of each aisle, ready to offer the Eucharist to the faithful, and Alberto allowed himself a sour moment to note that the traffic management inside the church was superior to that outside. He did not explore the thought further, however. In the pause just before the hymn began, a single word rang out from somewhere at the front of the church.

'FIRE!'

A man standing along the back, even taller than José, cried out an instant later. 'Her veil – the candles!' A shriek answered him, followed by a confusion of wails.

'FIRE! FIRE!' another voice shouted in answer. Alberto glimpsed a tiny flame licking up the side of a small cloth, but he could not tell what was happening. Someone knocked over a pew, and the three behind it fell backward like dominoes. Women screamed, men shouted, and thunder of ten thousand feet hammered against the stone floor.

Without looking, Alberto already knew that the door, bolted on one side, would be too narrow.

He was proven correct: people were already jammed in the space, shouting and pushing. A veiled, elderly woman fell to the floor and Alberto lost sight of her. More people pushed past him, their eyes crazed with fear.

'Slower! Slow down!' he shouted, to no effect.

There was one thing left to try. He linked arms with José and braced himself. His brother, terrified but trusting, stood at his side, his bulk acting as a barrier against the flow of people. Together, they pressed their shoulders into the advancing wave.

'Split them up!' he called out to José, hoping that his brother could understand him amid the cacophony. 'Break the flock into two.'

At the word 'flock', understanding dawned on his brother's face, and they leaned into the packed crowd.

Their temporary obstruction at last released the clog in the door; a second later, people streamed past them on either side. Dozens, then hundreds rushed out. An older man bellowed to the others to get out of the way, while a younger man threw his arms in the air with a wail, and allowed himself to be carried out by the people pressing against him on either side.

As the brothers strained to hold their place in front of the door, Alberto cast about to see what had happened to the fallen elderly woman. With his free arm, he pointed at a worried-looking young man in a striped shirt who was moving at a more deliberate pace than the others. 'You, in the striped shirt! Find the old woman on the ground!' The young man, surprised, turned his head to see whether Alberto was addressing someone else, and then searched the floor. Spotting the old woman under the collapsed pew, he pulled her out and helped her to her feet. They tumbled together towards the door.

Hundreds more pressed past, still terrified.

Alberto swayed on his feet, but José stabilised him, planting one foot forward and the other back, at right angles to each other. Together, they stood firm, a rock in the flood of people. Alberto's head ached, and his ears rang from the screams. He thought he would faint.

Then, in an instant, it was over.

The church was empty, except for a faint whiff of smoke and the smell of sweat and incense. A priest had stripped off his cassock and was using it to snuff out the remaining embers of the tiny blaze. Papers littered the floor, strewn among dropped shoes and a children's prayer book. Another priest wiped his forehead and walked toward the brothers.

'You were here by God's grace today,' he told them. 'From the altar I could see what happened.'

'Thank you, Father,' Alberto mumbled, studying his feet. Confident among his sheep and worshipped by his dogs, he'd always been bashful around strangers and authorities.

'How did you know to stand in front of the door like that?' the priest asked, brushing the dust from his vestments. 'You saved many lives, I believe.'

'Sheep,' blurted out José. He fell silent, looking to his brother for guidance.

'The animals flow faster through the gate when you split the flow,' Alberto explained at last. 'You just have to be able to stand there and defy them. Often, they don't even touch you as they go past. Seems to be different with people,' he concluded, rubbing a bruised arm.

The priest nodded. 'Come with me, my sons. We will eat together and celebrate your selfless act. For it was my predecessor, Peter, who said to the first flocks of our Church,

"And when the Chief Shepherd appears, you will receive the crown of glory, one that will never fade away.'"

The throng milled about on the plaza outside, crying with relief and wondering what had happened. The sun shone on the white domes of the Basilica, and six thousand souls sent their thanks heavenward.

The Coalbrook Deception

A story by Grace Chan

One evening in 1960 at the Clydesdale Colliery in South Africa, 437 men died in terrifying conditions almost 200 metres below ground, when 900 pillars caved in, suffocating or crushing the miners trapped inside.

It was one of the worst mining disasters in history. Tragically, information about several separate pillars collapsing, which resulted in the phenomenon of cascading pillar failure, was not recognised or put together in time to evacuate the miners. Or, if it was recognised, no one took action in the crucial window when it could have made a difference; supervisors shouted at the men to return to work.

This is us. In 1960, the global average temperature was 0.12°C above pre-industrial levels. Will we notice the obvious signs that surround us, and take action before it's too late?

It was the first time for either of them to go down in the rattling lift, and they stood side by side, letting no one know how afraid they were.

Sixty other men and boys jammed themselves in for the morning shift. Some were just out of school, and others had wrinkles in their skin as fine as spider's silk. They would have bid farewell to the sun as they entered, but it was already shrouded by the thick, black cloud of coal smoke that billowed from the great engine that powered their descent.

Nels and Victor Nkwinika faced the accordion doors, their backs rigid. Skinny Victor stared ahead, while stout Nels squeezed his eyes shut. 'Clear!' rasped old Milton Mnguni. The top of the door closed from above, meeting its counterpart in the middle, and the cage was complete.

Milton caught Victor's eye, gave an outrageous wink, and smiled as he manipulated the pedals.

Caught off guard, wiry Victor guffawed, startling his brother out of his stupor. He was still smiling as the powerful lift began its rapid, 200 metre journey downwards, and muttered something to Nels in Xitsonga. The latter craned his neck upwards to see whether the old operator was still at it. But the world above was gone as they rushed into the mouth of the mine.

When they emerged ten hours later, the light had already given way to the inky darkness that exists only in a South African night. Filthy, bone tired, and at the edge of their nerves, the boys alternated between boasts about the exploits of the first day and unexpected silences. Old Milton fell into a comfortable stride with them as the three walked down a dusty track back to the hostels.

'That first time down the mine; it's not easy,' he told them. 'I remember it. Where have you come from?'

The two looked at each other before answering; it was a habit they had. 'Caputine,' Victor replied.

'Where's that?'

'To the East.' Nels was the one to answer this time. 'Where the Portuguese are.'

'Ah, yes, so-called "Portuguese" East Africa,' Milton snorted. He chatted as they walked, slow and steady, never changing his stride; it was surprising how much stamina he had for a man of his age. The boys, for all the exuberant foot races of their childhood, struggled to keep up. 'And you're – brothers?' Milton asked. 'Close together, from the looks of you.'

This time their silent conference lasted longer. 'We are brothers of the same father,' admitted Nels at last. 'Born in the same month. But my mother and our father died in the last epidemic, and Victor's mother sent us here. She was our father's second wife.'

'Oho,' Milton chuckled. 'When I was younger, I thought of taking a second wife, but it would have been a big mistake! I am already suffering from the tongue of the first one, and it only grows sharper with age. Not to mention the fact that the church says it's a sin.' The boys offered a polite laugh in response, and Milton sang the first lines of a bawdy song in Hlubi. The brothers couldn't understand the lyrics, but they gathered from his tone and gestures that it was meant to cheer them up. Their faint smiles went unnoticed in the darkness, but after Milton had sung through the refrain, they joined in as best as they could, their confident harmonies offering a warm contrast to his hoarseness.

A small wooden church stood at the edge of the village where the miners lived. 'The men here are formidable singers, you know. They will appreciate the two of you,' Milton told them. 'Will you come on Sunday? My voice is no use to them any more; if you opened up my chest, it would look like the inside of a termite mound.'

They already missed the camaraderie of their congregation back home, but they hesitated to agree. 'We will think about it,' Victor said. 'Our – my mother might not like it, with our father so recently dead.'

'Yes, you must consider what your mother might say, if she were at hand!' cried Milton. 'But remember, boys here become men within a short time. Then it is she who will ask you for permission. Sleep well,' he said. 'Brothers should look after each other, whether awake or in dreams!'

As the old man walked away towards his hostel, Victor reverted to Xitsonga, speaking in a low voice. 'Does he know?'

'How could anyone not know?' Nels replied. 'Our mother thinks that by making you grow your hair out like a mushroom, and by feeding me until I'm fat, our faces will be disguised. But a man like this Milton Mnguni, he sees everything.'

'At least you are being fed! I wish it were me. Instead, you enjoy everything while I starve.' Victor's voice was bitter.

'I'm the one who must invent the memory of a false mother. In any case, it is better to starve a little than to dine on clay,' Nels retorted.

Victor looked away; he knew what Nels was speaking of. Superstitious about the misfortune that would follow, too many of the women in their village who bore twins put a lump of clay in the mouth of their newborns, or abandoned them to the elements.

Although the practice was dying out, the untimely death of their father had revived their neighbors' ancient terror of twins. A few days after his funeral, at their mother's insistence, they were climbing the ladder onto the roof of a rickety bus. She had disappeared into the cloud of dust that they left behind.

Half a year passed, and Milton Mnguni said nothing to make them suspicious. They learned to stay separate from each other. Victor cultivated a deliberate growl to his voice and kept away from church; Nels practiced his high tenor in the choir, and ate as much as he could.

Before work, Nels hung around the creaking, powerful lift and pestered Milton with questions about the operation of the tubs and the administration of the tally board. Below, Victor learned to distinguish pure coal from the slag that was good only to be crushed and carted away, and hours with the sledgehammer hardened his scrawny arms into steel bands of muscle. He volunteered for night shifts and slept in the afternoon sun, darkening his skin to a deep wenge. He met Nels only on Sunday afternoons, during their precious hours of rest.

'Why do we bother?' he asked Victor as they sat in the tiny miners' bar nursing bottles of warm beer. A woman came to their little metal table, gave an inviting smile and shook her belt made of bottle caps, but the boys were absorbed in their conversation. 'We make all this effort to look different from each other, just so we can work in the same place, but I seldom see you as it is. Why don't you go to another mine somewhere? Then nobody will know I exist and we could both be free.' The woman pouted and danced to the next table. Her hips moved in time with the rhythm of Lloyd Price, playing on the scratchy record player in the corner.

'How do we know there is a job available at another mine?' Nels pointed out. 'And how much do we need to pay to find it? Our mother sold half of the items in our household just to get us here.'

'Still. Aren't there mines in other countries?' Victor asked, lifting the bottle to his mouth. Nels saw his brother's ropy muscles move beneath his skin and wondered at the transformation.

Nels swallowed the rest of his own beer and gnawed on a strip of *biltong*. 'Milton told me he was put to work abroad after the war. He was in *Wales* for ten years. But his lungs were ruined, so they sent him back. That's why he operates the lift now.'

'He's kind to you,' Victor said. 'He likes you. Maybe he can find us a job in *Wales*.'

'I doubt it. Anyway, who wants to work with a bunch of *umlungu*?' Nels startled himself with his own daring and glanced at the bar door with its fluttering pennants.

Victor laughed. 'No reason to be nervous; none of the *umlungu* hang around this bar.'

Nels nodded. 'Anyway, Milton says that when you're down in the mine, everyone is the same color.'

'You're beginning to sound like him,' Victor teased.

'Ha! You're the one whose voice is getting to be more like a *ngongoni* every day. Do you still remember how to sing?' Nels gave a friendly punch to his brother's arm. 'Oww!' he cried, rubbing his knuckles. 'Even your arms are made of hard coal now.'

'I'll toughen up my arms as long as you toughen your mind. Keep learning what you can from old Milton.'

Within another six months, the mine supervisor had accepted the situation that already existed in practice, and assigned Nels to be a part-time apprentice to old Milton. He learned the details of weighing, lift operation, and coal grading. It gave them more time to talk. Nels perched on a little stool next to Milton, ready to jump up and fetch a piece of chalk or a drink of water if he wanted them, and to entertain him with questions when errands weren't needed.

'I was with the men working in Section Ten today, raising the roof,' he told the older man.

'Top coaling. It's a common practice. How did it go?'

'I don't know; I'd never done it before. But the pillars look taller and thinner than they did before. And some of the coal we cut is different to what we usually cut – not as hard.'

'It's a lower grade of coal. The power stations will take this rough stuff now. There was no use for it in the early days.'

'But the pillars are thin and weak. Some of the men were talking about it. Should they be worried?'

'It's hard to tell,' Milton replied, reflecting. 'When I was in *Wales*, they used wooden pit props to support the roof. You could hear them groan and creak if there was subsidence in the rock above, and the sound of it would give you time to get out and avoid a collapse. But here, the pillars are carved from the rock itself, and they're meant to be in place for years. The pillars in the south and west sections of the mine have been standing for decades.'

Nels raised an eyebrow. 'So how do you know if something is going to go wrong?'

Milton stared off into the dusty camp for an eternity. 'I'm getting thirsty. Can you fetch me something to drink?'

Nels knew when it was time to stop asking questions and start watching.

Christmas came and went. It was only a few days after the holiday, and Victor's section team were walking toward the lift with a heavier stride than usual. As they waited for their turn, a cutting machine operator commented, 'You're Nels's brother, aren't you? I know him from the church choir. He's quite the singer! The church was packed for the choir service. What a pity you never join us.'

'Me? Oh, I have no voice for singing. Maybe, maybe he got it from his mother. Meanwhile, all my mother gave me was my bad luck with love.'

The operator laughed. 'And it looks like Nels's mother taught him how to enjoy a good dinner, as well! If he met a hippo in the river, I don't know which one would make a meal out of the other!'

Victor's polite chuckle was ripped out of him, as a thunderous roar sounded, and a blast of wind knocked the entire group to the ground.

The noise subsided, and he lay on the hard floor of the mine, astonished, waiting for the pain to hit. Within a moment, he felt the throb in his backside and his shoulder blade, but he was not seriously injured; his predominant feeling was surprise. The men around him struggled to their feet one by one and stood in silence, listening.

There was nothing.

Victor shook his head to clear his ears, but heard only dripping water and the normal sounds of the mine. A moment later, the creak and grind of the lift resumed. It arrived, and the man in front opened the accordion doors with a rush of and rattle of metal. They entered without a word, alert and silent.

They were halfway to the top when Victor spoke. 'What in the hell was that?'

'Pillar collapse. It happens sometimes.'

Victor mastered his shaking limbs, but could not prevent his heart from pounding so hard he was sure the others could hear.

He had to wait six days before he could see his brother at the little miners' bar, and tell him what happened.

'Did someone inform the inspector?' Nels asked. He'd already chewed through three pieces of *biltong*. It was becoming a nervous habit. The woman with the bottle cap belt sniffed and ignored him as she passed their table.

'Yes. He said it was a pillar in Section Ten,' Victor said. 'They had cut it too thin, or maybe the coal was too weak. It was just a fluke that no one was directly underneath. They're giving the instructions to check the other pillars now.'

Nels shook his head. 'Where are you working on your next shift?'

'I don't know. We're assigned day by day. I don't suppose you and Milton have anything to do with it?'

'No, the boss is in charge of all that. I've never even seen the entire mine; it's more than a mile and a half from end to end.'

'Sometimes it feels like longer,' Victor admitted. 'But even more so, for you! You spend your days with Milton, weighing coals and taking notes; you probably couldn't run from the eastern to the northern section without stopping for breath.'

'I'll race you now, and win, too!' Nels boasted.

Victor stared at the door and the sunshine outside. 'We're no longer kids, Nels. We don't need to run foot races.'

Nels stood up and threw a little money on the table for the drinks. 'Maybe you've already become a man, Victor, but I'm not. I'm just as scared as I was when I was a child. Come on. Run a race with me to clear our minds. If nothing else, it will give me a chance to practice not looking like you!'

Victor smiled at last, and Nels understood what he had been missing; his brother hadn't laughed since Christmas. 'Fine!' Victor said. 'But I won't go easy on you. See that chinaberry tree over there? First one to touch it and make it back to the bar door is the winner!'

'You're on!' said Nels.

'Go!' cried Victor, and the two scampered towards the tree, laughing as if they had nothing else in the world to worry about.

More than three weeks passed, and Nels spent much of it in deep conversation with Milton. For the first time, he heard darker stories of Milton's time in *Wales*.

'It's not how much you know about any one thing; it's how you put the information together.' The old man paused to cough. He hacked and spit for a full minute, recovered himself, and continued. 'I was a young, stupid kid, and I only paid attention to myself. Sure, I noticed my throat hurt after I'd been working a long shift. But if I'd talked to the others, and seen that it was happening to more than one of us, I might have noticed the damage it was doing to me. To all of us.' He coughed again. 'That's the great sorrow of age. You know enough to no longer fixate on a single antelope, but to look at the entire herd. But you no longer have the energy to chase down even a single one.'

'I'm sorry to hear it.'

'You know, I was a singer when I was your age, same as you. They invited me to sing in the *umlungu* choir, with the other miners. It could happen like that here, one day.'

Nels remembered what he had heard from the other men and shook his head in doubt.

It was late afternoon when they felt, rather than heard, a rumble below, and the alert buzzer began to shriek. Milton turned to the lift operation levers. 'Start checking the tally board when they come up.'

Both levels of the double-decker lift were packed with men, dusty, frightened, and trembling. 'It was Section Ten, in the northern part,' one of them told Milton, throwing the cage doors open. 'Another pillar collapse, I assume. Knocked us off our feet again.'

'Anyone hurt?'

'No. We were well away from that area.'

An hour later, a new group emerged and Nels checked each of them as they placed their tags on the board. 'Yet another pillar,' an older man explained, nursing a bruised shoulder.

'Section Ten?' asked Milton.

'No, Section Nine.'

Struggling to track the tags, Nels could not see Milton, but he heard something in the old man's cough that stopped him in his tracks. He turned back to the top of the lift shaft just as a third group was emerging, this time a roof cutting crew, boisterous and defiant. 'Phew!' one of them cried. 'Thought we were done for! It was worse than my mother-in-law's shout, followed by her breath!' The group was laughing in relief and punching each other in the arm.

The supervisors were shouting, 'Back in the mine! There's work to be done.' The men were milling about, uncertain, buzzing with rumors.

Milton shook his head. 'One pillar collapses, we can blame it on the particular composition of the coal in that particular place. But three of them – each one might be weakening the next. I saw it in Wales, once. The pit props fell, one by one, like a row of drunk men standing side by side, when one falls and knocks down the rest, all in a chain.' He paused, and reached for the heavy black phone. 'I believe we should call the inspector. He might want to check on the safety of the other pillars this very evening.'

Nels was frozen, but only for a moment. He searched frantically through the big board for Victor's name and work assignment. 'Milton, it's what you described,' he said.

'What's that?'

'You're seeing the big picture, but you're taking no action. Do whatever you can right now to stop the supervisors – you need to keep these men who have already come up from going back down. But send me down now.' Before the older man could respond, Nels was at the lift, ripping open the accordion doors. With reluctance, Milton pressed the pedal and the machinery groaned. As Nels descended, he heard Milton beginning a long-winded discussion with the supervisors.

The cage door opened in the dimness below, and Nels tore out of the lift into the tunnel toward the eastern section of the mine, the miner's battery bouncing against his hip. Within moments, he was panting from the exertion, but there was no choice: it was his brother in there, his twin, the one person most like him in the entire world.

He tripped and grazed his hands on the rough floor, but couldn't see the scrapes in the dimming helmet light.

It was a mile and a half from the northern gate to the eastern work area, he remembered. I can make it. It's no longer than any foot race we ran as children. He remembered to take deep breaths, the way he did before singing a long note. His lungs and his legs burned, but he kept running.

The routine noises of a team at work told him he was close to the destination. As soon as he thought he could be heard, he shouted. 'Get out! Victor! All of you! The pillars in Section Ten are collapsing. Get out! Victor!' He stopped, and leaned against the wall, heaving. 'Get out! Roof fall! Victor!'

The men stopped, confused. 'Is something happening?' one asked.

But the moment Victor saw Nels's face, he sprang into action. 'It's my brother. Come on! Let's get out!'

The two boys sounded the alarm to the rest of the team, and before long the deafening machines were rumbling to a halt. The men shouted to each other, 'Don't rush, but don't waste time. Let's go!'

Nels knew, rather than felt, that Victor's arm was propping him up as he ran back with the other men, all the way toward the lift entrance. The eerie silence of the mine was like nothing he had heard; not a single machine was humming or roaring, not a single hammer or shovel was tapping or clanking. Only the tramping feet and the cries of the men, encouraging each other to make haste, were audible. Fine dust hovered everywhere.

Victor and Nels were in the last group to the surface, standing with grim expressions just inside the door on the lower tier of the lift. The two brothers held each other's arms, their heads tilted upwards. Evening was falling as they emerged, and the red sun was sinking behind the trees. Nels staggered to the tag board, ensuring that every man was accounted for.

Victor walked towards a small grove and collapsed on the ground, looking up at the sky. A single star was visible in the darkening gloom. A few minutes later, another star appeared, and the faint light of a third emerged. Nels finished the tally and dragged himself to join his brother, flopping onto the coal-stained earth.

They didn't know how long they had been sitting in silence when the roar began. A massive column of dust thundered up and out of the lift shaft, covering the terrified men. Incredibly, it continued for twenty minutes, as the collapsing mine pillars fell like dominoes, shunting the air out of the way and out through its only route of escape. The men scrambled to a safe distance and stood in awe, wondering what dread fate they had avoided.

When at last the roar ended, Milton, his mouth and nose covered with a dusty cloth, emerged from the lift operation room.

He came to the grove where the two brothers were lying, and painfully sat down next to them. 'After this,' he said to Victor, 'I hope you will at last stop pretending, and agree to sing in the choir.'

'What?'

'Nels saved 1,000 men today. They will not care that you are twins.'

'How –" Nels couldn't finish his own question.

'Voices like your brother's don't appear often in our choir,' Milton said, still addressing Victor, 'and God has granted us two of you. Come and sing, now.'

'You knew?' Nels asked. 'You knew we were twins.'

'How could I not? You may have deceived others, with your big belly and puffy hair, but I am too old to be fooled by such tricks. Moreover, I heard you both singing under your breath that first morning, as you were waiting for the lift.' Milton's scratchy voice traced the outline of a melody as he repeated the old lines: "'I was foolish to marry hurriedly / I wish I had stayed / At my mother's house / I would not be experiencing such anguish! / I was foolish to marry / What sorrow is mine! / Now I have conceived in twos ....'"

Nels shook his head in wonder. 'It's the song our mother used to sing when she was sad. We must have been singing it to calm our nerves. But I didn't know you could understand Xitsonga.'

Milton shrugged. 'I have learned many things in my life. After all, it's for the old to know things, and for the young to act.'

'When we have a reason to do so,' Nels replied.

'You had an excellent reason today,' Victor said. 'And you were willing to go.'

'You were willing to listen.'

'When we have those who are willing to listen, and those who are willing to act,' Milton said, 'it gives me hope for our future together. Now, let us be silent again, and watch the stars come out.'

The Flixborough Legacy

A story by Grace Chan

On the first of June, 1974, disaster struck the town of Flixborough, in north Lincolnshire, England, when a chemical plant exploded, killing or injuring more than half of the people on site. According to the campaigners of the day, 'the shock waves rattled the confidence of every chemical engineer in the country.' A simple case of negligence. But how could it have gone otherwise? And how would that have affected our world today? In that year, the global average temperature was 0.3°C above pre-industrial levels.

This is us. Individual decisions never occur in a vacuum — and neither do their far-reaching consequences.

'Auntie Nell! It's me, your long-lost nephew, come to stay.' Jimmy stood at the worn, wooden door, uncertain about whether to enter, as the rain spit and drizzled outside.

'Come in, come in. Get out of the wet! Oh, and look at you! You're already a man grown! I remember when you were ....' She made a vague gesture, not much above her waist. 'Set your wellies over here.'

Jimmy laughed as he doffed his mackintosh and struggled out of the big boots. 'I'm already thirty-five, Auntie Nell! And who's this?' He leaned down to scratch the cat's head, found a peg inside the closet door for his coat, and lugged his overstuffed duffel bag into the warm kitchen. There, he breathed in a delicious mixture of sage, fennel, and sizzling fat. Sausages. On the small television in the corner, Keegan's second goal against Newcastle in the Wembley final was being shown for the hundredth time. The crowd roared.

'The cat? That's Felix, there. Now, I've put you in the box room. The bed's a bit cramped but you'll be alright. It's upstairs to the left.'

'I've been at too many boarding houses to complain, Nell. But I don't suppose I could convince you to make a toad-in-the-hole for me some evening? I've not been home to have one from my Mum, not in an age.'

'That's what we're having for tea tonight.' She switched on the oven light and leaned down to peer inside. 'It's almost ready. You've arrived not a moment too soon. Come, come, come. Now tell me again, what is it you're doing here in Flixborough? The trawlerman's life in Grimsby isn't for you, then? Not that I'm not glad to have you. It gets lonely here.'

Jimmy grew pensive. 'The fish stocks aren't what they used to be, Nell. To tell you the truth, I'm the last of the men there to throw it all in.'

She nodded as she brought out two old plates and various mismatched cutlery. 'So I've heard. It's just as well, Jimmy. That's no kind of life. A dangerous job, and a tough one. I've been wanting to know when you'll settle down. Is that why you're back?'

He laughed. 'There's a girl out there for me somewhere, Nell, but I haven't found her yet. For now, I've got a job. It's at a scaffolding company, handling a contract at the Nypro plant.'

'Oh, that place. I can see it from the bottom of my garden. The noise of the factory doesn't bother me – my hearing isn't quite what it used to be – but it smells something powerful.'

'Hence the scaffolds: they're doing repairs,' he replied.

'Don't you miss it, though? The sea. Your uncle Mark, he spent his whole life as a trawlerman. You always took after him, you know. His mother told me that when he was a little boy, he used to dress up in his father's breton cap and yellow overalls, and tell the world he was going out to take in a haul of fish. And I'll be blessed if he didn't do just that.'

'The new job pays well enough to make me forget all about the sea. I'm the charge hand, the head of our team here.'

'Well, now, don't be getting above yourself. You may be the boss of your scaffolding crew, but while you're here, I've got plenty of jobs for you. There's the greenhouse that your Uncle Mark put up. It's nothing but a bunch of big tatty holes now. My tomatoes hardly came in at all this year.'

The box bed was more comfortable than he had expected, and Jimmy adjusted to the new routine. The greenhouse was another story, however. His uncle had extended it several years back, with two ill-fitting parts at different levels, so that Nell could grow onions in a raised bed, while the lower bed was tall enough for tomatoes. But not all was right.

'It's the wind that breaks the connection between the two parts of the greenhouse,' Jimmy told his aunt. 'The air pressure on each section is different. They move separately, and the plastic tears. I've tried all types of reinforcement, and it rips every time. The two pieces need to be separate. It's broken three times already. But it's more than that.'

She gave him a keen look. 'Something more than your uncle's old greenhouse?'

'Right you are, Nell. It gives me a bit of a worry about a piece of work we put together a few weeks ago, down at the factory. They've taken out one of the big, corroded reactors. And they needed a bypass connection in the meantime. But the reactors are at different heights, so there is a dog-legged piece of pipe connecting one vessel to another. They used these big accordions – bellows, they call them – to connect the pipe to the reactors, to allow it to move a bit. At its heart, it's not so different from your greenhouse here.'

Nell sat back in her flowered chair, with its chintz almost worn through. 'Are you saying the pipe down at the factory will break down, just like my greenhouse?'

'I don't know. But it might.'

'Will you speak up, then?'

'It's not my place to tell them how to run a factory. I'm not one to go with my boots on when they're in there with their tweed jackets, leather elbows, and pipes.'

As she always did when she was pondering a problem, she shuffled to the sink, filled the kettle, and put it on the hob. 'Come have a cup of tea, Jimmy, and we'll think it through.'

They talked long into the night. It was a funny thing about his aunt Nell. She never gave him advice, outright, except when it came to finding a nice girl, or looking after his good-for-nothing younger brother. But after they'd had a good chat, things always became clearer.

The next evening, he was shaking out his umbrella as he entered his aunt's house. 'I spoke to the boss today,' he told Nell. 'It wasn't near as bad as I thought.'

'Then there was no danger, after all?'

'Oh, there was danger, all right! They shut down the entire operation within the half hour. But nobody blamed me. No, when I took the boss down to the scaffold, and showed him the rub marks on the planks, where the ties were shifting, he got a right worried look on his face. I led him past the bellows, and he went grey as ash, and shook my hand, and ran back to the office as fast as I've ever seen a man run who was wearing a tweed jacket.'

She nodded. 'Just as I said. He saw it for himself, and that was all that was needed.'

'There's going to be a hearing.'

Another nod. 'You'll need to polish your shoes, then.'

The day of the hearing came, and it was like nothing Jimmy expected. The men who questioned him had no nonsense about them, and they kept at it for more than an hour. But he found their discussion confusing. Although something had gone wrong, they did not find fault with any individual. Instead, they spoke of things like 'process', and 'systemic risk', and 'built-in safety features' and 'culture of transparency'. But it was clear his alert to the foreman had profound implications. A huge, flammable vapour cloud would inevitably have found a spark to ignite it, ending in a vast explosion. The expert showed a map, with circles on it drawn in red pencil. Thousands of buildings crowded inside the outer circle. And inside the innermost circle, covered in the darkest red, Jimmy recognised Nell's house and garden.

A grave man with thick, horn-rimmed glasses spoke. 'There's more to operating a safe plant than a regular equipment inspection and a safety test. We need men to keep their eyes open, and to have the bravery to speak up, including to their superiors. Gentlemen of the committee, and lady, I should say, I would like the Factory Inspectorate to investigate this incident as if it had indeed all gone wrong. As if we were all sat here today mourning the loss of hundreds. I urge you to take this opportunity, to make the name Flixborough famous – because it's here that a new industry-wide improvement must begin, one that prevents future calamities, as this one has been averted.'

A fair-haired young man in the gallery, his eyes wide set, with the hint of a tilt to them, listened to the expert's speech. Alexei's teachers kept suggesting to him that whenever he found out about any public speech, lecture, hearing, or event going on, that he make a point of attending and listening to it. 'As an English learner, you'll find there's no such thing as too much exposure to the language.'

It was different advice from that of his English teachers back home in Moscow. The teachers in the UK were kind, but odd; and he heard and read little of the capitalist propaganda that he had been led to expect by his Soviet minders.

Indeed, what he wanted most of all from his study trip was to find an English girl, since everyone said they were 'liberated'. Alas, none were to be seen at this obscure hearing about a chemical plant – an ex-fisherman, a factory boss, and several stuffy academics. A week prior, he had seen a promising young woman with long, ironed hair at the lecture on rose cultivation over at the crumbling manor house, Bailey Hall, but nothing came of it. He haunted flower shows for the next month, hoping to catch another glimpse of her; instead, he was drawn into an extended, one-sided lecture on hybrid grafting by a befuddled, white-haired man convinced Alexei was from Scotland.

Overall, the cultural exchange had made an enormous improvement to his English, but to his social life not a bit   .

Months later, after his return to the Soviet Union, Alexei found it difficult to secure a position that made use of his English skills. He and the other 150-odd student cultural ambassadors had been selected for the exchange because of their political virtue. But upon the end of the program, their very contact with Western, capitalist ideas rendered them suspect.

He cast about in several academic and administrative roles, always trusting the Party to find what was best for him. In Minsk, he met Alina, a girl from a good family, whose father had fought against the Nazis. She was an electrical engineer.

More than a decade after he completed his degree, he and Alina got a placement in a backwater power plant in the SSR of Ukraine. People spoke a strange kind of Russian there. It sounded odd compared to his own, a pure Muscovite variety. They insisted it was a distinct language, in fact. His role was to translate technical documents, a job he was eminently suited for. He also stayed on hand at the plant, often taking the night shift, to act as an on-call translator whenever someone needed to check the specifications of a piece of imported equipment, or refer to one of the many written scientific papers obtained from Western sources.

Alexei found it difficult to form friendships in his new city, Pripyat. People were narrow-minded, suspicious. But after several months, a few of the longer-term residents opened up.

'I've been here since the early days,' a pale, dumpy man told him over a glass of vodka. 'They were just building it, then. We moved here from Lvov.' He pronounced it L'viv. 'It wasn't much of a place for a family, then. Now, there are all sorts of things available. The amusement park is scheduled to open soon. If you and your wife are having children, to contribute to the glorious future of the eternal October Revolution, there will be plenty for you to do.'

Alexei could not figure out whether the man was mocking the glorious October Revolution. He stayed on the topic of the amusement park. 'I passed by the construction site; there's a Ferris wheel going up.'

'May his most Holy Saint Lenin allow us to live to see the day!' the man commented, this time with a clear undertone of sarcasm. He drank down the rest of his little glass of vodka and ordered another. It was cheap in Pripyat, like most staple goods.

Something in the older man's tone bothered Alexei. 'You sound as if you doubt it will happen.'

'Oh, the Ferris wheel will go up, all right. They said it would be done by May 1986, and here we are, a few days away. But who knows whether we'll still be around to ride on it.'

'Are you feeling ill?' Alexei examined the man. His pasty complexion and fleshy jowls did not speak of robust health.

'I feel fine. And if you'll buy me another vodka, I'll feel better. No, it's the plant. Nothing ever goes wrong there, because in the workers' paradise of the Soviet Union, nothing is allowed ever to go wrong. But I've been working on nuclear plants ever since Obninsk, and I am telling you that one of these days, a little problem, a little overload here, a budget cut there, and we will all —' he made a little exploding motion with his hand. 'Poof. Well. In any case, "Don't be sad, don't be angry, if life deceives you!"'

Alexei knew that the older man was quoting Alexander Pushkin, his own namesake. He countered with a quote of his own. '"Better the illusions that exalt us, than ten thousand truths."'

The man peered at him. 'You think so? A model of Soviet youth. I wish you and your beautiful wife every good fortune in life.' He swallowed his last drop of vodka, his unsteady feet bringing him out to the cold, rainy April night.

The following week, Alexei arrived at work for the night shift when he heard about another power plant in the region, which had suffered from an unplanned failure. Smug, he recalled the old man's pitiful accusations: the fact that he was hearing about this failure now was proof that the system was working, as there had been no cover-up.

It was an annoyance, however. The failure of the other plant meant that his own plant, Number Four, would need to keep running until the local population turned off their lights and their electric stoves and the local factories ramped down for the night. They hadn't been able to run the safety test they'd been planning for that day as part of their annual shutdown.

'I don't want to see this test delayed a minute longer,' instructed the square-faced woman who oversaw the day shift. 'It's the third time we've attempted it. If our test isn't successful, our managers will lose their bonuses, and believe me, no one here wants that to happen.'

The group of night shift workers listened stoically to her harangue. Alexei watched the group. He saw concern in the eyes of several. What would this test involve? Most of them were younger, straight out of school. Although he had spent the last several years immersed in technical documentation, he was not up to speed on the practicalities of shutting down and restarting a nuclear reactor.

As the day manager stepped down and handed over a hasty briefing to the night manager, Alexei approached one of the worried operators. 'Comrade. Tell me what you are afraid of.'

'Nothing at all, except looking like a fool.'

'What do you mean?'

'Ask any man or woman here whether they know how to run this test. I know my own section and nothing more. And our night manager has been placed in this godforsaken city, in this godforsaken plant, on this godforsaken night shift, for a   good reason.'

'What reason?'

'Because he doesn't know what the hell he's doing, either.'

Alexei thought back to the hearing in England. 'We need men to keep their eyes open, and to have the bravery to speak up, including to their superiors,' the old capitalist had said.

If the stakes were high at a little chemical plant in England, how much higher would they be when a nuclear reactor was involved? Thanks to his knowledge of English, he had access to certain documents about an incident in Pennsylvania, in the United States. A near miss.

He would not let a similar incident in Chernobyl embarrass the great Soviet Union. He entered the office of the day manager, catching her off guard as she loaded a large bottle of pear brandy into her purse. 'It's a gift of appreciation from the workers!' she explained.

'Comrade!' said Alexei. 'I am sorry to inconvenience you. But I would like to ask you to follow me, and observe for a few minutes. Please.'

Grumbling, she followed him as he led her to the group of night shift workers, who were in a huddle, attempting to understand the instructions for the test. 'I would like to ask you some questions.'

'What is it now, "Professor"?' They teased him because of his foreign experience, but he recognised grudging respect behind it.

'Could I ask you: who here has experience in conducting the test we will attempt tonight?'

The men and women looked at each other, and did not speak.

'Let me ask another way. Is there anyone here who has ever participated in a similar test?'

Again, they remained silent, shuffling their feet. One blurted out, 'Seryoshka told us a little about it. But I've never done one.'

Alexei addressed the day manager. 'I am sorry to be the one to show this to you. However, it's clear we need your help to manage the test.'

She gave an audible, pointed sigh, and walked back to her office, where she placed her purse back on the desk. 'Listen, everyone!' she bellowed from her office door. The day shift workers, who were already at the exits, paused. 'Nobody leave. According to this clown here, we all need to do a double shift, because our comrades on the night shift don't know how to read a sheaf of instructions.' To the instant groans and complaints of the group, she replied, 'We'll get the thing done, and then you can drink yourselves into oblivion tomorrow morning. But in the meantime, let's get to work!'

She turned to Alexei. 'You've put me in an awkward position. I was ready to go home and enjoy a glass of this very nice brandy with my family. But since you've gone and blabbed about this situation to everyone, it means now I'd be the one responsible if the idiot night crew does anything wrong. So you can finish out your shift tonight, but I don't want to see you on these premises again after tomorrow morning. Ever. Is that clear?'

Keeping his face impassive and his back straight, Alexei nodded, and cried out. 'Thank you, Comrade! Long live the glorious October Revolution!'

Would the future be simple obscurity for him, working in a menial job? Or worse – the gulag? He would have to inform Alina about what had happened. As a Soviet citizen, she would agree that what he did was right and necessary.

He hoped it was worth it.

The next morning, a little more than 1,100 kilometres to the west, a young doctoral student in physical chemistry at the

Academy of Sciences in Berlin-Adlershof in East Germany woke up to a chilly, beautiful April sunrise. Her husband pulled open the blinds of the tiny window in their little apartment in Mitte. 'Angela, time to get up! Can't you hear the birds singing?'

It was a gorgeous day, and she was in a good mood. Many people had already cleared out before the May 1 holiday, which was just a few days away, and the younger students were already frolicking on the lawn. Her thesis on quantum chemistry was nearing completion. Yes, everything was looking fine. She had received preliminary approval to travel to West Germany to attend a congress, and later to Donetsk for a language course. She hoped to hear about exciting developments in nuclear power.

An extensive network of nuclear power plants, safely operated, managed by professionals, cheap, clean, and free of smoke and emissions, would be the future of East Germany. Perhaps all of Germany, if it were ever to be united again.

Or all of Europe.

She was certain of it, and nothing short of a catastrophe could convince her otherwise.

Above all, they must move away from their old-fashioned dependence on filthy coal, not to mention the instability of oil from the Middle East. The other viable option, natural gas from Russia, was perhaps cleaner than coal, but could not be called a realistic alternative.

As she entered the main building in the *Gendarmenmarkt*, a jovial professor greeted her. 'Mrs Merkel! When can we expect to start reading about you in the news? Perhaps with a new plan for the future of our nation?'

She laughed. 'Let's see! I need to defend my dissertation first. But you are right; I have been thinking about something I like to call the *Energiewende.*'

'The energy transition? I'm sure we'll be hearing more about it before long.' He beamed and entered his classroom.

The sky, vivid blue, remained clear all day, without a single cloud to interrupt it.

The Morton-Thiokol Challenge

A story by Grace Chan

On a bright January morning in 1986, millions of American school children sat at their desks, ready to watch a beloved teacher become the first civilian astronaut. Instead, they watched in horror as the beautiful spacecraft was enveloped in smoke and fell to Earth in pieces, thanks to a weak rubber O-ring seal made inflexible by frigid weather.

The explosion of the NASA space shuttle Challenger was more than a tragic accident that cost seven lives. The catastrophe created a grim milestone in the long decline of the American space program that had once united that nation, and in a larger sense brought an end to the golden age of American optimism.

Politics and personal influence forced the launch to go ahead despite engineers' recommendations. Yet a keen understanding of politics and personal influence can also halt a disaster in the making, even at a planetary scale. In 1986, the global average temperature was 0.6°C above pre-industrial levels.

This is us. It should have happened then. What might happen next?

11.45 pm, Monday, January 27, 1986

'And I'm sorry to say, Mr President, that no matter what, tomorrow evening at six I'll be on the air with CBS News. In fact, I'd advise you to rip up the draft of your State of the Union address, the one you probably have on your desk right now.'

The President sighed. 'All right. Fine. I don't like how you've gone about it, but by God, you've got your way, Senator Glenn. I'll tell Beggs to cancel.'

'You mean Graham. You may have forgotten that Beggs is on leave, thanks to accusations made by people in your administration, that he is overcharging the government.' John could not keep the bitterness from his voice.

'Point taken,' said the President. 'And hell, I'm regretting taking that call from Don; he's the one who said I should listen to you. Now: you've done your job. It's time to get off the damn phone, and let me do mine.'

'Yes, Mr President.'

9.30 pm, Monday, January 27, 1986

Two hours earlier, John had grumbled as the phone rang. 'Another telemarketer!' he muttered to Annie.

But the voice he heard on that cold Monday night in Concord, Ohio, was the last one he expected.

'I'll be a monkey's uncle!' he cried, when she explained why she was calling, long-distance.

He resisted her request at first. He parried, and she insisted. Then she pulled her trump card.

'I am sixty-eight years old already, and I am going to retire this year,' said the voice from the cordless phone. 'And that makes me far too old to accept any of this nonsense. You were all too ready to ask me to check every calculation with my own hands, to make sure everything was in order, back when it was you yourself going into space. So I expect you to offer the same considerations to your successors.'

'Yes, Ma'am,' John replied, with a mixture of amusement and concern, when her harangue concluded. 'Thank you for calling. I'll see what I can do.'

'Remember: the thing about mathematics is, it doesn't matter what your politics are. It's either right or wrong.'

'Yes, Ma'am! You have a good evening, now.'

As he collapsed the antenna and hung the phone back on its cradle in the kitchen, he called out to his wife. 'You'll never guess who that was.'

'Hm?' Annie had never been much of a chatterbox, because her stutter, but she had a presence that commanded any room.

'Katherine Johnson.'

'Who?'

'Mrs Johnson, the mathematician, the one who worked with us on the Mercury missions.'

'Oh?'

'She's been having a talk with a fellow called McDonald, down at Morton-Thiokol. Where they build the solid rocket boosters.'

'I thought, I always thought she – was worth listening to.'

Annie had long ago given up the idea of acting as the perfect housewife and mother; indeed, both Lyn and John David were now in their forties, and John David had children of his own. Still, despite her gruelling work in disability activism, she kept their sprawling ranch house on the Scioto River spotless. And as she grew older, she developed more decided opinions about who did, and did not, merit her husband's time. Her laconic comment was a ringing endorsement of Mrs Johnson.

He continued, 'Well, yes, normally speaking, I'd have to agree with you there. And I've listened to her plenty of times. She said this fellow MacDonald has concerns about the launch tomorrow. The launch they're doing with that civilian, you know, the teacher.'

'Yes.'

'They're talking about more than a billion dollars wasted, if they abort it now. Not to mention the President wants it to headline his State of the Union address. MacDonald couldn't convince Jesse Moore or Gene Thomas to listen to him, so he's gone off the darn reservation.'

Annie gave him a disappointed look. Back in the earlier part of the century, the Burke Act dispossessed her grandfather from his place on a reservation, and he experienced terrible suffering during the Great Depression that followed. She would not tolerate any such language in her own house.

'I'm sorry, Annie. What I mean to say is that this fellow MacDonald, he has a darn fool idea that the weather will be too cold. Too cold! Why, the main combustion chamber reaches, what, six thousand degrees Fahrenheit!'

'Why?'

'Why is he worried? She says, that he says, there have been problems with the seals. Which, come to think of it, are what stops the exhaust gases from leaking into the joints.'

'Oh?'

'Now, you know very well I'm a pilot and not a rocket design specialist. But, now that you mention it, if he convinced her, maybe there's something to it.'

Annie took her time clearing the glasses and cocktail napkins that John's guests had left in the living room. She sensed when her husband needed time to think things through.

It was an odd thing to admit, but she envied Mrs Johnson. From an early age, Annie did everything she could to do what was expected, or, if she did what was unexpected, to do it within the acceptable norms for a middle-class white woman in Ohio. But Katherine Johnson, from the age of fourteen, tossed aside all expectations of what a Negro girl could achieve in those days, and lived her life as she saw fit. Katherine Johnson, she suspected, through the rigorous application of analytical geometry, had gained the respect of her husband in a way that she herself could never hope to.

She put the glasses in the dishwasher, dropped the paper plates into the trash compactor, returned to the living room, and asked her husband. 'What happens – if?'

'If I don't escalate it? Well, if I don't get involved, and everything goes as planned, then an old woman might be angry with me, and the President gets to boast about it in the State of the Union.'

'But?'

'But if something happens, and I knew about it, and was in a position to do something, then, gosh darn, if my constituents got wind of it, then there goes the election.'

'And?' She took off her apron, hung it on the back of the kitchen door, and sat next to him on the sofa.

'I know what you're thinking. It's not just about my constituents. I ought to be asking another question: what would John David say? For that matter, what would little Zach say?'

'Zach, he watches – every launch.' It was true. Zach was as space-mad as any little boy in the nation, and proud of his illustrious grandfather.

'Darn it, Annie! I'm convinced you and Mrs Johnson have been conspiring against me! The problem is that you're both right. As usual. Although I'll need to find a way to get through to him.'

'Yes.'

'But to tell you the truth, Annie, in the back of my mind, I've been thinking. We've had triumph after triumph in this effort. But there will come a time when something happens, and we'll have a tragedy that goes along with the triumph. And I guess that's the story of all mankind.'

'But.'

'But I don't want to be the one who failed to act, just at the moment I could have made a difference.'

Annie disappeared into the study, and, when she returned, handed John his well-thumbed Rolodex. She had already flipped to a card about two-thirds through the sheaf. It held the number of the President's Chief of Staff.

7.45 pm, Monday, January 27, 1986

Two hours before John spoke with Katherine, a group of men in Ogden, Utah, were sitting together in a meeting so tense that Bob was afraid they might come to blows.

January was cold in Ogden, cold and dreary in a way that was unthinkable in warmer states. The thick, grey clouds blanketing the mountains drove out all thoughts of winter merriment.

The Morton-Thiokol factory had completed the construction of the Solid Rocket Boosters more than half a year before, well ahead of schedule, in good time for the July launch as planned. The same type of boosters propelled nine missions, all successful. And in the burning heat of the summer desert, no one worried about the flexibility of rubber in cold temperatures. On the contrary: the greater concern was a slight charring they'd observed, they supposed was caused by the tremendous heat of the fiery combustion of 500 tonnes of propellant. The repeated delays, from a variety of factors, gave them time to conduct additional tests.

Nevertheless, Bob knew that Roger was terrified. The call Cecil arranged earlier in the evening with the client made his fears concrete. Robert and Joe could not have made it more clear: they did not have the data to guarantee how tight the seal would be at temperatures colder than fifty-three degrees Fahrenheit.

'It's Florida!' argued one of the local men. 'How cold can it be?'

'It got down to twenty-five there last night,' Cecil shot back. 'It's Cape Canaveral, not Cape Verde.'

Roger thought the call had ended with a recommendation not to go ahead in the absence of sufficient data. But to his surprise, Mulloy, the NASA man, called back an hour later, saying that he'd discussed it with the Mission Management Team Leader. 'Sure,' he said, 'if you insist, we'll check the temperature of the SRBs. But you know that's not part of the Launch Commit Criteria. Aldrich won't take it into account.'

'You're not required to check if the Solid Rocket Boosters work before deciding to risk the lives of the seven people sitting on top of them?'

'You know that's not what we're talking about. We're talking about a vehicle that has shown reliable performance on nine separate launches. And we don't see any reason to keep the entire country away from a mission that they've been waiting for, for more than half a year now, just because you want to put on your fur coat!'

That was how they all talked: never 'I', always 'we'. You never knew whether you were talking to a man or to a committee.

Roger walked over to where Bob was sitting, typing something into the computer terminal. 'I don't like this. Not one bit.'

'Have you talked to Allan?'

'Down at Kennedy Space Center? Yes. That's the reason Cecil arranged the telephone conference to begin with.'

Roger pushed aside a stack of paper, and sat down on Bob's desk. 'You and I both know this is dangerous. And we've both been trained to escalate our concerns through the proper channels. But when that isn't working, there's got to be another way!'

'Fine. You tell me, then: who's got the power to stop this?'

'The President could do it.'

'Do you happen to have his home number?'

'Sure, no problem, I'll just check the White Pages. No, damn it! I don't have the President's home phone number. And I'm not going to send a telegram to 1600 Pennsylvania Avenue.'

'Who does?'

'Damned if I know. Nancy, I would imagine. Or maybe the Speaker of the House, or the Senate Majority Leader. Someone like that.'

'Hey, you've given me an idea – John Glenn! He's not just an ex-astronaut, but a current senator as well. Too bad he's a Democrat, but if anyone could convince the President, he could. Do you know anyone who knows him?'

An unexpected voice spoke up from the next desk. 'It's not about who knows him. It's about who he'll listen to.' Mike Kozuma, a senior engineer, finished off his can of Tab and gave it an expert toss into the trash can at the end of the corridor, where it sank with a resounding clunk.

'He wouldn't listen to you, by any chance?'

'As if! The Japanese-American guy is always invisible. I mean, every man, woman, and child in America knows Christa McAuliffe's name, but not a single one of them can spell Ellison Onizuka.'

Bob and Roger looked at each other. 'Okay, I'll bite,' said Bob. 'Who's that?'

'A Commander in the US Air Force, an astronaut on the *Discovery* shuttle, and, as it happens, one of the mission specialists who's scheduled to go up in tomorrow's launch.'

'So what do you suggest?'

'One of the folks at NASA told us that John Glenn never went on a mission unless the flight path was checked by a particular woman who is supposed to be a mathematical genius. She's an old Black lady, and still works at NASA.'

'And unlike the President,' Bob realised, 'I bet her number is in the White Pages.'

Bob was already calling Allan MacDonald, and Roger was already dialling information. 'Hello? I need all the area codes for the suburbs surrounding Washington, D.C.' Within fifteen minutes, the phone was ringing in Katherine Johnson's kitchen.

4.30 pm, Monday, January 27, 1986

Yet it was only a few hours before that the Morton-Thiokol engineers grasped the true gravity of what might happen.

Discussions among engineers can go on forever when the topic is trivial: a debate about the best brand of wire strippers is as likely to produce a generational feud as a consensus. But unlike politicians, when the matter is serious, they will come to an agreement with surprising speed.

'The seals have come close to failing before,' Bob Ebeling said. 'More than thirty percent of the rubber was burnt out in a test that took place under similar conditions.' The other specialists agreed: this was not the occasion to be ignoring risk factors.

However, there was a problem: try as he might, Bob could not find a hard-and-fast rule to stop a launch if the temperature dropped below a particular level.

Roger Boisjoly argued that a written rule shouldn't be necessary. 'We have evidence of the leakage. We've all seen the blowby on the earlier flight. What more are they looking for?'

'That's the issue. The previous flights were fine, so why should this one be any different?'

'It's too cold. We think of the O-rings as being soft, like slices of pineapple, but at that temperature they'll be more like a frozen bagel.'

'I'm beginning to think you shouldn't have skipped lunch.'

'I'm beginning to think the idiots at the Kennedy Space Center shouldn't have skipped Physics 101.'

Someone came back into the room with a relieved look. 'Thank God. We've got a new conference call scheduled. Tonight at seven. We'll explain what's going on. They'll understand. But be prepared to stay late tonight.'

Bob let out the breath he didn't know he'd been holding, and reached for his phone. Darlene didn't like it if he came home late without telling her in advance.

'Honey, I'm sorry to do this to you again, but it's important.' He spoke a few quiet words into the handset; the other engineers teased him for deferring too much to his wife.

'That's all right,' she replied. 'I know there's a launch tomorrow.'

'Not if I can help it.'

'What do you mean?'

'There's no way those losers should be trusting the O-rings in this cold weather. If they go ahead as planned, the whole shuttle's going to blow up.'

'Are they going ahead?'

'I hope not. They're going to have to turn on the launch pad fire suppression system as it is, meaning the whole thing's going to be covered with ice. And we have no idea what that'll do to the thermal heat shield. We're having a conference call tonight to explain it to them.'

She was silent for a moment. 'I hope it isn't you who ends up as the loser in all this.'

'If the thing blows, we'll all be losers. We'll lose our jobs and who knows what else.'

'That's not what I mean. A loser, in my mind, is somebody that doesn't do anything, and, worse yet, they don't care. I want you to try your best, and if it doesn't work, you will know that you did something and you cared. And that's my definition of a winner.'

'Thanks, honey. You know that if anything were to happen, I'd regret it my whole life. But tell me, do you need me to pick up anything on the way home?'

'A gallon of milk, if it's not too late. And be careful on the roads after it gets dark. They're expecting flurries tonight. It's going to be cold.'

'So I hear.'

11.52 pm, Monday, January 27, 1986

'Get me Graham,' said the President. 'We're calling this thing off.' He slammed the receiver into the cradle.

He scowled, picked up a sheaf of papers from his desk labelled 'STATE OF THE UNION – DRAFT', and began to delete lines with a red pen.

The Country Woman

A story by Grace Chan

One of the most invasive plants in Southeast Asia is the water hyacinth – known as bèo tây in northern Vietnam. Originating from Brazil, its insidious expansion around the world has made it into a major weed species in more than fifty countries. Once established, it chokes off lakes and rivers, out-competes local flora, blocks commerce and takes over entire biomes. Pollution from sewage and fertiliser runoff exacerbates its disastrous spread.

While it is almost impossible to identify the moment in intercontinental exchange that brought it to Southeast Asia centuries ago, it is possible to envision alternative management and moderation tactics.

This is us. In 1990, the global average temperature was 0.45°C above pre-industrial levels, and greenhouse gas emissions were already at historic levels for the time. Today, will we look for alternatives to manage the deadly impact of climate change on those most affected by it?

Nguyễn Thị Na was thirty-one years old, and she hated her name.

It was a name borne of brutal efficiency. Nguyễn was the most common family name in the nation, Thị marked her as a girl, and Na was the name of the humble custard apple. In the village, where such names were common, she'd thought nothing of it. But in Hanoi, her more sophisticated contemporaries bore exciting names evoking the grandeur of Vietnam: Hoa Lan, the delicate orchid, or Quang Trung, the ancient hero. In the city, both her accent and her name marked her as nhà quê – a country bumpkin. Whenever she heard the term, muttered by derisive shopkeepers or shouted by swaggering teenagers, she seethed.

'Look at all of them,' scoffed a woman selling tea as Na passed, staggering under a load of vegetables from the market. 'Pretty soon they'll take over the entire city.' What irony! Na thought. The tea-seller had arrived in Hanoi less than a decade before.

In this time of Đổi mới, or Renewal, the national government was embracing reform and opening doors to the rest of the world. A decade and a half after the American War, it was time to find a new way forward. But back in the village, Na's elder brothers were doing their best to wrest a living out of the land, and for the last year she'd been stuck in her cousins' house in Hanoi. There, she cleaned floors, washed clothes, and emptied toilet pots for the old couple and for their arrogant son, Minh. The man's greatest achievement was the contract he'd signed for his small trucking company with the local district government. But despite the fact that he, like the tea-seller, had been in Hanoi for just five years, he and his wife took special pleasure in contrasting their rustic relatives' life with the glamour of the big city.

Na saw little enough of the glamour, for her job never ended. No sooner had she swept the tile floors of the narrow concrete house, it was time to wash the clothes. Throughout the wee hours of early summer nights, she sat by the pump for hours, stewing in resentment, waiting for water to trickle from the ancient city pipes so that she could fill up basins for the family's needs. Then, in the late summer, when heavy rains created treacherous puddles that filled entire streets, she spent nights sweeping water out of the front door with a broad broom. Minh's wife was the worst, taking every opportunity to call her lazy, slovenly, or dishonest. 'Do you expect me to believe that in the market they charged you three thousand đồng for this pitiful bunch of greens?' she spat. 'It should have been no more than two thousand! Either you're colluding with the seller or telling me an outright lie, but either way you're pocketing the difference.'

In this particular case the accusation was true, but how else could Na hope to save any money for her future? Her cousins provided room and board, and an escape from the penury of the countryside, where she'd never even held fifty thousand đồng in her hand at once. She didn't receive any wages – she was just helping her family, after all.

Yet she didn't want to grow old scrubbing men's underwear.

Her cousins seldom bothered to climb to the roof of the building, accessible only from a rickety ladder in the back. There, Na pounded the clothes in the washbasin, and hung them to dry on a metal wire sheltered by a piece of corrugated iron. When it rained, the water hammered on the makeshift roof like the jackhammers that tore up the streets with their incessant construction.

Yet from this eyrie also came her great solace: a view of the shining waters of West Lake, stretching northwards like a vast mirror ringed with a lush green frame. A narrow causeway spanned the southeast corner, dividing it from the smaller Trúc Bạch Lake. The slipper-shaped Hoàn Kiếm Lake just south of the Old Quarter was more famous, with its ancient turtles and associated legends. But Na disdained the crowds of tourists who gathered there on Sundays, buying cheap trinkets and taking photographs.

In November, when the summer heat dissipated and the rain ended, she stole moments walking back from the market to gather long stems of water hyacinth from the shores of West Lake. In the South, she'd heard, the fast-growing plant was used for making baskets and wicker furniture and not just for pig feed. In the evenings, she wove the strands together as she sat on the roof. It was a meditative act, and she could imagine she was still at home, with a beautiful future before her.

Most people called water hyacinth a weed, an invasive plant. She'd seen a news article about the many failed efforts to uproot it or poison it with herbicides. But Na appreciated its tenacity and its relative abundance. At the pond back in her village, more than two hundred kilometres away from Hanoi, the spindly reeds they used for baskets struggled to keep up with demand. For decades, villagers had taken every opportunity to pull the reeds from the marshes and ponds when they had a moment. They took pride in their skills, selling their hampers and wickerwork to outsiders. Indeed, nowadays, as the population of the village rebounded, lack of reeds was the only thing holding them back from selling more. The older villagers lamented the villagers' industry, and hearkened back to a time when reeds grew all over the village, as plentiful in the winter as in the summer.

Na was unconcerned with such things, since she knew old people loved to complain; instead, as she gazed across West Lake, she thought back to the spring days when flowers bloomed, and young women plucked magnolia blossoms to put in their hair. There was a time when she had done so herself. But she reached twenty-two or twenty-three and was still unmarried, and they started to call her ế – unsold goods. Not that there had been any opportunity to wed, with so many of the villagers related to her by blood.

In the city, meanwhile, few people knew how to make a basket the way they did in the village. People worked in offices or shops or in small workshops, and if they needed a basket they bought one woven of sedge from Đông Xuân market. As a result, the water hyacinth was thickening its green frame around West Lake. Soon, no shining mirror would remain, only a swath of vegetation choking the lake.

As she walked past West Lake on an afternoon in early December, an unusual sight greeted her: two foreigners, crouched next to the shoreline. Were they Liên Xô, perhaps, Soviets? She'd seen some in the centre of town, with their grim faces and pale eyes. But these people were different, with hair like rice straw. She stopped and asked another village woman passing by – one from her own region – what the two were doing. The other woman shook her head in bafflement, and they both stared with frank curiosity. The older of the foreigners, a man, held a technical instrument in his hand, and frowned at a pipe sticking out from the bank.

To her astonishment, the other foreigner, a woman, addressed her in passable Vietnamese. 'Hello, sister! Do you know where this pipe comes from?'

Incredulous, Na looked at the other country woman and laughed. Should she answer? And if so, how should she address this person, whose age and origin she could not determine? The other country woman prodded her in the side, encouraging her to respond.

'Hello ... Madame,' Na said at last.

The foreign woman smiled. 'No need to call me "Madame". I'm from Thụy điển. Svenska. This man is a scientist. He wants to know where the water from this pipe originates.'

Na hesitated; was this proper? Sensing her reluctance, the foreign woman assured her, 'We're working with the district authorities,' and pointed towards two Vietnamese men inspecting something further along the shoreline. Na recognised one of them from the neighbourhood – Mr Thắng.

Na didn't know where the country Thụy điển might be. 'The pipe just drains out the gutter,' she explained, and gestured at the streets that ran alongside the lake. 'It's from up there.'

The two foreigners conferred for a moment and the man frowned again. The woman asked, 'Are you sure it's not a sewage pipe? These plants wouldn't be growing here if it were just rainwater.'

Confused, Na said, 'There's sewage in the gutters, too. I empty the toilet pots into the street every morning. Where else would it go?'

The woman translated, and the man shook his head in disapproval. 'Thank you,' the woman said to Na. 'I'm afraid if this continues, the water hyacinth will get out of control. There's too much pollution here and it makes the weeds grow too fast. But we appreciate your help. Oh, by the way – what is your name?'

'My name's Na. Nguyễn Thị Na.' She didn't know why she'd blurted out her full name; she was flustered by the entire experience.

The woman smiled. 'A good name! Easy to remember.' A moment later, she called out to Thắng and the other Vietnamese man, handed Na a few small bills, and waved good-bye.

'How much did she give you?' the other country woman asked as Na pocketed the money, amazed at her good fortune.

'Two thousand đồng!' Na responded. It would be enough to buy a steaming bowl of Huế-style beef noodles from the shop on the corner, but she knew that the other woman would want a share for her part in the effort. She took one thousand đồng from her purse and handed it over, and the woman hurried away toward the market.

Na, too, was in a hurry: for the amount the straw-haired woman had given her was not two thousand, but one hundred thousand, more than she'd had in her entire life. She knew what to do: she walked south and east for half an hour until she reached the state-run Hanoi Department Store in the centre of the city. There, she'd heard, one hundred thousand đồng in the right hands would allow her to sell her baskets to the general public on the third floor. It was even possible that one of the foreign visitors, now increasing in number, would want to buy one. Other than the kickbacks to the official who controlled purchases there, it would be pure profit: the raw materials, after all, were free.

Within two weeks, her cousin's wife noticed what was going on. 'Where have you been? Constantly up on the roof, and neglecting the cleaning! Our house looks like a dump! Maybe that's the nhà quê standards you're used to, but we have different expectations in the city.'

You were transplanting rice seedlings a few years ago, thought Na, and now you're too proud to weave a basket.

Na gave a deferential smile and apologised. 'I'm too stupid.' But she spent the next hour on the roof assembling a wicker chair, ordered by a foreign ambassador who liked the hamper he'd bought earlier. It sold for 100,000 đồng, an unbelievable sum, and she kept the cash tucked into her pillow beneath the sink. Her cousin Minh didn't believe in luxuries, so she slept on a pallet in the kitchen on the ground floor and tucked away her bedding by day.

A week later, she ran into the other village woman at the market, the one who had watched as she spoke with the foreign scientists from Thụy điển. The woman, named Anh, was several years younger than Na but just as skilled in weaving and wickerwork. A plan formed in Na's mind.

For three days, she visited the market to buy vegetables at different times of day, looking for someone. At last she spotted him: Thắng, who worked for Ba Đình District and had been the host of the two foreigners inspecting the lake. She addressed him with the polite 'elder brother' pronoun, even though she suspected he was several years younger than herself. Indeed, he had a chubby, baby face and a haircut that made him look too boyish for a district official.

'Hello! Have you eaten yet?' she began.

Suspicious, he gave a perfunctory reply, 'Thank you, I have. I'm not interested in buying anything.'

'Don't you work for Ba Đình District? I have an idea for managing the water hyacinth on the lake.'

'Eh? What's that?'

'Will you have a cup of tea with me?'

It was an unorthodox request, but Na was convinced that their interests aligned. She saw him struggling to decide, and smiled. 'It won't take more than five minutes.' Some city people could be disarmed by a country person's open face; they thought all nhà quê were ignorant fools. But she could read and write just like anyone, and although she didn't have much education she never missed a page of the newspaper Lao động when its pages were posted in the display frames next to the district offices.

He gave in at last, and followed her to the small shop at the side of the road.

Over the bitter tea – Na suspected the tired leaves had already brewed several pots – they exchanged names and ages. To her surprise, they were born in the same year. But she continued to address him in the formal way, out of deference to his position, as she explained what she wanted.

It would not take much. If he was willing to give his official support to her little enterprise, prevent the police from harassing those who gathered the water hyacinth, and help her find more retailers to sell the resulting baskets, she knew that their collective efforts would make a serious dent in the invasive water hyacinth of Trúc Bạch Lake. 'That's what happened back in my village,' she said. 'Once people started buying our baskets, the weeds disappeared; they'd been gathered to near extinction.'

'Would your labourers root out the water hyacinth for free?' he asked. She chuckled inside to hear him refer to 'her' labourers, as if she were a hardened capitalist.

'Yes. But I'm concerned that once people see what we're doing, we'll get stopped by the police. If you can keep us undisturbed, I can offer you a cut of ... five percent of the profit.'

'Fifteen percent would be fair,' he countered. His face grew thoughtful. 'The national government has declared next year, 1990, the "Visit Vietnam Year",' Thắng mused. 'We could showcase your baskets and wickerwork as a characteristic craft of this region, and promote it to foreign tourists. And at the same time, this could help us get rid of the damn water hyacinth.'

'What about in West Lake?' Na dared to ask.

'That's not in Ba Đình District,' he said, shaking his head, 'so I can't help you there. Yes, I know it ought to be obvious that Trúc Bạch Lake and West Lake are part of the same ecological system, but that's not how government departments are organised. Still, if we succeed here first, I'm sure they will want to know more from us.'

Na was delighted to hear him use the word 'us' to refer to the two of them. 'There's one more thing. I heard from that foreign scientist that the sewage from the gutters is making the water hyacinth grow out of control.'

'It's true enough! The pollution is getting bad.'

'But where else will people dump their toilet pots if not for the gutter? We wish we could have a modern toilet in the house.

Isn't there someone in your district who can work on this problem?'

He snorted. 'The water and sewer pipes here were built decades ago, back when there were only eighty thousand people here, not two million. They say the government of Phần lan will come to repair it for the entire city, but nothing has happened. Anyway, from your point of view wouldn't you want the pollution to continue? It would mean more raw material for you.'

Na grew serious. Something in his boyish face softened her attitude toward the embattled lake. After all, the sight of it had soothed her aching emotions many evenings as she sat on the roof chapping her knuckles in the washbasin. 'Call me nhà quê if you like – it's true,' she said. 'But I also see how beautiful this lake is, and I don't want it to be strangled. The water hyacinth will grow fast enough to meet our needs without getting help from our manure.'

Thắng gave a kind smile. 'My family has lived in Hanoi for generations, and I know that our nation is independent today because of everything the country people have done for us. It will benefit all of us to have you in the city.'

Smiling in return, Na replied, 'For this statement, I will allow you ten percent of the profit. But that's all!'

Thắng stood. 'I agree to your conditions. But I will add one more: let's meet here again for tea next week.'

Na felt as if she were gliding over the sidewalks on the way home – she had entered into a dangerous conspiracy with the fresh-faced Thắng, and it had taken her to an unknown plane of existence. Yet instead of frightening her, it gave her a thrill of pleasure. Here at last was something new, something that could provide a future.

The delightful sensation lasted until the moment she returned to her cousins' house.

'Here I am, starving for dinner while you're enjoying yourself with some strange man!' shouted Minh's wife as she opened the door. 'Everyone saw you. What are they going to say about our family?'

'We were just having a conversation –'

'If that's how you're inclined, then you might as well go "work" at that hotel they're building for foreigners. After all, by this time next year they'll have plenty of men coming through town who are looking for experienced women.' Turning to her husband, she continued, 'These village people really are animals.'

Na apologised again and again, and rushed to the little kitchen to prepare dinner with the vegetables and tofu she'd purchased at the market. The kitchen occupied the back half of the ground floor of the narrow house. Despite a tendency to attract cockroaches it was superior to that of any of their neighbours, boasting a rice cooker and a two-burner electric stove imported from the Soviet Union. Using an electric stove meant she had to time her cooking with care to avoid the brown-outs that plagued Hanoi, but on the other hand it spewed out none of the toxic gases that coal stoves did. She'd used the latter often enough in the past. Whenever she put the small cylinder of compressed waste coal into the 'beehive' clay container and set it alight, she had to wrap her face with a cloth to avoid the smoke.

She served dinner to the family. When they were finished, she retreated to eat her own meal, wash the dishes, and figure out a way to solve her problem.

Even if Thắng cleared the way for her and Anh to gather water hyacinth and produce wickerwork, how could she find the time and space to do it, considering the burden of her duties at home?

She slept little that night. There was some irony in the fact that her thin pillow no longer offered any comfort to her aching head because it was full of money: bricks of 2,000 đồng notes packed the flimsy nylon cloth until it was as hard as a concrete block. During the hours when she did sleep, her dreams disturbed her.

By morning she knew what she had to do.

The weather on the day of her liberation was glorious – sunny and cool. Without a word to Minh, his wife, or the old couple, she stole out of the house at dawn. She walked to the northern side of Trúc Bạch Lake, where an old shed stood empty. The early morning sun glittered on the surface of the lake, rippled by a gentle breeze. A vendor strolled past, basket on her head, singing, 'Hot bread! Hey, hot bread!' Na could smell the crisp loaves through their burlap covering. Far off, another cried, 'Will anyone scoop rice?' Three girls in blue and white school uniforms cycled past her, their heads bare and their hair shining. Na refastened the ties of her hat under her chin; the sun was still low, but she didn't want any freckles.

She soon reached the abandoned shed, and spoke with the owner next door. He didn't believe her at first, but when she produced her bricks of currency, his greed overcame him and he stretched his hand out to accept the money. Within a few hours, she and Anh had cleaned out the rubbish and were hard at work in the shed weaving a set of low stools.

They'd been labouring for a week when Minh and his wife arrived, bitter and reproachful. 'How could you leave your old cousins so helpless?' he asked. 'You know how much they depend on you.'

'I'm sure you'll find another girl from the village,' Na replied, her eyes never leaving the long stems of water hyacinth spread out on the floor in front of her.

'They've sacrificed so much for you, offering you room and board for months, teaching you everything about how to manage in the big city ...'

'Yes, I'm grateful to them,' she admitted.

'You need to be with your family. You're coming back with us now, then,' Minh's wife declared, her already-sharp eyebrows becoming sharper.

Na felt her resolve weakening. It was true her elderly cousins needed help. It wasn't their fault that Minh and his wife were so useless.

Just as she thought she would give up, stand and follow the couple back to the narrow concrete house, Anh shouted to her from across the room.

'Boss! Are these visitors customers? Do they want to buy something? Or do they need a job? We need more workers, you know.' Anh made a deliberate choice to emphasize her country accent, making it almost unintelligible to the city folk.

Anh's cry jolted Na from her trance. A smile stealing onto her face, she asked Minh's wife, 'My colleague reminds me – do you need a job? We can't offer wages, but we can pay you by how many pieces you produce, or how much water hyacinth you collect.'

Minh sputtered, 'What! Do you think my wife – how could you – this woman – !' He used the most formal pronoun to refer to Na, as if they were perfect strangers and not part of the same family. Na chuckled inside and watched them depart with enormous satisfaction.

'Thank you, Anh,' she said. 'You've saved me from a serious mistake. Will you stay here for a little while? I have an appointment to drink tea with Mr Thắng.'

Four years passed. The water pipes were replaced in one neighborhood after another and a new sewage system spread throughout the city of Hanoi. The area of Ba Đình District near Trúc Bạch Lake still used the old system, and its residents grew impatient. A campaign appeared on televisions and in newspapers, paid for by the Finnish Aid Agency, encouraging the citizens of Hanoi to conserve water. Na heard through the gossip network that the old couple had passed away at last, leaving Minh and his wife in charge of the household.

As Thắng had predicted, their success in gathering water hyacinth from Trúc Bạch Lake was noticed and the little enterprise received the go-ahead to apply the same system to the larger West Lake. Now that large sections of both lakes were cleared of water hyacinth, they enjoyed an unprecedented boom in tourism – meaning that the poor quality of the water became more obvious. Calls to limit the influx of pollution became more urgent, and the city's government invited experts from the university to create a comprehensive plan.

More foreigners appeared on the streets of Hanoi: not only those from Sweden, but from France, Japan, and even America. Na had encountered many of them, since her baskets, chairs, and hampers were in every shop in the tourist areas of the Old Quarter of Hanoi. Copycats sprang up throughout the city, but as the first mover, Na had established a brand before the others and could command a premium for her goods. The local retailers called her by the familiar moniker 'Aunt Na', but the foreign customers knew the goods by their brand name, THINA. It was a good name, easy to remember.

At last, the day came when a group of her gatherers arrived back at the THIBA warehouse empty-handed. 'Aunt Na,' a young woman said as she entered her office, 'there's almost none left. What shall we do?'

'What, no water hyacinth at all?' she asked, looking up from her desk. She was knee-deep in paperwork, negotiating the contract with that foreign furniture company from Thụy điển – she'd long since learned to call it by its proper name, Sverige. The company, which sold discount furniture and household items all over the world, had first commissioned her to produce wicker napkin rings, and things had progressed from there.

'Well, there's still some left,' said the young gatherer, 'but it's harder to find. We've been getting it from the river, too, but it's not enough.'

Na knew this moment would come, and she was ready for it. 'It's time to expand.'

Anh, poring over employee contracts at her desk on the other side of the office, looked up in surprise. 'Expand? How can we, if there is no water hyacinth to supply our factory?'

Na gazed into the distance, as if looking across the span of West Lake's shining waters. 'Do you think Hanoi is the only place in Vietnam where water hyacinth grows? We will go into the countryside. Local gatherers will find it in their lakes, and be grateful for the income. The fishermen will thank us for clearing out their ponds. Remember, I have already engaged my older brothers for this purpose, to find gatherers throughout the region.'

The young woman examined her feet, anticipating the inevitable next statement from this crafty factory owner, Aunt Na – that her services in Hanoi were no longer needed.

Na continued, 'We will keep half of our gatherers here in Hanoi, because water hyacinth always regrows in a year, no matter how much you remove. And we will put the other half to work in the factory to meet rising demand from the foreign buyers. We'll need to have an apprenticeship programme, of course.' Anh was taking notes, as she always did when her boss outlined a new vision.

The fax machine rang, screeched, and spat out a new order from an overseas buyer. Na realised she'd need another translator soon to handle the volume. There were more and more young people studying English at the national university nowadays and it would be easy to find someone. Maybe she could find a financial expert there, too; people were getting more sophisticated. They already had five cash counting machines, since most local transactions still used five thousand đồng notes and it was tiresome to count out currency worth five or ten million đồng.

She no longer saw much of Thắng. He'd bowed out after a year, citing the new anti-corruption measures that prevented

154

officials from engaging in side businesses, but he'd been good about keeping up his original commitments and the gatherers were only rarely bothered. Anyway, nobody wanted West Lake to return to the tangled, overgrown mess it once was. The private clubs, hotels, and leisure boating services surrounding the pristine lake shores were making too much money. Still, from time to time they had a cup of tea.

One piece of the puzzle remained. She picked up one of the two telephones on her desk and dialled a number.

'Hey, Minh!' she cried, using the familiar 'nephew' form of address appropriate to their family relationship. 'Do you have any capacity available? We're going to need to transport a lot of water hyacinth from the villages up to the city, and we'll need at least two or three dedicated trucks and drivers to start with. Let me know the best price you can offer.'

'Aunt Na,' her cousin replied, 'it's so good to hear from you! Of course; it would be an honour to become a service provider to your company. Tell me what you need.'

She gave him the details, told him to reply to her within the day, and nodded with satisfaction as she returned the telephone to its cradle. Her cousin, unsophisticated in business, would offer a better price than his competitors. And his wife wouldn't want to pass up the opportunity to sign up such a successful company as their client.

After all, THINA was one of the most famous names in Hanoi.

The Failed Protocol

A story by Grace Chan

On September 16, 1987, in Montreal, Canada, 197 countries plus the European Union signed an agreement to phase out chlorofluorocarbons – CFCs – and other substances that were creating a hole in the ozone layer, a crucial layer in Earth's atmosphere that blocks the sun's ultraviolet radiation. Because of their action, the ozone hole in Antarctica is now recovering, and ozone levels are expected to return to 1980 levels within the next two decades.

CFCs cause more than one kind of damage. It is well-known that UV radiation hurts both plants and animals directly. But CFCs are themselves greenhouse gases and contribute to global warming. Moreover, when UV radiation damages plants, it reduces their ability to absorb CO_2. Without the Montreal Protocol, as it came to be called, these substances would therefore create a significant additional increase to existing global warming, around 2.5°C within a century – above that caused by fossil fuels and other emissions.

This is us. In 1987, the global average temperature was still just 0.48°C above pre-industrial levels. Will we learn the lesson of the Montreal Protocol, and the extraordinary power of international cooperation to avert disaster at a global scale?

The sun had risen half an hour ago, and the heat was already enervating. João Ribeiro sat on a disintegrating plastic chair on the weathered, wooden porch of his small farmhouse, slapping at the stinging insects and praying for a breeze. 2009 was turning out to have the hottest year he could recall in Mato Grosso in all his forty-two years.

He heard a rustle, and young Francisco emerged from the overgrown path. João felt his gut twist. As soon as the teenager was within earshot, João shouted, 'Nothing today!'

'What? I thought they'd be ripe by now!' Francisco responded, wiping the sweat from his face with a dirty sleeve long enough to hang past his spindly wrists. His expression was hidden by the broad visor of his cap, but João heard the disappointment in the young man's voice.

'I can't hire pickers if there's nothing to pick.'

'Your trees aren't bearing this year?'

'We got a few. Small, scorched fruit. But the thieves took them before they were even ripe. Stripped the branches bare,' João explained. 'Dogs didn't catch them in time.'

'What good is a guard dog anyway, if it can't chase off a mango thief?' Francisco grumbled, scuffing his boots against a felled log.

João shrugged. 'There are more thieves than dogs.' He glanced into the thicket. Instead of the deep, vibrant green he remembered from his youth, he saw sickly vines choking even sicklier trees.

Francisco sat on the cracked edge of the porch, his narrow shoulders sagging. He threw his worn backpack onto the dirt in front of the house and glanced at the shrinking shadows. 'It's gonna be bad today.'

'I heard on the radio that the UV index is going to be over eighteen by late afternoon. But the signal went out before I could hear more. It happens all the time, now. My friend José, down at the junk shop, said the UV is messing with the reflective bands in the atmosphere.'

João's explanation meant nothing to the young man resting on his porch. 'I might get work in Campo Grande, but I can't afford the bus there without wages. And it's too far to walk.' Three dogs of indeterminate parentage had run in from the orchard to investigate the newcomer. 'Hey, Amarela!' Francisco smiled, reaching out to rub the muzzle of the yellow one. 'Did you miss me? Have you had your puppies yet?' The dog's tail wagged furiously the moment she recognised the young man, but she yelped and cowered when his hand made contact with her nose. 'What's going on, girl?' Francisco asked.

'Sunburn,' João replied. 'This one's got guard dog in her blood somewhere, so she's always out patrolling during peak UV hours – whether or not I want her to. But I don't have the heart to keep her chained up. Hell, I wish I just could let her do her job! Not that it would make a difference. All three dogs together can't stop a gang. Not a hungry one.'

'What do you feed them?'

'Bush meat, mostly. They eat better than I do, sometimes.' João smiled, thinking of past feasts. 'I'm sorry I can't give you any work. But I can give you some coffee   .'

Francisco nodded, and took hold of a crumbling plastic chair leaning next to the front door. He removed his hat, revealing a peeling face.

'Don't use that chair – it'll crack under your weight. Use the wooden stool.'

Francisco laughed. 'I'm skin and bones, Senhor Ribeiro! You could put me on a crumpled up copy of *O Diario* and it would look the same after I got up.'

'Still. I left it outside for too long and the plastic got weak. It's the same with the greenhouse. I got some solar panels installed on the roof, because they told me the extra UV light would boost the photovoltaic cells, but it also burns them out more quickly. Not to mention the plastic mulch covers on the fields. They don't even last a full season any more.' João entered the house, leaving Francisco to examine the crumbling chair. He pitied the scrawny boy, who was a reliable picker and stayed sober most of the time. There was little enough reason to interact with the world these days unless you had some kind of buffer, and he appreciated the boy's honest acceptance of what was going on around him. If there had been any mangoes left, he would have been happy to keep Francisco on through the rest of the season, and when the avocados ripened he could pick those. But for now, it was far too early, and the green fruits were still small and rock hard.

João struck a match and lit the fire on his little stove. For years he'd been telling himself that he should upgrade to something better than a camping stove, but the crops were getting worse every year. Money spent on a new stove meant less for lime and phosphate, absolute necessities for soil that was less than one percent organic matter.

In a few minutes, he brought a large mug out to the porch. The young man held it with both hands for a moment, and blew on the tarry black liquid with cracked lips.

João peered at the boy's face with concern. 'Looks like you got a bad case. Did you get caught out?'

Francisco nodded and sipped from the mug. 'I was picking at the de Souza farm and they don't have sirens, and it was so hot I didn't want to put my covering on. So it was already nine o'clock in the morning by the time I noticed, and by then the bastard had already done his work.' He gestured with an elbow to the rising sun.

'When I was little, we used to be outside all day,' João mused. 'If it was too hot, we'd just take off our shirts and run around in a pair of shorts. My brother had a football, so he would call us all out to play. When school was out we'd stay on the field all day, sweating and yelling. I don't remember ever getting a single sunburn.'

João's brother had succumbed three years ago, as so many did, to the damage of a lifetime of too much exposure to the sun. The cancer had started as a mole on the back of his neck, the normal kind of blemish a man gets when he's in his thirties, but it had turned red and angry within a few months. By the time he agreed to ask a doctor about it, there were no options left, and he was gone soon afterwards. The farm was too big for one person to run, but João didn't want to sell it. Besides – who would want to buy it, with its dilapidated buildings, soil full of plastic shreds, and tired equipment?

At least the coconut trees were still producing. But he no longer had the energy to climb up to get them, and you never knew when seasonal pickers were going to show up. The spotty communications networks were getting worse, so word of mouth had again become the best way to get workers.

The panting dogs surrounded Francisco, their tongues lolling in the heat, and flopped down in the shade. In the morning, the porch faced away from the sun, but afternoons could be dangerous. Francisco discovered a stick in the dirt beside the porch and threw it as hard as he could. The dogs, yelping with joy, galloped after it. Amarela returned first, her tail wagging so hard it shook the rest of her body. 'Good girl!' said Francisco, giving a gentle pat to her shoulder.

Francisco took another sip of his coffee. 'It was the Canadians who did it, you know.'

'What?'

'All this. It's the reason the sun is so bad, now. Why you can't stay outside during peak UV any more. Why it's so hot all the time.'

'Where'd you learn that?'

'A picker at the de Souza place told me. Maybe I never went to school like you did, but I keep my ears open. He told me the Canadians put some chemicals into the air, and it made a hole in the sky that lets in all the UV light. They had a big meeting in Montreal and that's where they decided everything.'

João guffawed. 'Montreal! You're talking about that big meeting they had, years ago, when they tried to get people to stop using – what was it – CFCs, a kind of chemical. They use it for refrigerators and air conditioners, and for spraying things. People use them so much that they've made a hole in the – in the air, and it lets the UV through. I remember that meeting; I watched it on TV with my brother. It was a big deal at the time. All the countries were there, even our own President, José Sarney, before he was voted out. It wasn't just Canadians, though. Montreal just happened to be where the meeting was held.'

'It was us, too? Our politicians did this?'

'Yeah. They had a chance to stop it, but the whole meeting came to nothing, all because of some little thing they couldn't agree on. So they gave up. And here we are.'

'Just because they couldn't agree on every single thing?'

'Yeah. What a waste.' What a waste, indeed, João thought. A turning point in world history had ended up in this young man's mind as a shadowy conspiracy by a group of Canadians. Neither of them had ever met anyone from Canada, he'd wager. Not that João would refuse a ticket there, himself – he'd always wanted to see snow before he died, and he wondered whether the world's rising temperatures would make it impossible.

Scowling, Francisco flung the stick with even more force this time, sending it over the tops of the little mango saplings. The dogs tore through the orchard in joyful pursuit.

The young man had a good arm, for all his skinny build, João realised. Left-handed. He looked too skinny to be a good footballer, but he might do well in some other sport. Joao had seen an American game on TV once there the players threw a small ball with incredible speed and then sprinted around a diamond-shaped arena. There was a time, once, when a boy could go abroad to pursue such dreams.

Several minutes later, both men leaped to their feet when they heard the distant yelps change to barks. '*Porra*,' said João. 'They're back.' He kept his voice low.

'What do they want?' Francisco whispered. 'There're   no more mangoes for them to steal. And it's too early for the avocados.'

'That's what I'm afraid of,' João responded, his voice still at a murmur. 'What they'll do when they figure that out.'

Francisco jammed his hat back on, its clunky visor casting a shadow over his dark eyes. 'They might have seen the stick I threw. Have you got anything?'

'There's a machete on the stump over there next to the coconut tree. I've got my shotgun in the kitchen. Wait for me.' João slipped on a long-sleeved cover and a broad hat as he prayed that the squeak of the front door wouldn't be loud enough to alert the intruders. He couldn't hear their voices, only the dogs' barks, so he hoped they were far enough away that they had not heard his. When he re-emerged, pouring a handful of cartridges into his pocket, Francisco was already moving toward the noise behind the saplings. Guided by the sound of the dogs, they crept around to the other side of the thicket until they could see the gang from the back.

Five men crouched in close conference with each other, clothed in tatters, their faces covered in lesions. The three dogs surrounded them, growling, tails still.

'He's by himself. How much of a fight can he put up?' whispered one of the men, scratching at the peeling skin on his neck.

'He's going to come at us with a shotgun if we're not careful,' their leader replied. 'We need to get into the barn, take whatever we can, and leave. Propane. Phosphate. Seed. Just make it quick. And God damn – can't someone do something about this damn dog?' Amarela was within biting distance. A man in a long-sleeved T-shirt picked up a thick branch and whacked her across the nose. She howled and slunk back three lengths, then continued her low growl.

Behind the thicket, Francisco put his lips to João's ear. 'The sallow man in the middle with the sunken eyes – the leader – that's Rui. He's Senhor de Souza's nephew. He just came back from Campo Grande last week. I saw him while I was picking there. And the tall one, I know him, too; he was picking with me.'

João's face darkened at the name of his neighbour and rival. The de Souzas were still planting on twenty hectares of land that João's own father had cleared. The whole de Souza family felt no compunction about claiming Ribeiro land as their own. Before he could respond, however, Francisco snuck over to the left side of the thicket. Thrashing through the vines to create noise, he strode out in front of the men. 'Hey. Everything good?'

'Beautiful,' replied Rui, with an ironic glance at the sun, now peeking above the line of saplings. 'What are you doing here, kid?'

'Looking for work. Honest work.'

'Does Ribeiro have money to pay you?'

'No, which is why I'm out here talking to you. He has nothing to pick, either – apparently *someone* stole it all.' He held the machete loosely in his left hand.

João, from his hiding place in the thicket, saw Rui de Souza put a hand behind his back and clutch a revolver tucked into his belt. A moment later, everyone else saw it, too, as Rui pointed it directly at Francisco, his sallow face twisted   . 'This has nothing to do with you, kid. So why don't you move along and find your "honest work" somewhere else? And while you're at it, I'll take that machete. We might get a few *reais* for it.'

João could see Francisco's thin shoulders and narrow hips relax, as if he were about to dance a *lambadão cuiabano*. 'All right,' the young man said. 'This whole situation isn't my fault, but I'm in it anyway.' He crouched down and placed the machete on the ground, to one side. In the same motion, he picked up something dark green and hurled it at the gang leader's hand with crippling force.

'*Filho da puta!*' the man shouted, dropping the gun. Behind him, João sprang from the thicket to retrieve it, as Francisco picked up the machete again. The other four men spun around in astonishment, to find themselves facing the twin barrels of João's shotgun.

'Here – Francisco – take the revolver. *Caralho!* Was that an avocado you threw?'

The young man shifted the machete to his right hand and grabbed the gun with his left.

João addressed Rui, keeping the shotgun level. 'You're Fernando de Souza's nephew?' The man nodded. 'You must be new around here. He and I have had our problems, but he knows I've never stolen from him. Let's not make things any worse than they already are.' Amarela now stood at João's side, her growl subsiding to a rumble.

'Look,' Rui responded, 'we've got people to feed. My sister, Noemia – well, we're looking for work too, '"honest work" like this kid, but there's not much available. The last time we had a decent crop was five years ago.'

'So why shouldn't I just shoot all of you? Then you wouldn't be hogging all the food and Noemia could have your share.' He stepped forward.

'Senhor Ribeiro,' said Francisco, 'we need to get into the shade.' None of the men dared look toward the sun, but the tension grew. 'Come on,' Francisco gestured with his machete, 'at least let them sit on your porch.' João sighed and acquiesced.

At a nod from their leader, the five gang members shuffled towards the farmhouse porch. Under the protection of its roof, the man with the peeling neck spoke up. 'Are you going to shoot us or let us go?'

His shout, and the crack of the plastic chair as it collapsed, startled the entire group and set the dogs barking. A shard of plastic skidded across the boards, and the man cursed. In a flash Rui grabbed for the revolver, but Francisco held it tight, his eyes never leaving the gang leader.

'To answer your question, I'm still deciding,' replied João. 'You don't seem to have a lot of respect for my property. What I should do is teach you a lesson – maybe tell you to strip, and make your way back to wherever you came from as best you can. But peak UV starts in less than an hour, and I don't know if you would make it. Besides, it looks as if you've had enough radiation already.'

The man in the long sleeves spat on the ground, startling the dogs, who stood in a watchful circle. 'It's not just the UV – it's the heat. Every time one of those damn rich people in Campo

Grande turns on their air conditioner, it makes that hole in the sky bigger, and it makes the greenhouse effect worse, too. It's a degree and a half hotter than it would have been.'

'Oh, so you're the scientist who knows so much!' João snorted. 'Are you the one who told this poor kid that it was all Canada's fault?' He fingered the trigger of the shotgun.

Francisco spoke up. 'Senhor Ribeiro, you told me it was everything together, all the countries, who had that meeting in Canada. And then they gave up.'

'That they did,' said the man in long sleeves. 'My father told me about it, may he rest in peace.'

'It seems to me,' said Francisco, 'that we're having a meeting right now. Do you want to give up, too?'

João felt a surge of shame. It wasn't the kid's fault he'd had no education; few young people did, these days. And he had a point: there was no use in creating further rancour with a family he was already fighting against. Both the farms were in danger. Twenty hectares of land would make no difference when the fruit it could produce was stolen before it could ripen. Or if there was nothing to steal. When Francisco confronted the men, he had said something: *this whole situation isn't my fault, but I'm in it anyway.*

João stood. 'Rui, we'll be keeping the gun for now. You go tell your uncle that I want to talk to him. Any time after dusk, today, tomorrow. I'll expect him here. We need to decide what we're going to do. Together. And we're not going to give up just because we don't agree on every single thing right from the beginning.'

Rui raised his hooded eyes. 'That's it?'

167

'For today. But we have a lot to work out. And I don't want to see your gang back here pilfering avocados, either. Remember, between the two men living here,' he glanced at an astonished Francisco, 'and the dogs, we'll be keeping a regular watch. If, at that point, any of you want to hire on as pickers, I think we've still got a chance to get a decent price for the crop. This year, anyway. So you'll get wages. But for now, let's all go back to what we were doing before this. Trying to stay alive.'

The five men grumbled as they slunk from the porch into the trees, and soon there was nothing left of them but the black revolver.

'Did you mean that?' asked Francisco. 'When you said I'd be living here.'

'If you agree to it. My brother's room has been empty since he died. And you look like you could use something more substantial than a cup of coffee.'

'I haven't eaten in – a while,' the youth confessed.

'I'm a decent shot with this thing,' João said, gesturing to his shotgun, 'and I bagged a wild pig a couple of days ago. If you fetch a canister of propane from the barn, we can put together a good meal. And we can think about how to survive. For now.'

The Archivist

A story by Grace Chan

The world remembers March 11, 2011 as the day of a triple disaster: first, an earthquake so violent that it literally affected the tilt of the planet; then, a deadly tsunami that decimated Japan's coastal populations; and then, at the Fukushima Daiichi Power Plant, the worst nuclear incident since the Chernobyl disaster of 1986.

Japan is widely regarded as one of the safest and most conscientious societies in the world; it is therefore easy to conclude that this disaster could not have been prevented or lessened by any means. However, not only did the proper means to prevent the nuclear incident already exist within Japan – they were already in place nearby and were successful at another location.

This is us: In 2003, the global average temperature was 0.56°C above pre-industrial levels, then the second highest temperature on record. The dangers were known then, and many systems were already available that had the power to mitigate that rise. Since then, we have learned more, and developed even better solutions, but progress has been too slow. When will we learn from history and make the changes needed?

'Yuriko-chan!'

So startling was the shout from her office door that Yuriko Kimura forgot to respond with the expected 'Shhh!'

A moment later, she was trying to hide her discomfort with a forced laugh as the gangling, unkempt man crushed her in a fierce embrace. 'They should not let a noisy man like you into my library, Oniisan!' she whispered in mock rebuke.

'It would be unkind to keep your big brother Daichi away from you! I was already away for five years when I was at university in Germany and Australia. And here you are with your archive, just as solitary as ever, Imōto. At least it's cooler in here than it is outside in the sun!'

Yuriko surveyed her orderly, peaceful archive. Crumbling maps were unfurled and weighted on felt boards, years of corporate meeting minutes sat in neat stacks, and glass cabinet doors encased ancient land registry records. 'Yes, but you returned to Japan more than three years ago. And if I felt comfortable talking to people, I would have a different job. Historical archivists are also important to large companies like TEPCO, you know.'

Her brother laughed. 'You spend more time with people who died fifty years ago than you do with current members of our society now in 2003. Who's your latest boyfriend – and which century did he live in?'

Yuriko blushed. Her older brother's quip had come closer to reality than he realised. For the past several weeks she had been obsessed with the intense study of a man named Yanosuke Hirai, born in 1902.

Over lunch at a small hot pot restaurant near the TEPCO headquarters, she told Daichi about the famed engineer. 'He built the Onagawa power plant in Miyagi Prefecture, as well as the plant in Niigata. He worked with Yasuzaemon Matsunaga, the man sometimes called the "God of Electricity."' She beamed as she described Hirai's many achievements, from his technical expertise and deep sense of responsibility to his powers of convincing others around him. 'He cared deeply about designing for safety from earthquakes and tsunamis. The Niigata earthquake of 1964 caused the soil in that region to liquefy all the way down to ten metres – but the power plant there was safe, because years earlier, he had built a caisson to a depth of twelve metres! And although large-scale tsunamis are rare, he believed we should always be prepared. Let me list some of the major tsunamis for you. In 1420 –'

Her brother broke in. 'No, no, Imōto, that won't be necessary,' he smiled. 'Your passion for obscure topics is as strong as ever.'   .'

'So what are you going to do with all this knowledge about Engineer Hirai?'

'Is it necessary to do something with such knowledge?' she asked. 'I thought that its acquisition and organisation should be sufficient.'

He shrugged and took a long pull at his beer. 'It's up to you, I guess. Meanwhile, you haven't asked anything about me and my life.'

'Oh! I am sorry.' She paused and remembered the sentence he had taught her. 'Have you ... been doing anything interesting lately?'

'As a matter of fact, yes, I have. I am running for office.'

Yukiro was puzzled. 'Why would you want to do that? I thought you were an environmental activist.'

Daichi laughed again. Yuriko could never understand why he so often found her funny when she was not attempting to joke. He sipped his beer again and continued, 'I understand it's not the kind of thing that's up your alley. Never mind; ten people can be ten different colours. But anyway, I'm not exactly running for Prime Minister; I'm going to be seeking a seat in the Fukushima Prefectural Assembly, in the Iwaki constituency.'

'I see.' Yuriko lifted her teacup and tried to think of something suitable to say. 'Did you know that when Engineer Yanosuke Hirai was Director at the Construction Site of the Kurobe Hydroelectric Power Plant, he argued with the predecessor of the Toyama Prefectural Assembly there? He wanted to maintain operational safety despite wartime operations.'

'No, I didn't know that. Thank you for sharing. Maybe if I win my seat, you'll help me understand more about power plant safety, so I won't have to argue with the power company.'

She frowned. 'Why would you be required to argue with the power company? Oh – I see, another joke.'

After lunch, she was happy to return to the quiet Corporate History Department where she spent her days. The noise of the restaurant was exhausting, although she was careful to let no one see how it affected her. But she couldn't forget her brother's question: what would she do with all her newfound knowledge about Yanosuke Hirai?

It was true that TEPCO operated a power plant in Fukushima Prefecture. Perhaps she could share Engineer Hirai's story with the other employees of the company.

Thinking about what to do, she wrote an email to her colleague, Akana Kobayashi in the Corporate Publicity department. Kobayashi-san had always been very kind to Yuriko. She knew, from Yuriko's complaints, that every time an office moved, many historically important papers were scattered, lost, or discarded. And with the move to electronic communication, it was getting more difficult every day to preserve important records. Kobayashi-san had therefore stepped in several times to save these precious documents and hand them over to Yuriko to be archived.

Now it was Yuriko's turn to pay back the favour. Kobayashi-san had been asking for ideas for the employee newsletter, and Yuriko would volunteer to write an article about Engineer Hirai.

Only a few minutes passed before she received an emailed reply. 'Did Engineer Hirai work for TEPCO?'

Although Yuriko could not understand why this mattered, she explained that he didn't, but that he was a hero of the electrical power world.

Again, the reply came back in minutes. 'It's a good idea. We'll write a series of articles about "Heroes of Electricity,"' suggested Kobayashi-san. 'We can start with that man you called the "God of Electricity", then we can do a piece about Engineer Hirai, and after that we will feature some of the prominent engineers from our own company. Would you be willing to write the first two, and perhaps the others as well?'

Yuriko was pleased with the assignment and fell to it with zeal. Within a few days, she had written more than 15,000 words about Engineer Hirai and the 'God of Electricity' Yasuzaemon Matsunaga, and emailed them to Kobayashi-san.

'I am very sorry, but the articles are too long,' came the response. 'Can you cut them down to around 2,000 words each, please?'

Yuriko rocked back in her seat, brooding. What could she cut, and what must she keep? Engineer Hirai, was famous for his powers of persuasion, would have known; otherwise, there is no way he could have convinced impatient, cost-conscious boards of directors to spend money on the twelve-metre deep caisson in Niigata or the fourteen-metre high seawall that protected the Onagawa Nuclear Power Plant from tsunamis.

Safety measures like these, she thought, are what separated him from others.

She clicked 'Save As' and created a new document.

Almost a year and a half had passed before she saw her big brother again. This time, as he entered her library he tiptoed in an exaggerated manner and winked at the secretaries, making them titter. The performance was lost on Yuriko, however, who was peering at an old map on one of the large, tilted tables.

As she submitted to his hug she asked, 'Did you know that the great Jōgan tsunami of 869 travelled seven kilometres inland?'

'No, Tsunami-chan, I didn't know that. Are you ready for lunch?'

'Yes. You told -me you would arrive at 12:00 noon, and it's now 12:06pm.'

Daichi winked at the secretaries again. 'Good! Let's go.'

As they walked to the same hotpot restaurant they'd eaten at during his last visit, he asked her for any news.

'I recently published six articles in our employee newspaper about the heroes of electricity.'

'Very impressive!'

'I saved a copy of each article for you.' From her black leather bag she drew a multi-ring binder, its plastic sleeves labelled and colour-coded.

He glanced at a few of the labels as he leafed through the binder. 'Thank you! These are from your company's employee newsletter – is it okay for me to read them?'

'Yes, the newspaper is also distributed to workers and their families.'

'I've got to be careful now that I'm an elected official, you know!'

'Oh, yes. Congratulations! Have you been doing anything interesting lately?'

'I'll tell you about it after we sit down.' They had arrived at the restaurant. Christmas decorations hung on the walls, and a strawberry shortcake sat in the display case; the pre-holiday shopping bustle was at its peak.

Yuriko asked, 'When will you read my articles?'

'Not before I decide which beer to order. Excuse me!' He addressed a waitress. 'I will try this new "Draft One" drink from Sapporo; I heard it's trendy. How about you, Yuriko-chan?'

'I would like to drink tea as usual.'

'So, let me tell you what's interesting in my life at the moment.'

'Yes, please.'

'It turns out that serving on the Prefectural Assembly has been an eye-opener. In certain ways, it has a lot in common with my previous job at Friends of the Planet; we were always trying to get the attention of someone who has real power, and always finding that the decisions were made before we were involved. Nothing different there. In another way, however, it's completely different: it's far more serious. I feel I have a responsibility to the citizens of Iwaki constituency.'

'Responsibility is one of the core principles that Yanosuke Hirai espoused.'

'Ah, are you still researching that 100-year-old engineer?'

'No. I have moved on and I am now focusing on other topics. There is a certain atmospheric effect ....'

They continued to talk as they ate. Despite the noise and visual clutter of the restaurant, Yuriko was happy; her brother Daichi was content to let her talk about her interests, and didn't mind that she had ordered the same meal every time they met, while he always preferred to try out whatever was on special. She wished he would come down to Tokyo more often. 'When will you read my articles?' she asked again.

'Probably on the train on the way back. Is that fine with you? he replied.

'Yes. When will you come back to Tokyo?'

He paused. 'Well, I want to be back in Fukushima for New Year, if that's what you're asking. Keiko's parents want to see all their grandchildren together, and the twins are already two years old. Do you have someone to celebrate with?'

'No, I will stay at home, as usual.' Yuriko's apartment was as organised as her archive. Since their parents had died a decade earlier, she had lived alone in a clean, sparse, high-rise building about forty-five minutes from the TEPCO headquarters by train.

Daichi nodded, and finished his soup.

Five days later, however, Yuriko received an unexpected call. 'Imōto, can you come to spend the New Year with us after all?'

'Why?'

She heard him chuckle on the other end of the line. 'I read your articles, and I'd like to talk with you about them. I want to know everything there is to know! And Keiko says you're welcome to join us at her mother's house.'

'Very well. I will prepare.'

The train from Tokyo to Fukushima sped past grey-brown fields on the left, and the slate-blue sea on the right. At the edge of the ocean's horizon, the pale sun showed its yellow face. To pass the time, Yuriko noted the models and identification numbers of each of the slower trains as her faster train whizzed by.

Daichi met her at the station and grimaced as he picked up her heavy suitcase. 'You do realise you're only invited for three days, don't you?'

'Yes. My return ticket is at 11:56am on January 2, 2005.'

'Good. Oof! This bag weighs a ton. Good thing I brought the pickup.'

The bed of Daichi's little kei truck still bore the sign of his previous life, a painted logo in the form of a green ring. He hefted her suitcase into the back. 'Anything delicate in here?'

'No, just books.'

'Good. We're not expecting rain, but your bag might get bumped around a bit.' He got into the driver's seat and started the engine. After several minutes of silence, he asked, 'Have you been reading the news about Indonesia?'

'Yes. It's the most powerful earthquake ever recorded in Asia, and the death toll is expected to reach 200,000.'

'That's what I wanted to ask you about.'

'I can direct you to several newspapers that are covering the story.'

'Thank you. But what I really want to know is – could the same level of damage happen here?'

She thought for a moment, and then spoke for several more.

At last he pulled the truck into a narrow street lined with two- and three-story buildings. Daichi turned off the engine and removed the keys. 'Here we are.'

Climbing down from the cab of the little truck, Yuriko concluded her response to Daichi's question. 'A tsunami can affect any part of the coast, depending where the quake is. But you told me last time we spoke that you didn't want me to go through all the previous tsunami incidents.'

'Well, I've changed my mind. Now I want to hear about them.' An older woman appeared at the gate and the two bowed to each other with friendly smiles. 'Okāsan!' cried Daichi. 'This is my younger sister, Yuriko Kimura. You may remember that you met each other at our wedding.'

'Of course I do. How are you, Yuriko-chan? Your nephews will be pleased to see you. Try to forgive them for being a little bit noisy!'

Yuriko bowed in turn. 'We have met on two occasions, and the most recent one was on Saturday, January 26, 2002, when my brother was in Tokyo with you. It was five degrees Celsius that day.'

'Now I'm the foolish one!' said Daichi, pointing to his nose and laughing. 'I'd forgotten.'

After dinner, when the boisterous children were finally asleep and the rest of the family had retired, Daichi quizzed Yuriko long into the night. His newfound interest in tsunamis was equalled only by her own. 'So explain to me – why would Engineer Hirai insist on building a seawall of fourteen metres at the Onagawa plant while the one at the Fukushima Daiichi plant is only 5.7 metres?'

'He researched the history of tsunamis in Japan and observed that waves of ten metres or higher have occurred up and down our coast. In some cases it was before recorded history, but biological markers such as tree lines provide a clue. Perhaps the engineers in charge of the Fukushima plant did not do the same research.'

'Okay, fine. But why not higher? This past week, the people of Aceh in Indonesia reported a wall of water thirty-six metres high.'

'The geology of our tectonic plates differs from that in the Indian Ocean. Most of our geologists agree that an earthquake stronger than 8.0 on the Richter scale is unlikely.'

'But not impossible.'

'Not impossible. But even if we experience a quake of 9.0 or higher, the undersea conditions are not the same. Therefore,

Engineer Hirai determined that fourteen metres was a suitable height.'

Daichi sat back on his heels and contemplated what he had heard. 'Your articles were really well-written, Yuriko-chan. I'm sorry I called you Tsumanarai-chan for so long. They were really interesting.'

'I've brought several books for you,' she offered, reaching into her heavy valise, 'about the seismological history of Japan, principles of industrial safety, and operational issues at nuclear power plants.' She handed over a stack of dense and weighty tomes.

'Oh, my,' her brother responded, looking through them. 'I'm never going to be able to get through these before you go back to Tokyo.'

'You don't need to return them. I bought them for you.'

Daichi examined the books, each of which had cost tens of thousands of yen. 'Thank you. You really are my favourite sister in the world.'

Yuriko frowned. 'I am your only sister.'

'It doesn't mean you can't be my favourite,' he replied, touching her sleeve.

She was relieved; at last he had remembered how much she hated his spontaneous hugs. It was a habit he had picked up while overseas.

Yuriko could not decide, the following spring, whether she was surprised to read about her brother's fiery speeches in the news. She had suspected that he would make use of her information to put pressure on the Fukushima Daiichi Power plant to build a higher seawall, although she had not imagined he would make it the centre of his platform.

What did surprise her, however, was that her profile of Yanosuke Hirai was picked up and reprinted by *Yomiuri Shimbun*. She was pleased to be credited as the author, a 'noted historian'. In a moment of boldness, she bought another copy of the newspaper, cut out and mounted the story on archival card, and hung it on the wall of her office.

Within the year, a new seawall began to rise along the coast, surrounding the Fukushima Daiichi power plant. Yuriko clipped these news stories as well, and saved them in a new box file tucked away in the 'Special Projects' section of the archive. She wrote an email to her brother, congratulating him on his success. He answered only with 'www'; she hoped that meant he appreciated her note.

Although she continued to make an annual New Year's pilgrimage to see her brother and his family, she was always relieved to return home to the peace of her apartment. Even her work was more hectic than before; she was often asked, now, to write a piece for one outlet or another on some historic figure from industry. Kobayashi-san encouraged this, saying it would help the company's public relations efforts.

Meanwhile, Daichi's party was voted out of office, and back in again a year later; she could not keep track of the reasons.

And then, in 2011, the impossible happened.

'The consensus was 8.0 at a maximum,' she explained to Kobayashi-san, from the Corporate Communications department. Her embattled colleague had fled to Yuriko's archive for a few precious moments of sanctuary, among the deluge of media queries. 'Although researcher Yasutaka Ikeda stated in 2005 at a conference in Hokudan that we should prepare for a 9.0 quake, his opinion was not taken seriously.'

'But your family is safe?'

'My family? No, my family is dead.'

'Don't you have a brother in the affected area?'

'Oh, I understand. Yes. He's my favourite brother. But their house is located far from the coast, in a modern building in Fukushima City. They suffered some damage to their furniture, but nothing serious. And you?'

'My family lives here in Tokyo. But my team and I are exhausted. We're updating our website every hour with detailed information on the expectations for the resumption of power services, and the damage to the Fukushima Daiichi Power Plant. It shut down safely, but the third floor sustained structural damage and we don't know when it can start up again. I've had to come here to get away from them all.'

Yuriko frowned. 'So the seawall was ineffective?'

'Ineffective! On the contrary, without that seawall, the water would have flooded the turbine and reactor buildings! I can't even imagine ...' her voice trailed off, lost in contemplation of the horror that might have been.

'And what about Onagawa plant?'

'Same. They're safe, but they've also shut down. I'm afraid the region will have serious blackouts for some time. We won't have enough power for all the air conditioners in a few months. If they aren't able to start up again, it's going to be a long, hot summer.'

Yuriko commented, 'Our elders and ancestors endured many summers without air conditioning. We can learn from their wisdom.'

'It's true,' Kobayashi-san replied. 'They knew many things we have forgotten. Say, that might be a good topic for an article in our employee newsletter at some point after this crisis calms down. Want to write it?'

Yuriko nodded again. 'Perhaps. But I think there is a more timely issue. Our power plant has survived a tsunami thanks to its seawall. But what about all the other nuclear plants around the world that are located next to oceans? The sea levels are rising, because of *global warming.*' She used the English word. 'When that happens, what will protect them?'

'This is an excellent question,' Kobayashi-san replied, 'but today, I need to deal with the website. Still – promise me you won't forget this?'

'I will not,' Yuriko promised.

She turned on her computer and opened up a new folder. 'This one is even more important. Engineer Hirai would have known.'

The Manilamen

A story by Grace Chan

Hurricane Katrina, one of the most devastating tropical storms of the modern era, caused 1,392 fatalities when it struck the Gulf Coast of the United States in August 2005. A particular tragedy of the storm was its impact on the elderly: around 215 bodies were discovered in nursing homes and hospitals in New Orleans, having perished from dehydration or the stress of evacuation. Hundreds of other patients and residents suffered without power, food, or fresh water for days.

The impossible situation meant that for many caretakers, nothing could be done to save the residents. But in other cases, the scale of devastation might have been lessened by using the resources at hand.

This is us. In 2005, the global average temperature was still just 0.71°C above pre-industrial levels. Will we work within the constraints of our current situation and find resourceful ways to mitigate the damage on our planet and on ourselves?

'Are the diapers here yet?' Marco asked. 'Mrs Robillaux on Ward Three needs to be changed.'

Dolores shook her head, her dark ponytail swinging. 'No. But Gabriel's gone to buy the incontinence pads and some other stuff from the Walmart. He said it's Friday already, and he's done with waiting around for supplies.'

184

Marco snorted. 'Good luck trying to get that reimbursed!' There was bitterness in his voice; his fifty years had taught him never to trust the boss, whether it was back home in the Philippines or here in New Orleans in the United States. But perhaps Gabriel was still young enough to believe in people's fundamental goodness.

A buzzer sounded. Mr Laplace on Ward Two wanted something. 'Okay, Boss, Mrs Robillaux will have to wait a little longer,' Marco told Dolores, 'so I'll take this one in the meantime. And let me know if Joseph shows up; he's on for the two to ten shift, but nobody's heard from him.'

'Oh, he'll be here,' said Dolores. 'I'll hand him his own backside wrapped in a catheter if he doesn't show. And he knows it. I owe him a couple of write-ups as it is.'

Marco laughed and lumbered off to Ward Three. In every room, the television was blaring. He wished he could turn them down, or at least wear earplugs. But the residents, many half deaf, needed the volume high. And they needed him to be alert to their needs. One was in constant pain, another was disoriented, and some were just lonely. Mrs Picard's children had never once visited her in the two years he'd been working at Folded Wings Nursing Home, here at the edge of the city. It was an odd place: the repurposed terminal of a small, private Louisiana airport originally constructed for oil millionaires in the 1980s, and abandoned in the wake of 9/11 and the dot-com bust. Some residents thought they were waiting to board; they made repeated requests for their gate number, but their flights never arrived.

At least there was something interesting to watch on TV today other than soap operas and game shows. Instead, it was all about the weather.

'Katrina was declared a Category Three storm at five o'clock this morning,' an excited blond woman in a raincoat was saying. 'St. Charles Parish, St. Tammany Parish, and Plaquemines Parish have ordered a mandatory evacuation of all residents, while Jefferson and St. Bernard Parishes have made recommendations for voluntary evacuation. Tolls are now suspended on the Lake Pontchartrain Causeway as well as the Crescent City Connection, to speed up evacuations.'

Hmph! Americans were spoiled, Marco thought to himself. He remembered the many typhoons, most much stronger than this storm, that had ploughed through Luzon year after year. It was as predictable as a daytime soap: a tropical depression would form somewhere in the Pacific Ocean, build in strength, and make its inevitable beeline for the northern Philippines.

Bwisit, he thought, but didn't say it out loud, even 14,000 kilometres away from home – you never knew when and where you'd find a Filipina grandmother ready to scold you for using foul language. He chuckled to himself.

'What's going on with you this morning, Mr Laplace?' he cried as he entered the room and turned off the call switch. It was sad, the way these old folks lived, far from their families, with buzzing 1980s lighting overhead and the stink of disinfectant permeating the ward. Meanwhile, the August weather outside was sticky and unbearable, and the creaking air conditioners strained to keep up.

He took in the room at a glance and understood why the old man had called him. The upper half of Mr Laplace's bed was

186

tilted up, allowing him to sit up and read and watch TV during the day. But over the course of the morning, the old gentleman had slid down so far that his spindly legs were bent against the footboard, and he couldn't reach the grab bar above him to pull himself up. 'Oh, I see it. No problem, sir!' The old men liked that, when you called them sir. 'Let me get you set up, there.' Marco's broad smile shone in his bright brown face. Mr Laplace was as light as a sheaf of rice straw after the paddy had dried along the summer roadsides. 'Is that fine?'

The man responded only with a vacant stare, his jaw open and a thread of moisture hanging from it. Marco said, 'May I?' and wiped his mouth. Mr Laplace was not the best company, but he was better than some of those in Ward One, the Memory Ward. Alzheimer's, Parkinson's, or other debilitating maladies had robbed them of any vestige of their Southern charm. Some felt free to address him with whatever racial slur first came to mind.

'The National Hurricane Center has issued a Hurricane Watch from Morgan City,' the blond weather girl was saying, but Marco wasn't worried. The two-story cinder block building was sturdy enough to withstand high winds, although he wondered how the hangar, the former control tower, and the five-story parking garage would fare. The oversized garage was not part of the airport; it was the first phase of an adjacent shopping mall complex that was never built and now stood as a monument to the developers' arrogance. Nobody had been up to the control tower since the airport had gone bust four years back.

In any case, there were two backup generators in case the power went out.

His immediate concern was the buzzer – no, make that the three buzzers – now sounding. And he hadn't even properly started his afternoon rounds yet. Three workers handling sixty-two residents, most too frail to take themselves to the bathroom, was criminal understaffing. But that was all Medicare would cover, so they were told. The owners of Folded Wings Nursing Home, who lived somewhere in Florida, did not share the full details of the accounts with the staff.

Meanwhile, Gabriel still wasn't back from the Walmart, and he was worried Mrs Robillaux, already suffering from diabetes and other complications of obesity, would end up with another urinary tract infection if he didn't change her diaper soon.

Residents with infections often got confused. That very morning, one of them, a wrinkled, brown-skinned man with an infection around his ostomy port, claimed to be a deserter from a Spanish galleon. He grasped Marco's wrist with an ancient claw. 'They're going with General Jackson! But they'll never make it out alive,' he cried, before demanding to know why he hadn't received his portion of Jell-O that morning. It was nothing like Mr Jerome's ordinary personality; he had been a counter-culture warrior of some kind in the late 1950s, a graffiti artist and a hippie, and was more apt to rage against the machine than to dwell on Spanish galleons. Maybe Marco would ask the old man about it once the antibiotics kicked in and he recovered his senses. Despite being confined to a wheelchair, Mr Jerome was normally one of the more mobile residents, restless, pushing himself through long-abandoned corridors to explore the bowels of the old airport.

Marco was planning to tell Gabriel about it when he arrived. But the mobility van didn't pull into the runway-turned-

188

driveway until after one o'clock, and as Marco helped Gabriel unpack his purchases he saw that the younger orderly had more to tell.

'It was a madhouse there, man!' Gabriel said, hoisting a bale of bottled water over his head. 'People were stripping the shelves bare. Milk, water, flashlights, canned goods, cereal boxes, you name it.'

'Looks like you were the one doing the stripping.'

'I'm lucky I got all this stuff as it was.'

'What, you think the hurricane's going to hit us that bad?'

'I'd have bought the last canoe if some woman in front of me hadn't've grabbed it right out in front of me. That woman was a beast, man,' he mused. 'This storm is a beast, too.'

'My shift's over in half an hour anyway. I wonder if Joseph will show?' Marco hustled inside to avoid the rain, which had begun to splat on the steaming tarmac in huge drips. The wind was rising.

'Christina should be here for the two to ten shift, anyway,' Gabriel said. 'Miss Reliable!'

Marco knew what Gabriel was thinking, because it was on his mind, too: the abandonment laws. Even if their shift had ended, if the other workers didn't show, they needed to stay or they could be prosecuted. Marco didn't particularly relish the idea of driving back home to his trailer and riding out a hurricane alone, but it would be better than spending the storm at work. He was already bone tired. He'd arisen before dawn to make the six to two shift, and the previous day he'd pulled a double shift, six in the morning to ten at night. Dolores would be pulling a double today.

'Come on, man, help me with this crate of Ensure,' Gabriel was saying. As they emptied the van, Marco told him about old Mr Jerome and his delirium.

'Oh, I know what he's talking about,' Gabriel responded, to Marco's surprise. 'The old guy's a Pinoy like us, yeah?'

'Yeah.'

'Then he's talking about the Manilamen.'

'Men from Manila?' Marco asked.

'Back in the 1700s,' Gabriel explained, 'Spain owned half the world, right? The Philippines, Mexico, and Louisiana right here, too.'

'Not the French?'

'Not at that point. The Spanish took Filipinos as slaves to work on their ships. But some of those guys escaped, and ended up here. And they ended up fighting for the United States in the War of 1812 under General Jackson, and becoming war heroes. Everyone called them the Manilamen.'

'Wait, which war was that?'

'The War of 1812? It was the one fought in 1812, dumbass. America versus England.'

Marco shook his head. 'How do you know these things?'

'You never go online? You never heard of Wikipedia?'

Marco shook his head again. 'I don't have internet in the trailer. So, what, you think maybe Mr Jerome was one of them?'

'What? No, it's 2005!' Gabriel hooted. 'He'd have to be like 200 years old. He's ancient, but that would be a stretch.'

'Well, you never know. My friend told me about this one old Indian guy –'

'The Manilamen, though, those guys were hard core. Just set themselves up in the bayous of Louisiana, picked up right where they'd left off in the Philippines. Built a whole village called St. Malo, full of houses that looked just like *báhay kúbo*. The palmetto rotted, so they had to replace it every other minute. No mattresses, so they made them out of sailcloth and Spanish moss. No bed frames, so they put the mattresses on shelves on the walls. Then half of them went off to become pirates.' Gabriel was flushed with admiration for the ancient deserters.

Dolores emerged to help them cart the goods to the kitchen on the top floor of the low-slung building.

Two o'clock arrived. To their surprise, both Joseph and Christina arrived on the dot. 'Okay, I'm outta here!' Marco smiled, heading for his moped.

'Wait.' Dolores's voice held a note he'd never heard: fear.

He stopped. 'What do you need?'

'If we have to ...'

'If we have to what?'

'You heard. They've already evacuated some of the lower-lying parishes. If we have to go, there's going to be no way the three of us can handle everyone.'

'If it comes to that,' Marco said, 'then five of us won't be much better than three.'

'I'm asking you to stay. For a while.'

Marco glanced over at Gabriel, who hadn't made a move towards his own truck. 'Come on – you don't seriously think – ?' The younger man studied his own shoelaces, his hands pushed deep into the pockets of his uniform. 'Well, that's *bwisit* if I ever heard it. Fine. I'll stay. For a little while. But then I'm out of here.'

Friday night and Saturday had passed into Sunday morning, and Marco was giving grim thanks to Gabriel for his foresight. The five staff members stopped speaking of shifts, and instead held impromptu meetings to distribute cereal and Ensure, allocate bottled water, and feed the generators. The kitchen was useless without power or water.

The last thing they'd seen on the news, before the electricity went out in the wee hours of the morning, was that Katrina had been upgraded to a Category Four. This type of hurricane in the Atlantic was far more frightening than a TCWS Number Four back home, although Marco supposed they were equivalent.

'We don't know how long this will last, and our fuel might run out before the power comes back,' Dolores had said at breakfast. 'I say we stop everything but the most essential electrical services – I'm talking about medically necessary equipment – and only use one generator for now.'

'All right, *Nurse* Dolores,' said Marco. Despite the rain and wind, the heat was oppressive inside the concrete building, and they would suffer without the air conditioning. But he knew she was right. Back home, he'd lived through enough power cuts to understand that it was better to have too much fuel left over when the power came back than it was to run out too early.

The good news is that the antibiotics were doing their job with Mr Jerome, who was back to his lucid self. He'd awakened in the dark and shouted for Marco when he found that the call button didn't work. The old Pinoy remembered nothing of his dream forays with General Jackson and the other Manilamen, and was now restlessly wheeling himself up and down the sweltering halls. Marco was concerned that the old man's dogged infection would return in the sticky heat, and returned to Mr Jerome's room to remind him to take the full course of medication. Would their doctor arrive for his usual Tuesday visit? Anything might happen before then. Marco decided he'd leave and head to the Superdome as soon as he'd checked on Mr Jerome.

As he neared the room, he passed the Folded Wings Nursing Home signboard. 'Mr Jerome! Is this your work?' he shouted to the old man, now absconding in his getaway wheelchair. Someone had taken a can of spray paint to the sign, covering the word 'Folded' with an artistic rendering of the word 'Flooded'.

'Me?' the old man spun around and gave an innocent grin. 'How could I reach it? I'm stuck here in this chair.'

'You think it's going to flood?'

'I worked on the levees during Hurricane Betsy back in 1965. I always expect a flood.'

'Has it ever happened since then?'

'No, but only because every time a hurricane happens, thousands of people in Louisiana pray to Jesus for the levees to hold. Still, if I were the Lord, my patience would be getting exhausted by now.'

Marco laughed. 'Mrs Picard has a radio and some batteries. She's in the common room. Do you want to go over there and listen? It might keep you out of mischief.' The common room had once been a lounge where rich men and women waited for their private pilots to whisk them around the world; now, the faded brown furniture provided a shabby but serviceable gathering place for the residents of Folded Wings.

He heard the wind and his sinking heart told him the moped wouldn't make it. *Bwisit.*

In the meantime, Marco, Dolores, and Christina headed to the old terminal warehouse and gathered all the trollies, trucks, and hand carts they could find. Gabriel found a mini forklift in the hangar, and, to Marco's surprise, had hot-wired it within a few minutes.

'You really think we're going to use that?' Marco asked.

'No,' Gabriel grinned, 'But you never know.'

Mrs Picard's radio confirmed what they'd been suspecting all along: that all Orleans parish was now under a mandatory evacuation order.

'And how exactly do they expect us to evacuate?' Marco asked the other staff, who were all squatting in the corner of the common room. 'We've got, what, four of our own cars, each of which can carry two or three people plus the driver – that's eighteen at most – along with my moped and a mobility van that can fit one wheelchair max. So eighteen spots, for sixty-two residents.'

'Only three cars, actually,' said Christina. 'Joseph gave me a ride to work, because I didn't think my old Chevy could make it. And don't forget, Joseph's truck only fits one person in the cab other than the driver.'

'How many of the residents can walk?' asked Gabriel.

'What, we're going to ask them to walk?' retorted Marco. 'You heard the National Weather Service. Anyone without shelter is going to face "certain death." How far away is the Superdome, anyway? There's no way they could make it.'

'The wind won't affect a cinderblock building,' Dolores said. 'We'll be okay; we're not in a trailer park and this isn't a tornado.' Marco spared a thought for his trailer as he glanced outside. How would he get to the Superdome now?

Gabriel continued, 'No, I wasn't suggesting anyone walk. I'm thinking about what happens if it floods. We need to get the residents up to higher ground.'

Mr Jerome's warning about the Lord's impatience rang in Marco's ears. 'What higher ground?' he asked.

Gabriel stood up and assumed an unmistakable air of command. 'We need a better contingency plan. Dolores, how many wheelchairs do we have?'

Marco was surprised how quickly Dolores, Gabriel's nominal boss, accepted the upending of the ordinary hierarchy. 'A dozen,' she replied. 'And as to your earlier question, no more than two thirds of the residents are fully ambulatory. There are twenty in the common room now, but that's including the ones like Mr Jerome, who don't walk but can operate their own chairs. So if we're moving them anywhere, we need at least two dozen more chairs. And I think some of them wouldn't survive a car transfer. I don't know how we'd even get them into that jacked-up truck of yours, Gabriel.'

Gabriel ignored the slight.

'Okay. Moving by car is out of the question, so we'll stay here and work with what we have. Also, it won't hurt to let them know we're here. Go find Mr Jerome and ask him for his spray paint. And then find a way to get onto the roof of Ward Two – that's the biggest flat area, with the gravel covering – and paint HELP on it, as big as you can make it. Do it one line first, because we don't know how much paint is left in that can, and then thicken the letters up so they're more visible. Wear a raincoat, and take a couple of the medical restraint straps to tether yourself to the railing – you don't want to get blown away.'

They all flinched at the sound of breaking glass. A piece of flying debris had struck the far window of the common room.

'I think we can transport at least three people on a luggage cart if we nest them like bobsledders,' Gabriel mused.

'Where would we take them?' Joseph asked.

'Step one will be to get them to the base of the control tower,' Gabriel replied. 'After that, we would need to carry them up the steps one by one.'

All five of the staff looked out the big window at the old runway, and beyond it, the squat, broad control tower. Almost invisible in the downpour, it stood at the very opposite end of the old airport premises, nearly half a kilometre away from where they were sitting.

'*Bwisit*,' said Marco, out loud this time. He saw a twitch of Dolores's mouth that might have been a smile, but the faces of the others remained still. 'Is the control tower big enough?'

'We'll be packed tight, but I think so. We only do this,' Gabriel reminded them, 'if the flood reaches us.' The rain was cascading in sheets, flowing across the old runway tarmac at an alarming speed.

'Fine,' replied Marco. 'It's good to have a plan.' He eyed Gabriel's muscle truck out on the lot and wondered where the younger man kept his keys.

It was pitch black when Gabriel shook Marco's arm. Amid the shriek of the wind, he felt he had slept for less than an hour; he had been dreaming of peanut butter. At home, they would take enormous bags of their roasted peanuts to the man in the centre of town who had a grinder, add sugar, and return with delicious, oily jars of sweet peanut butter. Marco didn't care for the American supermarket brands.

Gabriel shoved half a peanut butter flavoured granola bar into his hand as he roused him. 'Let's go. The flood walls are gone. Christina heard it on the radio.'

'What time is it?' asked Marco, his body begging him to stay put.

'Five thirty. The water is going to reach us soon. We've got to move the residents.'

Marco struggled to alertness. 'Do we have the luggage carts?'

'Dolores and Joseph are getting them. We'll ask everyone who can manage it to propel themselves, and for those who can't, we'll push them in relays.'

'Okay.'

A few minutes later, they were leading a procession down the halls of the old terminal, past the common area and towards the main hangar. 'The windows in the kitchen upstairs were blown out! And the roof came off Ward D late last night,' Gabriel shouted over the noise of the wind.

Mrs Picard was pushing Mr Laplace's wheelchair, while Mr Jerome moved his own wheels. 'Take the left-hand side; that's where the ramp is.' The men nodded their heads and followed his lead toward the main hangar.

The floors were thick with broken glass, and the view from the old hangar's windows was a shallow, rising lake, stretching as far as the eye could see. Debris floated in the filthy, wave-capped water.

They arrived at the control tower. The door at its base was chained shut and a padlock.

'*Putang ina mo!*' Marco cursed. 'If it isn't one thing, it's another.'

Mr Jerome rolled in from the rear and examined the lock. 'Gabriel, gimme that,' he instructed, pointing toward an old aluminium beer can in the corner. 'Dolores, Christina, I need something I can use as a wave rake. Either of you got a bobby pin?' With a quizzical expression, Dolores reached to the back of her head, pulled out a brassy black little object, and handed it to him. A lock of hair came loose and floated to her cheek.

'You think you can open this?' asked Gabriel. 'If so, I'm gonna go back for the others.'

'This brand of padlock is infamous,' Mr Jerome chuckled. 'Back in the day, we called it the toddler's starter lock. It might take me a minute with my arthritis, but let's see.'

Gabriel nodded and motioned for the other staff to follow him back to the main wards. 'Okay, folks, let's —'

'Got it!' cried Mr Jerome, as the padlock clicked open.

The staff hooted with laughter. 'Fantastic, Mr Jerome! Okay now,' Gabriel called out. 'Those of you who think you can climb stairs on your own, please get going. Slowly, one step at a time, holding the handrail. Everyone else, stay put. Christina, stay here. We'll be back.'

Half an hour later, they returned with the last group of their bizarre cargo: two, three, and even four residents on a single luggage cart, crying or singing hymns. One was mumbling, 'Just let me die here,' but most showed more determination than they had in all the time Marco had known them. The staff had put as many supplies as possible into the upper baskets of the luggage carts, and stuffed their pockets with what was left.

Marco had something else in his pocket. Gabriel's keys.

Although the filthy water was still rising steadily, he was certain Gabriel's big truck could get him to safety and higher ground. The giant Ford was a monster, built for harsh conditions, and anyone who wanted to evacuate had likely already gone, so the highways, while awash, were probably clear of traffic.

The Superdome was only thirty miles away. He could make it.

This whole thing was hopeless anyway, he rationalised. They'd never get the non-ambulatory residents up those stairs. Plus, it wasn't his shift, and Joseph and Christina were both there, so he couldn't be prosecuted for abandonment.

He needed to save himself first.

Most of the ambulatory residents had already disappeared up the stairs, climbing as though struggling through a flood of molasses. Christina and Marco were already beginning to help the next group of residents up: those with some mobility but who couldn't manage steps alone. The third group waited. It was the smallest, thank God. Some were weeping but most sat silently on their luggage carts and in their wheelchairs, to be helped or carried one by one. It was eight flights to the top.

I can't do this, Marco thought. I'm fifty years old and my knees are already shot. There's no way. I've got to look after myself. You can't save everyone.

As Marco hesitated, Mr Jerome wheeled up beside him. 'Are you a Manila man?' he asked.

Marco froze. 'What?'

'Just making conversation while I wait my turn. I wondered if you were from Manila, or from somewhere else.'

'Oh. I thought you said something else.'

'I was born in Urdaneta, you know,' Mr Jerome continued. 'They call it Urdaneta City now, but it was just a town back then. In Pangasinan, a few hundred kilometres north of Manila. It's been a long journey for me, in more ways than one.'

'I guess so.' Marco felt the keys in his pocket and glanced out the window. 'How long since you've been back home?'

'Home to Urdaneta? I never went back. Once I decided   to come here, I was all in. If you keep telling yourself, "Oh, I'll stay for a little while but then decide later," it means someone else is deciding things for you. When I make a choice, I stick to it.'

Marco thought of the 'Manilamen' Gabriel had told him about. Having escaped from their galleons and found a place to settle down, they should have left well enough alone. They didn't owe anything to anybody. But they'd gone on to fight in the war, and become heroes. What had gone through their minds when they first escaped? Why had they decided to leave their huts in the Louisiana wilderness? He imagined the Manilamen returning after their service to General Jackson, heroic in victory, only to find their huts overtaken by rot.

'And besides,' Mr Jerome was saying, 'now this is my home. Home is the people you live with, the people you work with, who've sacrificed their time and money and effort for you – they're the ones you owe your loyalty to, not the place you were born or the house you happen to live in.'

'Didn't you have a family here? Weren't you married?' Marco asked, curious.

'I'm what they used to call a "confirmed bachelor",' Mr Jerome replied, with a wink.

Before Marco could ask more questions, Dolores shouted to him, 'Come on, we need a hand here!'

With that, Marco's desperation left him, and he turned to do his duty.

Two exhausting hours passed before they finished carrying up the last resident. The wind made the entire control tower shudder, and the control room itself was cramped and dusty, barely enough for all the residents to sit or lie. But the structure held steady, and its top was positioned far above the deadly flood below. Mr Jerome, one of the last to be carried up, cried out, 'God bless late-stage capitalism!' Marco wondered what he meant.

Below, the big doors of the main wards were still holding off the flood, but water had already seeped into the hangar and was already a half a foot deep. Marco was about to nip outside and move his moped into the abandoned parking garage when Gabriel grabbed his arm.

'What now?' Marco asked.

'Mrs Robillaux. She's still in her room.'

With horror, Marco understood. Carrying Mr Laplace up those steps was one thing. But Mrs Robillaux was another story. It normally took four of them working together to get her onto their single bariatric wheelchair. The chair was currently in the repair shop.

Marco shook his head. 'There's no way we can get her up there.'

For the first time since the disaster began, Gabriel looked hopeless. 'I don't want to leave her there.'

'Would the top of the car park be high enough?'

Gabriel glanced out the window. 'Maybe. It's four stories up, probably twenty feet. But she couldn't stay there, man. It's exposed to the wind on three sides.'

'What about putting her inside your truck?'

'Yeah,' Gabriel nodded. 'We'll need the forklift to get her there, but I think she could ride out the storm inside if she had to.'

Without a word, Marco shoved a hand into his pocket, withdrew the keys, showed them to Gabriel and said, 'I won't leave anyone behind if I can help it. I'll get your truck. You tell Joseph and Christina and get that forklift started.'

'What —' Gabriel began, but Marco had already sprinted back towards the control tower.

It would be another two days before they released Mrs Robillaux from the truck, sobbing and disoriented. They'd had to tear out the back seats in a rush as she languished on the forklift, but there was just enough room for her, and the truck protected her from the elements. Twice, during lulls in the storm, Marco and Gabriel had climbed down from the crowded control tower and made their way over the floodwaters along a precarious service catwalk to the garage. There, they changed her incontinence pads and checked her supplies. But she had spent much of the time wet and miserable.

'It's okay, Mrs Robillaux,' Marco said. 'This will be over soon. They're coming to get us. A helicopter saw Joseph's sign on the roof, and dropped a walkie talkie down to us. But the wards are all under water, so we probably need to sit tight for another day or two.' The news only increased her tears.

'Have you heard from my children?' she wept.

'No,' said Marco, 'but I'll see what I can find out.'

The two men returned to the catwalk and Marco wondered again what might have become of his trailer. His moped, transferred at the last moment to the parking garage, was standing next to Gabriel's truck, leaning beside it like an old companion.

'Hey Gabriel,' Marco asked, remembering something. 'That village where the Manilamen lived, the one you were telling me about.'

'Yeah, St Malo. I remember.'

'Is the place still around?'

There was a wry look on Gabriel's face. 'Looks like they got wiped out back in 1915, and everyone scattered. Nobody's left nowadays.'

'What happened?' asked Marco.

'Flattened by a hurricane,' the younger man said, shrugging his shoulders. 'You can't save everyone.'

The Yellow Rat

A story by Grace Chan

The 2008 earthquake in Sichuan, China was felt a thousand miles away. By the time the final toll was counted, it was clear that more than 69,000 people had lost their lives.

Most of those affected were in no position to construct monumental fortifications or implement Herculean solutions. But when we listen and think ahead in places where others only speak and react, opportunities can reveal themselves that we would otherwise overlook. Not everyone will grasp these opportunities, but the one who does may come from anywhere.

This is us. In 2008, the global average temperature was 0.9°C above pre-industrial levels. As our climate changes, natural disasters are increasing around the world. Where will your opportunity come from?

The village had not changed since the last time Huang Ning was home.

In the industrial city of Dongguan, every week brought a new batch of migrants, a new group of workers, a new factory opening, a new chance. But back in Luobozhai, in Sichuan Province, it was the same as ever. Small, rainy, and boring. The name of the little hamlet itself was banal, laughable: Radish Village.

Ning descended from the rattling bus, annoyance and defeat showing on his face. As the bus pulled away, he kicked a clod of early spring mud, sending a squawking chicken running in the opposite direction.

His final pay cheque, including severance, was enough to buy one of the cheaper mobile phone models. In Luobozhai, however, no mobile phone tower was close enough for him to get a signal. Frustrated, he checked the phone again, but the characters 'no network' were all that showed on the little screen. He'd heard that the government was merging the phone companies into three large groups; maybe one of them would bring a tower to Radish Village. For now, the rest of the world might be living in 2008, but Luobozhai was stuck in the past.

Three other young people were in the same situation, including his younger sister, Huang Luo. All four left the village together on an over-crowded, long-distance bus to Guangdong Province, found work at a new electronics factory in Dongguan, and were all sacked together. Luo and the other two, disheartened, returned home right away. Ning swore he would find a new job, and stayed for three more weeks, until his money ran out. But at last, he had to admit that he was a rare breed: a healthy twenty-five-year-old man in Dongguan who couldn't find work.

They were lucky to receive a final pay cheque. 'I've been keeping my eye on the American market,' the blunt factory boss told his laid-off workers. 'I think they're going to have a financial downturn, and that's where most of our customers are. This isn't the first time I've managed a business through difficulties: I was here during the 1998 crisis, the dot-com bust in 2001, and the post-SARS slump in 2003. So I won't risk keeping on extra workers, when the buyer might cut my contract at any moment.'

He was a fool! thought Ning, frustrated. According to the TV, both the Chinese economy and the American economy were as strong as ever. Was this not 2008, the year of the auspicious number eight? In a few months, the Summer Olympics would take place in Beijing for the first time, beginning on August 8. He was proud: at last, China was ready to step onto the global stage.

If only he could get a *hukou*, a residence registration, he would go to Beijing to find a job. No jobs were to be had in Luobozhai, and wages were pitiful for those jobs that did exist. How was he going to support his mother and four grandparents now? Giving birth to Luo twenty years earlier already strained his mother's finances; she tried to argue that even though they weren't members of the Qiang ethnic minority, they still had the right to a second child. But the village family planning council disagreed, and levied fines all the same. She never let Luo forget it, reminding her again and again how lucky her daughter was not to have been abandoned at birth, or given away.

Ning himself was not sure whether to feel guilty or resentful about having a second child in the family. Most of all, he wished he could have stayed in school, and not had to go out to earn. For as long as he was allowed to attend, he loved learning about science, dissecting creatures and finding out what was inside, and tinkering with batteries and resistors and electrical wires. If he had been able to stay for a few more years, perhaps he could have performed a more useful function at the Dongguan factory, more than cleaning the equipment. But when his father died, there was not enough money.

The morning after his arrival back in the village, a rooster's crow, followed by the clucking of chickens and the squeals of the neighbour's pigs, conspired to wrench Ning out of bed before it was light. The dormitories in the factory, crowded though they were, had never antagonised him like the cacophony of a working farm.

His mother was already up, squatting before a fussy little coal stove, persuading it to light. 'As long as you're here,' she nodded towards the bag of feed. It was the longest sentence she'd spoken to him since he returned.

He rose, scratched himself, and went out to tend to the chickens.

As he scattered the feed in front of their coop, he saw how agitated they were. Two wouldn't come out of the coop at all. Only one had laid an egg. It was a plucky little hen, smaller than the others, with soft grey feathers. He smiled and scratched her head. 'Good girl! What's wrong with the rest of them?' he asked Luo, who was standing in the yard, brushing her teeth.

'There was a little earthquake last night. Didn't you feel it?'

'No. I was too exhausted from the trip, I guess. Nothing damaged, though, it looks like.'

'It was just a shake.'

Minor quakes were a fact of life in Sichuan, an annoyance that kept people on their toes, but posed no real threat to daily existence. Indeed, the last big one happened ages ago, seven years before Ning was born.

He listened to the clucking of the chickens and the chatter of the wild birds. Birds in villages and cities are different, he thought. Sparrows, crows, pigeons, swifts.

He brought the single egg back into the house and presented it to his mother without a word. Resigned, she nodded, and sat back on her heels. She tucked it away into a little cabinet.

That evening, as they ate a small meal of spicy noodles, with a few mustard greens on the side to provide a little variety, Ning asked his sister if she knew of anyone in town who might want to buy his phone. 'Without a connection, it's a useless piece of metal. But maybe someone who's travelling out of town soon will want it.'

'Don't you want to wait until the village gets a service tower?'

'We don't know when that's going to happen.'

Their mother picked at the greens, eating a tiny amount. Luo put another bunch into her bowl. 'You're too thin. These will be good for your blood.'

'We don't have enough for one person,' she grumbled. 'I don't know how we're going to feed three.'

'Are my grandparents well?'

'They have enough. Your father's father has a small   pension from the army, and their sow gave birth to three pigs this spring.'

'What about your own parents?'

She shook her head, dismissive. 'If they had a son, I wouldn't have to worry.' She drew out a single noodle from her bowl and ate it with deliberate slowness. 'You can visit them if you like.'

Ning nodded. 'I thought I'd go around the village tomorrow, and see if anyone might need help with harvesting the winter wheat. It's a bit early, but ...'

'I heard the Zhu tea farm is harvesting tomorrow,' commented Luo. 'You can try there.'

Big Zhu, the tea farmer, paid Ning a pittance, but was good for conversation. They smoked cigarette after cigarette together, as they gathered the tea leaves along with several other day labourers. 'Little quake last night,' Zhu commented.

'I missed it; I was asleep. To be honest, I kind of miss the ground shaking from time to time. But it spooked the chickens, that's for sure.'

'They always know about it first,' Zhu laughed. 'Hey! Focus on the top three leaves. Don't forget, this is the early harvest. We shouldn't pick the leaves lower down until later in the year.'

'Will do. By the way – what do you mean, they always know about it first?'

'Oh, everyone knows that,' Zhu replied with a breezy wave. 'Chickens, all kinds of birds, and the other farm animals know when a quake is coming.'

'I suppose I've heard that. My grandmother used to say the same. But I was never sure if it was just out-of-date thinking. We're a modern people now; we shouldn't be listening to old wives' tales.'

'I assure you, it's true, and the scientists at Peking University have proven it. Birds' ears are more sensitive than ours. Sometimes they'll know about a quake a good five minutes before it arrives.'

As the long day continued, the germ of an idea formed in Ning's head. He'd have to get a few long wires.

That night, he hung his head as he handed his paltry wages over to his mother, but glowered with defiance. She accepted them without comment and served a simple dinner to all three of them.

'Luo, you've been back for a few weeks now. Do you know where I could find copper wire?'

'Have you forgotten so fast? A couple of years in Dongguan, and you don't remember where Peng Ni's hardware shop is! When I came back home, it was easy for me to see that everything was where it had always been.'

'How would I know if it's still there?' he shot back. 'I've been home for a day.'

'Do you think you can sell him your phone?'

'No, I'm keeping my phone. I have another idea.'

The next evening, after a gruelling day cutting winter wheat, he dragged himself to the shack where Peng Ni always kept his shop. To his surprise, the door flew open, as if he was expected.

'Oh. You're not —'

'No. I'm Huang Ning. From down the road. We keep chickens.'

Peng Ni gestured towards the spare racks. 'What do you need?'

'I'm looking for wire.'

Peng Ni showed him spools of wire, drawers of connectors, switches, and toggles. He saw one piece that was decades old;

others were new, cheap and cheerful junk from the plant in Chongqing.

Ning looked through all of them, but had to concede. 'It's too difficult for me.'

'Maybe I can help. What do you need to do?'

'I want something that can throw a switch whenever it detects a noise.'

'Why didn't you say so!' He dug through a pile in the back of the shop, and found a small Zave sound sensor. 'Here you go. Ten yuan.'

'But I'll need a switch, too.'

They discussed it for a few minutes, and Ning brought out a piece of soft school notebook paper to draw a little diagram of what he wanted. Half scoffing, and half entertained by the young man's earnestness, Peng Ni offered to teach him the rudiments of circuitry.

'I won't be able to pay,' Ning confessed.

'If you strip this pile of old phones and cart them to the recycler, I'll let you keep a percentage of the gold he extracts. He lives in the next village over. Let me show you how.'

By the time Ning left, he knew he would be late for dinner. 'Don't tell my mother about this.' The older man smiled.

Luo, with sunken eyes, hemming a neighbour's dress, kept her head down when he arrived. 'We already ate,' she said. Their mother lay exhausted in the corner, on a pallet that served as her bed.

'Everyone is broke here.'

'Don't you remember why we left to begin with?'

The chickens had begun to lay again, after their little scare. Every morning, Ning fed them, cleaned their coop, gathered their eggs, and listened. He was convinced that they had at least a dozen distinct types of call. Perhaps more. One day, a new cry burst out, one that he hadn't heard before. A moment later, a swift, grey form snuck from the corner towards the brooding racks. Ning stood still, a large block of wood in his hand, for what felt like an eternity, and then struck. Bullseye!

He held the dead rat aloft by its tail, and crowed about his victory to anyone who could hear. He then recorded his notes about the chickens' cries in his little notebook, his pencil digging into the soft, grey paper.

During the day, he went from shop to shop, from farm to farm, finding whatever work was available. Sometimes Peng Ni would give him a phone to strip, or a tangled collection of wires and parts to sort through. As he sat prying metal loose with a pair of rusted pliers, he understood that this was another kind of education.

A week later, an old lady came to him with a request to deal with three rats in other chicken sheds. There was not much to talk about in a small village, and news of a vigorous, young rat assassin was spreading to every house. If it served to protect the flocks, the villagers could still dig out a few coins and dirty bills from under pillows or inside old tea canisters.

With the earnings from his rat killing, he bought additional bits and pieces of old wires or half-depleted batteries from Peng Ni. By running noise sensors, microphones, trip switches, and connectors throughout the village, within a month he put together a network of fourteen chicken coop monitoring stations.

Everyone knew him now. They no longer called him by his name, Huang Ning, which meant 'yellow mud', but by a new nickname, Huang Shu.

Huang the Rat. Huang the Weasel.

He didn't mind. It fit him, since he was born in the Year of the Rat. And sometimes he felt like a rat, stashing away bits and pieces of electronics in a corner of the house or in the back of Peng Ni's shop. He was learning more every day: his occasional visits to the recycler gave him a new appreciation for the vast variety of electronics that existed in the market. He determined that one of the discarded 'junk' phones from a city many kilometres from their village was a high-spec Japanese model, with more computing power than the old desktop his boss used at the factory.

Although it was good and dead, after an accidental plunge into a puddle, he kept it to one side.

Meanwhile, he monitored the chicken sounds day and night. He set up Zave sound sensors to activate whenever a coop became suddenly louder. In a moment, just by listening to the birds, he could determine whether the threat was a fight over chicken feed, excitement from the farmer's arrival, a rainstorm, a motorbike, a stray dog, or a rat.

No one, he mused, had ever listened to so many chickens for so long – and never not across such a wide area.

After drying the Japanese phone next to his mother's coal fire, he wheedled it back to life, although the battery was useless. It was a 'smart' phone, one of the first he'd come across: full of apps he'd never seen before, although most needed a live connection: games, entertainment, a notepad. He was fascinated by an earthquake warning app. He recognised certain Japanese characters borrowed from Chinese so many centuries ago. He smiled: looking out for earthquakes was a point of commonality between their two cultures. The Japanese were better at it, he had to admit.

He coaxed his mother, that evening, to tell him about the quake that happened before he was born. 'Can you tell us what it was like?'

'You don't want to hear about any of that.'

Luo piped up, 'Yes, we do. Do you remember it?'

'Remember it? Of course I remember it!' she snapped. 'It was the worst day of my life.'

They gaped at her.

'I was eighteen years old. I was going to be married that year. There was a man from Anshun, who was introduced by my father's old boss. He was the handsomest man I'd ever seen.'

'Did ... something happen to him in the earthquake?'

'No. But this entire village was devastated. Don't you know that since that day, my mother could never again walk as she used to? The house collapsed into ruins. But the worst part of all was that my older brother was inside when it happened.'

'You had a brother? We had an uncle?'

'Not after that day. If they'd had a moment's notice to get out of the building, maybe he could have been saved. But he and my mother were having a meal, and she was going outside to check on something, when it struck. It was like a thunderclap. The door frame was made of wood and stones, and it fell on her. It took them a day and a half to dig her out. The infection

215

in her leg almost crippled her. And they didn't dig out my brother until a week later.'

Luo and Ning sat, frozen.

'The man who was supposed to marry me took back his proposal, of course. My father spent too much money on my mother's medical treatment and on my brother's funeral, so I became too poor for a man like that. And a year later, when your father came here and offered to pay for our debts, it was my duty to go with him.'

'And the house was rebuilt?'

'No thanks to the village People's Committee! Those rats ate away every bit of spare money they could find. It took my father ten years to gather enough earth and stones to put it together again. He used whatever materials were at hand. If there's ever another quake, it won't be any different from the last one.'

Luo and Ning whispered long into the night. They worried they would keep their mother awake, but recounting the grim tale had exhausted her, and she fell asleep on her pallet in the corner, still wearing her clothes.

The next morning, after feeding the chickens and taking notes on the other coops, he was back at Peng Ni's shop. 'The Yellow Rat has arrived!' he shouted, by way of introducing himself. They sat together for several hours, going over Ning's plan.

'It's worth showing to the People's Committee,' Peng Ni admitted at last.

'My mother told me never to trust them.'

'Maybe, maybe not. It's their job to look after our village, after all. And they have access to the loudspeaker system.'

Over the past decades, the village leaders had installed a public address system whose blaring noise penetrated into every residence. In the afternoon, it played patriotic songs, announced important political topics, and gave advice on family planning. Every day at 4.00 pm, an enthusiastic voice cried, 'Villagers who want to get rich: have fewer children but grow more trees!' or 'Carry out family planning, implement the basic national policy!' Ning had never considered the system as a tool – the village residents ignored or ridiculed much of the content – but he understood the practicality of Peng Ni's plan.

The People's Committee laughed, but agreed to the idea, as long as they wouldn't be required to pay anything. 'We don't have the funds. But we've always heard the same thing, of course, and your idea has merit. If it really happens, then the worst that could go wrong is that people are a bit vexed, and have something to joke about; the best is that we save lives.'

Ning thanked them, and within days had put a basic system in place that connected to his chicken network.

Yet, after all the weeks spent on planning and rigging wires and sensors, Ning felt a keen sense of anticlimax as they made the final connection and ran a test. Seeing his glum expression, Chang, the People's Committee representative, said, 'Cheer up. Something terrible may yet happen!' and chuckled at his own joke.

'It's not that.'

'What, then?'

'What if our system works? If the big one comes, the village will still be destroyed.'

Comrade Chang became serious. 'Huang Shu, if your system works, you will be a hero of this village, and of all Sichuan Province. Buildings can be rebuilt; but remember, people are the most precious resource we have.'

It was less than a week later when, in an insane moment of cosmic synchronicity, Ning heard the chickens make a new sound.

Throughout the morning, there were rumbles of discontent among the flock. But as Ning relaxed after lunch, they made a more irritating babble. At first, he couldn't understand what he was hearing. Every sound sensor in the network was firing at once.

The birds' cry transformed to a wail.

He dropped his little ceramic cup and shouted to his mother and sister, 'Get out of the house! Now! Right now!' At the same moment, he took up the direct 'hotline' connection to the People's Committee office, and roared into the receiver. 'It's happening! Right now! Sooner than we could have imagined! Put out the alarm!'

Seconds later, an alarm siren sounded on every loudspeaker in the village. 'Earthquake warning! Get out of your houses! Earthquake warning! Get out of your houses!' it shrieked, again and again.

Ning's mother and sister came out into the yard, confused and annoyed, and asked what was going on.

Hearing the loudspeakers, people rushed into the street, shouting for others to follow.

And the world collapsed.

A violent noise like a highway full of container trucks roared through the earth, shaking the very land on which he stood. Waves billowed through the ground, as if it were the ocean itself. At first, Ning attempted to stay upright, but gave in to the relentless undulations, and fell to his knees. A pig shrieked next door, its scream worse than the sound of slaughter, and the chicken coop collapsed in on itself. Luo turned back towards their house, horrified, just in time to see the roof cave in. She and her mother both sat down heavily, and Luo held the older woman to her chest, cradling her as they felt the ground roll beneath them.

The quake went on as seconds ticked by.

Ning attempted to glance at his watch, but lost his balance and put his hand down. It had been at least a minute since the quake began. A utility pole swayed and then toppled. Across the small lane, he saw several neighbouring families sitting in their front yards, stunned at the chaos surrounding them.

At last, after more than two minutes, the roaring subsided. Vast clouds of dust floated everywhere, forming a haze that filtered out the sun. The stink of chicken manure, charcoal, and motor oil combined with that of burning rubber and plastic. Shouts came from across the street, as his swineherd neighbours tried to put out a small fire with an ancient extinguisher.

Stunned, he got up, and stood, unsteady for a moment, wondering whether it was he or the earth that was still swaying. The dust was settling, the finest particles still hanging in the air, while the heavier motes drifted downwards.

Where was everyone?

Ning heard a pitiful noise coming from one of the loudspeakers. It was emitting an incomprehensible wheeze from its felled utility pole. He turned toward the main road.

And then he saw them.

People.

His neighbours, standing in the dust, confused, angry, or terrified, but alive. Up and down the road, they were struggling to their feet, talking, shouting, crying. Mothers held wailing babies. Children clung to their parents' legs. An elderly man squatted on his heels, unwilling to rise.

Ning moved among them, reeling at the sight of so many collapsed houses, asking, again and again, 'Did everyone get out? Was there anyone left inside?' They shook their heads in a daze. They were all out. One had a scrape along her arm; another had bumped his head as he rushed outside. There were no serious injuries.

At last, he returned to attend to his own mother and sister, who sat, silent and confused, in the middle of the chicken run. Wordless, Luo gestured to the collapsed chicken coop.

A small, grey hen lay on its side, crushed under the weight of the corrugated steel roof. Ning lifted the bird and cradled it to his chest.

'It's a fortunate year for us, after all.'

Mapping Merapi

A story by Grace Chan

Mount Merapi, one of the largest active volcanoes in Indonesia, began a new series of eruptions in October 2010 that would become its largest seismic event since the nineteenth century. 353 people died on its slopes and countless thousands of livestock were killed, as pyroclastic flows devastated entire villages.

No human technology has the power to halt the enormous destructive power of a volcano. But the relentless development of new technical solutions holds enormous potential to mitigate the damage from destructive forces. Missing Maps and similar open-source mapping platforms were not introduced until 2014; but how many lives could have been saved if such systems were available at the time?

This is us: in 2010, the global average temperature had just reached 0.82°C above pre-industrial levels. Today, many technologies are already available that can stop and even reverse global warming. Will we have the political and social will to implement them?

It was only when the power went out that Respati turned off his phone, undressed, and tucked the mosquito net under the edges of his thin mattress. He should have logged off earlier; with an electric fan blowing directly across his bare skin, he might still have been able to fall asleep despite the heavy air that made his armpits stick and his neck itch. But in the total blackness and stillness of the tropical night, there were too many noises. The chirping of the geckos, the chattering of the macaques, and the barking of his neighbour's dog made it impossible to ignore the beads of sweat on his upper lip and the insecticide stink from the treated net.

The non-governmental organisation who had visited their village was a blessing and a curse: it was better, of course, to avoid the mosquitoes that caused dengue fever, but the treated nets they donated made him uneasy – what was he breathing? At the time, his mother had asked the charity workers for extra nets for the goats, but wavered when its acrid smell reached her nose.

And the foreign woman had encouraged Respati's sister to go to school. Still, he worried that she and the other girls would forget how to speak their own Javanese language. As it was, hardly anyone could write its beautiful, ancient script with its sweeping descenders.

Most importantly, however, Respati could not decide whether the NGO's transformation of himself had done more harm than good. The NGO had given him a mission and expanded his horizons far beyond the farm, their shop, and the village. Thanks to them, he now had a smartphone and a connection to the internet. But it had also given him an obsession that consumed the core of his days, a passion that kept him up in the blackest hours.

His new passion was maps.

Their system was brand new, but its network already reached into areas far greater than anything Respati had imagined.

It was simple, in a way. Volunteers from Europe, America, and elsewhere pored over satellite images of remote settlements like those surrounding Respati's village, and created maps of areas that had never been uploaded into the global database. Then, Respati and other community volunteers were paid a small stipend to verify their work on the ground, and add local detail such as neighbourhoods, street names, and mosques. In this way, over time, information about every square kilometre of Indonesia would be accounted for.

It was a noble cause, one that put Respati in touch with a world larger than his own. But his mother harangued him for all the time he spent on it, reminding him that his priority should be supporting the family, not wasting his efforts with some expensive electronic device that served only as a temptation for thieves.

As a mosquito whined outside his net, desperate to enter, he recalled their last conversation.

'Maps are important, *Ibu*. They connect us with the world.'

'What has the rest of the world brought us? All kinds of plastic junk and sweet foods that the children crave, and force their parents to spend money on. When I was a girl, we made our own toys – a bottle and a little pile of pumice pebbles was enough for us.'

'We sell all those plastic items and sweets in our shop, *Ibu*. And speaking of the rest of the world, my father's cousin in Yogyakarta is our connection to the suppliers. Without that income, we'd never survive on what we can grow.'

'Maybe if you spent more time on cultivation and less time worrying about maps, we could earn more from our land. When your father was alive, we managed.'

She expected this to end the argument, but his growing frustration made him press the issue. 'Fine. I'll ask him for advice when I visit his grave at *nyekar*. But *Ibu*, tell me this: without maps, how would we know which direction to pray?'

The question stumped her at first, but a moment later, she had found an answer: 'That's a matter for the imam.'

He would never convince her, he realised. But in a few hours, as the first shades of grey leaked into the blackness, they would rise and turn towards Mecca to pray, in the direction determined by some anonymous cartographers and stamped with the imam's approval.

The electric fan started to whirr again, and its faint breeze blew over his body: the power had returned. He slept.

When morning arrived at last, it was no cooler, and the exhaust from two-stroke motorbike engines pervaded the air long after the intrusive rattle of their motors had passed. Respati sat up and checked his phone. Two new quadrants had been mapped by overseas volunteers, and needed verification. The imam's call over his scratchy speakers roused his mother and sister, and they washed in haste before unrolling their small rugs. His sister, already wearing her school uniform, prepared a bowl of *nasi uduk*.

'I'll take the coconut cookies over to Bu Rati's shop,' Rumi told his mother. 'She said they need ten more cartons.' She nodded her approval. Their shop was making a slow expansion from retail to wholesale, with the help of a small trailer attached to the back of Respati's Honda Dream motorbike. He knew the roads and paths well, and could make efficient work of dispatching cartons of cookies, soft drinks, preserved fruit, stove lighters, bamboo fans, and safety matches to the tiny kiosks that formed the province's vast consumer goods distribution network.

The breeze on his face as he sped along the narrow path brought relief from the stifling heat. In the distance, Mount Merapi almost pierced the wispy clouds. He marvelled at the snow on its top, and imagined himself standing at its peak, shivering, as if the chill of a refrigerated delivery truck surrounded him.

Bu Rati thanked him for his prompt delivery and paid him on the spot. She must be doing well, Respati thought.

'Would you and your mother consider selling pesticides?' she asked. 'Several of the farmers in this area said they would buy from me if it would save a trip into town.'

Respati nodded. 'We're thinking about it. But we'd need to find a good supplier. We don't want to sell something that's expired, or something that doesn't have good safety instructions.'

'Fine. Let me know. And tell your sister to stay out of trouble!'

Respati laughed. His sister's virtue had been under the personal protection of kiosk owners all over the region since her *tedhak sithen* when she'd just learned to toddle, even though she'd never shown a shred of interest in anything but school, sweets, and games.

It was time to do the verification of the two new sections that had been mapped overnight.

He knew the areas, but not as well as those closer to his home. It would take him an hour of driving on precarious paths between rice paddies and along ledges to get there. Bu Rati agreed to keep his trailer at her shop for a few hours while he went on the excursion.

He shifted to second gear as the little Honda climbed through the hilly coconut groves on a smaller mountain opposite Mount Merapi, and swerved when a dog jumped out in front of him. At the edge of the new sector, he slowed to take photos and record names. If the street was unmarked, as it often was, he asked someone from the village. A hundred roads had the same name — 'central road' or 'mountain road' — but it was always an improvement over the anonymous 'unverified?' or 'possible dirt path' that existed on the website before he brought them into digital reality.

We're making a model of our world, he thought to himself, out of electricity and radio waves.

This area, high up the mountainside, was too remote even to benefit from a connection to the provincial power grid. A cell phone connection was out of the question. He would upload his information once he was back in his own village. But as he approached a cluster of buildings he saw a row of three low, concrete rooms with electric lights glowing from the interior thanks to a noisy diesel generator off to the side. A cleverly constructed roof of tar and woven thatch shaded two men inside, who were repairing the inner tube of a motorcycle tire. A third man held a mortar board and a trowel, and was repairing a long, ugly crack in the leftmost concrete wall.

The break was no doubt the result of one of the many little earthquakes that plagued the region. There had been a dozen in the past month, one nearly sending him careening into a rice field. He shook his head at the memory; he'd been lucky that time. Once a motorbike's carburettor is submerged, it will never be the same. He'd seen enough angry drivers pushing their bikes along the road after attempting to drive through a flood, sour expressions on their faces.

A row of glass bottles filled with petrol sat out front. Respati hailed the older of the men repairing the tire. 'How much for a litre?' The man's dark eyes, below a high forehead, gave him the impression of a wary lizard, but he relaxed at Respati's question and his open smile.

They haggled over the price, and Respati filled his tank. Respati tried to explain his mission, but the man was indifferent; when his wife set out a meal of *tumpeng* in the back of the shop, he gave only a half-hearted invitation for Respati to join him. Despite the growling in his belly, Respati thanked the man, took his leave, and got on his motorbike for the trip back.

An hour and a half later, he turned off the engine and shook out his limbs. His mother's cry emerged from the shop. 'It took you that long just to get to Bu Rati's shop and back? When are you going to water the goats?'

'I'll do that now,' he shouted in reply. First, however, he plugged his phone into its charger and made sure that the signal was connected. It would send background updates while he went out back to unfurl the long hose running from the cistern. He frowned as he remembered the row of three houses and the dish of *tumpeng*. The little settlement was known to the people nearby, and even to local leaders. It even had a name, according to the dark-eyed man with the high forehead.

But from the point of view of the rest of the world, the residents didn't exist, and would never receive the type of support that he and his family did. No foreign NGO would visit them. Still, despite their relative isolation, they were making their own way, buying and selling, and growing food. Would they be better off without interference?

He shooed off an over-eager nanny goat that was nibbling the seam of his trousers.

Back inside the house, he was satisfied to see his phone flashing with dozens of notifications. Good: his updates had been successful. He picked up the device and scrolled through the list.

His expression changed to concern as he saw the texts, however. One word stood out: EVACUATION.

'*Ibu! Di ajeng!* Look at this!'

Mount Merapi, quiescent for four years, was awake again.

It was absurd. He should have known. He shouldn't have had to wait for the government warning. The earthquakes should have made it obvious.

'Is it really necessary?' his mother asked. 'Four years ago there was an eruption, but we were never in danger. What does our imam say?'

'*Ibu*, one of these messages is from the imam. Come on, let's get ready.'

They packed as many of their possessions as they could into the little trailer, and moved all the unsold goods into the back of the store, covering them with a tarp.

Respati herded the goats into their ramshackle barn and stuffed hay into every spare corner. Thinking, he picked up the mosquito nets and tacked them over the doors and windows. 'I don't know if that will keep any of the ash out, but maybe it will buy you girls a little more breathing time.' He patted a hungry nanny on her muzzle and was rewarded with an affectionate bleat.

'I've called your father's cousin,' his mother told him as he emerged. 'I said they could expect us in Yogyakarta by late evening.'

'I don't suppose they were very happy about that.'

'What can they say? I hope it will only be for a short time.' She nodded toward Mount Merapi. Respati noticed that the clouds at its peak were now a peculiar colour, as if reflecting something glowing from beneath; was it because of the angle of the light, or had the eruption begun? He mounted the motorbike and his mother sat behind him. His sister, complaining that the goats would be left behind, took her place in front of him and he started the engine.

Despite the time lost in preparation, they were among the first families on the road. 'It will get worse once we reach the main road,' his mother predicted gloomily. But she entreated everyone they passed to get moving.

They had been driving for an hour when the noise began in earnest. In the early afternoon, they heard a roar like an angry peal of thunder, followed some time later by the first of a shower of choking ash. Respati's sister threatened to put the motorbike off balance, craning her neck to look behind them.

'Knock it off,' he shouted. 'You won't be able to see anything from here. And we don't want to die in a collision any more than we do in a volcanic eruption.'

His mother, unmoved, continued to pray.

They were descending toward the main road that led to Yogyakarta, a paved, two-lane strip frequented by delivery trucks. A long line of traffic was already visible from a distance, looking like a mottled river strewn with rocks. There were individual motorbikes, overladen with people and luggage, tractors, trucks, and even ox carts. Every vehicle was heading away from the mountains.

Respati slowed to observe the situation, then pulled to the side of the road.

'It will clear out eventually,' his mother said.

'By then it might be too late,' he replied.

'Is there another way?' his sister asked.

There it was: of all the people on the road, Respati should know best how to navigate the winding roads and unmarked dirt paths of the region. He took out his phone and was astonished to find a signal. He flicked through his mapping data and nodded to himself: they were close to   a sector he'd verified several months previously, and he was reminded of the new truck road that two village leaders had constructed to facilitate trade between them. It was ironic, he remembered, that each of the villages called the road by the name of the other one. We only define ourselves, he thought, as we relate to others.

'Yes. There's another way,' he told his sister. 'But for all our sakes, can you please stay still as I drive? It's going to be a bumpy ride.' Chastened, she promised, and he turned the motorbike toward the new truck road.

They had been in Yogyakarta for three days, packed into a tiny apartment that could not be expected to hold three more people on short notice. His mother was sniping at their cousins and stewing under their patronising comments, when Raspati saw a face on the television, with black, lizard-like eyes and a high forehead.

'I know him!' he cried.

A sober reporter was standing among a group of unhappy men in an emergency shelter, while an aid worker shouted in the background. 'My motorcycle repair shop, my coconut trees, everything was under the ash cloud,' the dark-eyed man complained. 'The trees will never recover.'

'And you and your family got out with minutes to spare.'

'Yes, thanks be to God. It was a miracle. The rescuers found our village very quickly, although we had no way to call them. Somehow they knew where we were, and they came to our aid. They said they found us on a map. It is the work of God, I am convinced! We are far away from the cities, so we thought we would be forgotten. But they found us.'

'A miracle indeed,' replied the reporter.

'But all my goats are lost, I am certain, down to the last one.'

A statistic flashed on the screen, showing the number of livestock estimated to have perished in the pyroclastic flows. Without warning, Respati began to cry. His father's cousin faced away, pretending to read a magazine.

With tears flowing, Respati moved closer to the television. *It was my maps*, he thought. The dark-eyed man, ignorant of the true identity of his saviour, was asking how much the government would reimburse him for the lost goats and burnt-out buildings.

How amazing, Respati reflected, that I should be here in Yogyakarta, and see an image that has flitted through the air like a sparrow. My grandfather would have called it magic. Yet how quickly we adapt to marvels, and render them banal! In a minute, the story of that dark-eyed man has transformed from a tragedy to a miracle, to a haggling session about the price of goats.

'Can you clean up that ash?!' his father's cousin shouted to his wife. Fine grit was filtering through the small apartment's air conditioning unit and collecting on the floor. The Yogyakarta Airport had closed the day before.

'That man doesn't realise it yet,' Respati said, 'but he and his family are only alive because they became part of the rest of the world.'

'Everyone's part of the world, whether they know it or not,' his father's cousin replied, annoyed. 'Now, isn't there something else we can watch?'

Inflammable

A story by Grace Chan

In early January 2025, wildfires ravaged Los Angeles with unprecedented savagery, lasting for weeks and devastating the area. Dozens perished, hundreds of thousands were forced to evacuate, and thousands of buildings were destroyed.

A wildfire is classified by insurance companies as an 'Act of God'. But can humans do anything to prepare for a future determined by the whims of the supernatural? While the weather is unpredictable, the impact of fire on a human dwelling is not.

This is us. In 2024, the global average temperature passed a terrible milestone: for the first time, it exceeded 1.5°C above pre-industrial levels. Are we ready to take the hard decisions that will help us get ready for what we are about to face?

The custom Silverado pickup pulled up to the curb. Maria opened its fire-engine red door on the passenger side, threw her bag into the footwell, and climbed up to the seat. 'Hey chico! How was the barbecue? Worthy of La La Land?'

'Epic!' Pedro laughed. 'You should've been there. The neighbours only called the cops a couple of times.'

'Not my scene,' she smiled in reply. 'And I'm glad this was the last one. You guys always end up arguing over the best way to get the grill going, and it makes us actuaries nervous.'

'There was some of that,' he admitted, 'but you know as well as I do that we'd be the best group to have on hand if anything went wrong. Anyway, as an actuary, you would've enjoyed some of it — everyone was taking bets about which neighbourhood was going to get hit first this year. It's gonna be a tough season.'

'Is there any other type these days?' she said. 'We're already seeing the first fires in the hills above San Fernando Valley.'

'Yeah. Well, someone else will have to handle it this time.' Pedro squinted toward the horizon. 'How many calls are we scheduled for today?'

Maria consulted her phone. 'Just two. Our first stop is at nine o'clock in Altadena. Allen Avenue.'

Pedro took a sharp breath. 'Oh.'

'I know,' Maria replied.

Pedro donned his sunglasses and pulled out into the street. They drove past row after row of empty lots. In some, a lone charred chimney or metal flagpole still stood, pointing upwards in defiance like a middle finger. On others, white paint dazzled their eyes in the bright morning. It had rained a little in the previous week, and green growth burst everywhere from the few trees that had survived.

Traffic being sparse, they arrived at the site within forty minutes. The lot was cleared and level, and little remained of the previous structure.

Pedro parked and pressed the button on the centre console. Maria watched as the entire side of the truck opened upwards. The driver's-side platform then pivoted to the left and descended to ground level. Pedro engaged the control on his right arm rest, and his seat – now revealed as an electric wheelchair – proceeded up the driveway towards the waiting group.

'Morning!' cried Lenny. 'Sorry I couldn't make the barbecue. You wouldn't believe how busy things have been lately. Let me introduce you.' He gestured toward two women in expensive outfits, the older one wearing a sour expression. 'These are my clients, Kristyn Martin and Ginger Alvarez – that's Krystyn with two y's, by the way – and these here are the twins.' Two six-year-old boys, dressed in oversized Rams T-shirts, gaped at the red Silverado in awe.

Ginger, the younger of the women, offered a perfunctory nod and explained, 'The boys were still toddlers in 2025, so they don't even remember what the original place looked like. We've been staying with my brother's family in Palm Springs the whole time.'

Pedro nodded. It was a common story. He turned to Lenny. 'Your company is the primary contractor?'

Lenny nodded. 'Yep. We're doing rebuilds on thirteen homes in this neighbourhood alone. The area got hit hard.' He scanned the street, where houses were in various stages of construction.

Pedro glanced over his shoulder at his truck, where the twins were running their fingers along the edge of the door, trying to figure out how it worked. With a smile, he clicked a remote, causing it to open again like the wing of a seagull, its silent hydraulics raising it in a smooth, single motion. 'Take a look inside if you want,' he said to the startled boys. 'Just don't drive away, all right?'

The red-haired twin giggled. 'We can't drive it away! There's no seat!'

'Not to mention the fact that you are not licensed to operate a motor vehicle in the State of California,' Pedro replied, 'unless the Emergency Code has a provision I'm not familiar with.'

'How come you're in a wheelchair?' asked the blond twin, wandering over from the truck to inspect the control panel on Pedro's armrest. 'Don't you have legs?'

Ginger reached forward in embarrassment to hush her son, but Pedro stopped her. 'No, it's okay. I've got both my legs,' he explained to the child, lifting a sneakered foot, 'but my lungs don't work very well. I can't walk more than a few steps without getting tired. So my chair helps me do everything I want to.'

Maria brought the topic back to the new house. 'Lenny, have you got a copy of the plans on you?'

Lenny laid a sheaf of drawings on a folding table. Maria explained to the clients, 'Between us, Pedro and I do four jobs. He looks at the fire durability of the building design and the accessibility for ADA compliance. I understand you will also operate a business at these premises?'

'Yes. I'll be moving my studio back here once it's finished.'

Maria nodded. 'Right. And meanwhile, I look at the insurability of the building, and assess whether the mortgage provider will accept the insurance cover and the details of the design.'

'Insurance cover!' Krystyn spat. 'It's taken us years to get a single payment out of those criminals. But maybe it's my fault – I was idiotic enough to imagine that when I signed up for so-called fire insurance that I might be insured for fire.'

Maria gave her a frosty look. 'The idea is that when the next fire comes, the new building is ready for it. Which means you don't need as much of a payout. It's the same in high flood risk areas; all new buildings have to be flood resistant or else they don't get insured.'

'Let's get this over with, then,' said Krystyn.

Lenny leaned over the table and highlighted the fire resistant features. 'We've got a metal roof with vent-free eaves, and we're using stucco walls for low flammability. The walls are fibre cement cladding with mineral wool insulation. Lightweight enough that it won't trap you in an earthquake.'

'What's the insulation facing made of?' asked Pedro.

'No facing. It's semi-rigid stone wool batt insulation. We've also got double-glazed, tempered glass windows. And the clients have agreed to install a ten-tonne water tank under the garden, replenished with rainwater and grey water from the washing machine and dishwasher. It can be used to damp down the house in case of a wildfire, and to water plants in the meantime – they're planting low, fire resistant species instead of trees, and using gravel mulch.'

Ginger added, 'We're putting in a lot of succulents.'

'What's the deck going to be made of?' Pedro asked, pointing at a spot on the plans.

'Concrete,' Krystyn replied, 'with an aluminium shade. Because according to some people,' she tossed her head toward Maria, 'regular sunshades that people in Los Angeles have been using for the past hundred years are no longer good enough.'

Pedro sat back in his chair, thoughtful. 'It looks like you're on the right track. But if you're serious about this, you'll put in roll-down metal fire doors from your roof overhang or along the side recesses, that can be automatically released and secured with a latch.'

The two women glanced at each other. 'Jesus H Christ. How much extra is that going to run?' Krystyn asked Lenny, and took a deep breath when she heard his ballpark figure. 'You're going overboard, here.'

Maria had seen it before and was growing impatient. 'Look, we've done the modelling. If you insist on continuing to live in this area, you need to understand that this kind of fire is no longer a once-in-a-lifetime experience. It's normal. And you need to build for it.'

'No, you're the one who needs to understand!' Krystyn shot back, jabbing her finger into the plans. 'We have been waiting for four years already, trying to get a permit to rebuild a perfectly good house that already existed, that was up to spec when it was built, that we bought in good faith. And now you're telling us when it's already halfway built that we have to go even deeper into debt!'

The boys hid behind Ginger's legs, their eyes wide.

Maria tried to hide her frustration. 'Don't blame me. I'm just trying to explain to you what will happen when the next fire comes. You can build up to code, and in all likelihood the structure will still be standing when everything around it burns down. But if you want to have a decent place to live when the ash settles next time, then you'll listen.'

'A decent — ! We have been staying,' Krystyn replied through gritted teeth, 'in a shoebox with my misogynist in-laws for the past four years. You cannot begin to imagine how much I want to have a decent place to live.'

Pedro swivelled towards the two women, inserting himself between them. 'It's not your fault.'

'What?' Krystyn replied, startled.

'It's not your fault, or my fault,' he pressed on. 'Not as individuals. I didn't get like this' – he gestured towards his body – 'because of some personal sin. Smoke inhalation is a risk of the job, and I don't know why it hit me worse than it did some of the other guys who are still out there. But sometimes we have to do things to protect ourselves and our communities, even when it's not our fault.'

'You were a firefighter,' said Krystyn. It was more a statement than a question.

He nodded. 'Fourteen years. It was the only job I ever wanted to do. Our crew was doing the containment on this street. I wasn't the only one to come out of it with a permanent disability; there were a couple of convicts working alongside our guys, and they, well, they finished their sentence early.'

'I'm so sorry.'

'Times change,' Pedro said. 'And sometimes the only thing we can do is to change with them. At least I got a sweet ride out of it.' He nodded at the pickup. 'And a buddy of mine gave me a good deal on the paint job. So sometimes there's a silver lining.'

'What's the silver lining here?' Krystyn asked.

Maria spoke up from the side. 'Goats,' she quipped.

'Goats?' asked Ginger. 'What, like the animal?'

'Under the provisions of the Emergency Code,' Maria said, 'the County decided that some areas will be returned to nature, and it turns out that the best way to manage them is with a herd of professional goats. They use a geo-collar that guides them to the areas that need to be eaten. Same principle as invisible dog fences, but more advanced. And kids love them. Every once in a while one will end up on a roof, but they're not like cats – they're good climbers. So you don't need to call the fire department to get them down.'

For the first time, they saw Krystyn's bitter expression soften. 'Goats, huh. We'll see.'

Pedro slapped his knees. 'Welp,' he said, 'let's go take a look. Lenny, lead the way.'

The group moved across the cleared site. Lenny showed them where the new structure would go, while Ginger pointed out where the garden would be planted, with wide strips separating any combustible plants.

Pedro took notes and made approving noises. The family had the right idea: the first line of defence was managing fuel – keeping the undergrowth down to reduce the magnitude of the fire upwind of any community that has been identified for protection. The goats would help with that.

Lenny said the new house's large-scale deluge system, fed by the underground tank, would be part of its second line of defence. It would be the kind that could sometimes put out the fire and would at least create a massive reduction in radiative heat. Pedro had heard that the city was considering a water curtain mechanism as well – a row of tall street lamps along the boundary road, every hundred yards, fed by the new water distribution system connected to the seaside drinking water plant. It was still tied up in budget discussions, but Pedro suspected that the looming fires in San Fernando Valley would force a decision soon.

The question in Pedro's mind was the third line of defence: would the homeowners commit to maintaining all the fire protection features throughout the year, even during the wetter months? That was the ultimate purpose of their visit, after all; everything else could have been accomplished from a desk. He had to assess the homeowners' willingness to do what was needed.

All of a sudden, Krystyn knelt down in a corner of the yard and picked up a small object half buried in the dirt. She remained silent at first, but tears flowed down her cheeks. 'Honey,' she called after a pause, 'you're not going to believe this.'

Ginger strode over, leaving the children piling gravel into little heaps. 'Oh, my god. Is that what I think it is?'

The off-road tires on Pedro's chair gripped the rocky soil as he made his way toward the two women.

Krystyn was holding a blackened box, just big enough to fit in the palm of her hand. Along its edges, Pedro spied a thin, shining line; the entire thing must have been silver, once, and was now tarnished beyond recognition.

'When we left,' Krystyn said, 'we had no time. I had my purse, and each of us grabbed one of the boys, and we just threw them into the car and drove. Every single one of my possessions was gone. My high school yearbook, Ginger's favourite sweatshirt, all the photos of my parents — we left everything behind. You tell yourself it's just stuff, that it shouldn't matter, and that we should be grateful we got out alive. But it does matter. And the one thing that I wished I'd taken with me was a jewellery box that my grandmother gave me when I was a little girl. It wasn't even valuable, but no matter how much money I had, I was never going to get it back. You'll probably think I'm stupid, but I've been dreaming about this box. I dreamed about it last night. And here it is.' She opened it delicately, her fingers caressing the little hinge. Inside, it was still silver, but whatever it had contained had burnt to ash.

She stood up straight. 'I know these fires are more than property damage. They've taken away our lives, our health,' she nodded at Pedro, 'and our memories. We'll do whatever it takes to stay ahead of the next one.'

Maria started to say something, but Pedro put his hand on her arm. 'Are you sure,' he said, first regarding Krystyn, then Ginger, 'you wouldn't prefer to move somewhere else? There aren't so many fires in Seattle, you know.'

'No,' Krystyn said. After a pause, she continued. 'This is our home. It isn't what it was before, but we know that. We're going to re-build it into something better.'

Pedro turned back to Maria. 'I think we can sign off on this project.'

Twenty-four months passed.

People no longer spoke of 'fire season' since the months with higher rainfall were vulnerable as well. Lacking any other response, they traded sarcastic memes, accompanied by the inevitable comment, 'Too soon?'

Two minor wildfires passed through Altadena as if on a whim, sparing the building site by a few streets. The workers scattered before the blaze, but returned a few days later after it was controlled. Maria made a casual comment, a month later, that the new house on Allen Avenue was complete and the family had moved in.

Somewhere in an upmarket Los Angeles emporium, an enterprising furniture designer created a stylish living room set in wire mesh and marketed it as 'L'inflammable', only to discover the actual meaning of the word a day after the launch.

The Altadena water curtain project was rejected on the grounds of its potential interference with people walking their dogs, and then revived a month later. A recent fire's near miss, next to the house of an LA County Supervisor, must have been pure coincidence. School fire drills now took place once a month instead of twice a year.

And then the big one hit.

The speed of the thing was unbelievable. Within a day, smouldering flames in wooded areas turned into rampant fire tornadoes, leaping like a capricious mountain lion from one neighbourhood to the next, swiping a murderous paw across houses and streets. Areas hit hardest in 2025 were devastated again, but this time the impact was even broader, destroying thousands of homes, offices, and public buildings.

Half a day into the new blaze, Pedro packed up and moved to his cabin. He got around too slowly these days to risk a hasty flight.

Someone said this fire had started in a backyard barbecue, but the idea was dismissed. No one would be foolish enough to risk the ruinous penalties imposed for illegal outdoor grilling. Those days were over.

Trees that had not gone up in flames six years before now formed giant torches that illuminated the night. Residents, pets, workers and even the working goats were evacuated. They hunkered down in shelters and were evacuated again as the safe areas became unsafe.

The fires took eight weeks to contain. Pilots in the sky and tank trucks on the ground battled in their respective domains. Exhausted, firefighters slept in between shifts wherever they found a flat surface. Even in areas not scorched by the wildfires, daytime temperatures soared.

At last, as the ash floated down to the charred ground below, the residents breathed. It was over, for now, and they returned to work. Pedro picked up Maria as usual, and after their first site check they stopped at a new Vietnamese vegan place for lunch.

'Remember that couple with the twins?' Pedro asked.

'The two women? Yeah. I remember one of them was a nasty piece of work, although she softened up a little when she found that jewellery box.'

'We'll be passing close to their place this afternoon. Let's take a detour and see how they fared.' Without waiting for her response, Pedro activated his turn signal and got into the left lane.

They craned their necks as he rolled along the street they'd visited two years before. To Pedro's satisfaction, while some buildings showed damage and the ground was scorched, most were still standing. He pulled up beside the sloping driveway, where a metal sign read 'Spark Community Design Studio'. Two gangling, eight-year-old boys were standing outside the front door of the stucco-faced building, staring at the sky; one held a controller. Pedro followed their gaze and spotted the drone hovering above.

It looked, Pedro thought to himself, normal.

He rolled down the window and asked, 'Are your parents' home?'

One of the twins, his blond hair now darkened to ash brown, stood for an instant in surprise, and then bellowed, 'Mom! It's the guy with the truck!' A moment later, Ginger emerged from the front door, a smile on her face.

'Hello!' she said. 'Come to inspect your handiwork?'

'You might say so,' he replied, a sheepish grin on his face. 'Looks like you didn't get hit too bad this time.'

She surveyed the house and yard. As promised, no lawn surrounded the property, only a garden consisting of low, wide-spaced rows of succulents and artistic arrangements of rocks and gravel. Several of the patches had escaped without major damage, but others were destroyed. Pedro noticed the pipes from the underground tank, well-maintained and clear of debris. The house itself also bore signs of scorching, but no structural damage. 'Nothing like the first time,' Ginger replied. 'We moved back in the day after they gave the all-clear. Same with most of our neighbours. Lenny and his company did the work on a lot of them, you know.'

Pedro grinned. 'Good for him.' As he tried to think of what else to say, Krystyn appeared in the door.

'It's you,' she said. 'I thought you'd show up at some point.'

Maria held her breath.

'We owe you,' Krystyn continued, 'a debt, and an apology. This last fire was tough, but we survived, and the place came through in one piece. For that matter, our insurance claim was resolved a lot faster this time, although I have to admit it was much smaller.'

Pedro nodded. Things had changed.

At last, Krystyn broke into a smile. 'Do you have the time? Come on in. I'll give you a tour.'

Is Disaster Inevitable?

Afterword by Steve Willis and Jan Lee

The average increase in global temperatures compared to the pre-industrial era smashed through the 1.5°C barrier in 2024 as if the human race hadn't even noticed anything was going on. Fossil fuel exploration, production, and combustion rose to historic highs. The brief dip in air travel during the pandemic became a distant memory. Cattle and sheep production, which have the highest emissions intensity of any agricultural commodity, continue to rise as global meat consumption soars.

Furthermore, the era of vicious cycles has begun. Hotter weather leads to greater use of air conditioning, which in turn creates higher demand for energy produced by burning fossil fuels. Changes in seasonal rainfall patterns, also the result of climate change, give rise to deadly wildfires which themselves are among the greatest emitters of greenhouse gases.

Given these realities, it is excusable to conclude that disaster is inevitable.

Yet the truth is subtler and more complex. On one hand, crises are bound to happen, which is why best preparation refers to 'when' rather than 'if'. Disaster readiness is a sophisticated craft that smart organisations and communities invest in over the long term. But on the other hand, examining how things might go right is less common than poring over how things went so wrong. For every disaster that occurred, a thousand others were avoided. It's worth asking: what happened when nothing happened?

When seeking to prevent such things in the future, therefore, it is important to examine how things could have gone otherwise. Could someone have spoken up at the right moment? Could crucial expertise have been leveraged from some unexpected source? Many such voices go unheard when they belong to marginalised groups. In some cases, nature itself – the flora and fauna that surround us – can be an untapped treasure trove of solutions. In other cases, the solution is already obvious but the right people aren't listening: could there be an alternative way to exert influence on those who hold decision-making authority? There are also times when a certain action, taken years before, provides a solution to the problem much later.

We have presented these stories – written 'by' Grace Chan (the protagonist of our earlier novel, Fairhaven) – as little mysteries. They explain in the first paragraph the real toll that a historic disaster wrought, and then leave the fictional characters in the story to discover what a solution might have been. We present these stories as a positive, Green Mirror alternative to the Black Mirror stories that cause such anxiety among their viewers. If any Hollywood agents are among our readers, we hope you'll think about this as a possibility!

But in a larger sense, these stories are not only mysteries but parables. Although none of them is 'about' our current climate disaster, *per se* – they are about earthquakes, sinking ships, and industrial explosions – each of the stories has a lesson to offer to anyone looking for ways to avert the worst effects of climate change:

- Speak truth to authority.
- Leverage the power of networks.
- Listen to nature.
- Look for expertise in unexpected places, and among under-represented voices.
- Prepare for calamities as if they will inevitably occur.
- When the standard methods fail, look for a workaround.
- When the stakes are high, act fast but act with care.

We therefore aim to help the reader who finishes this book come away with the conviction that, no matter how inevitable the disaster seems now, it is both possible and necessary to act to avert it.

In no way do we wish to second-guess the actions of the participants in the real disasters, who did their best with the information and materials available to them, and we mourn with those affected by the incidents described in the book.

Whether it is the colossal disaster of climate change that faces us now, or any smaller disaster, however, it's important to realise that it's not as inevitable as you might think.

Futility is the name of a book, written in 1898, fourteen years before the *Titanic* sank, written by a man named Morgan Robertson. The book was about a large ship, the biggest ocean liner ever built, and its name was the *RMS Titan*. In the novel, it strikes an iceberg in the North Atlantic, sinks, and all but a handful of the passengers perish. The book was written before the actual *Titanic* sank.

What a coincidence! Or was it? If the builders of the *Titanic* had read it, might they have thought twice about how to prepare for a disaster?

One often looks to the past and wonders, 'What if I had taken action back then ... how different our present would be!'

After you read these stories, we ask you to consider, 'What if I take action now ... how different our future will be!'

More information on actions you can take to help tackle the global climate disaster can be found at https://fairhavenclimatenovel.substack.com.

Acknowledgements

Although this is entirely a work of fiction, the authors have used real events to tell the stories. As a result, there are many ways in which this book departs from reality. Some are intentional and others accidental, but all errors are the sole responsibility of the authors.

Nevertheless, where a degree of verisimilitude has been achieved, it is with the help of our friends who have provided their services as consultants and accuracy readers. These include Bethan Clark and Leslie Smith on the history of Girl Guides; Lloyd Roach on knots (and horses); Corey Franklin on American history and racism; Thomas Sullivan on NASA missions; Phạm Đức Toàn on Hanoi in the 1990s; Jacob Goldberg on Autism Spectrum Disorder; Frances Luk on the Sichuan earthquake; Hans Leung on present-day Los Angeles; Luana Prado on mangoes and Brazil; Dhiny Nedyasari on Indonesian culture; Paul Christiansen on water hyacinth, and Jerry Joynson on a variety of technical solutions.

The authors would also like to thank Denise Baden of Green Stories and Habitat Press, the Hong Kong Writers Circle, the Lisbon Writers Group, and the Hong Kong International Literary Festival for their support in the drafting, publication, and launch of this book.

Finally, the authors are grateful for the forbearance and support of their families, who have many stories to tell.

References

Climate anxiety links
https://www.unthinkable.earth/resources?utm_source=substack&utm_medium=email

Links to information about the original incidents
https://en.wikipedia.org/wiki/Titanic
https://en.wikipedia.org/wiki/Great_Molasses_Flood
https://en.wikipedia.org/wiki/R101
https://en.wikipedia.org/wiki/1971_Iraq_poison_grain_disaster
https://en.wikipedia.org/wiki/George_V   https://en.wikipedia.org/wiki/George_VI
https://es.wikipedia.org/wiki/Tragedia_en_la_iglesia_de_Santa_Teresa
https://en.wikipedia.org/wiki/Coalbrook_mining_disaster
https://en.wikipedia.org/wiki/Flixborough_disaster
https://en.wikipedia.org/wiki/Space_Shuttle_Challenger_disaster
https://en.wikipedia.org/wiki/Pontederia_crassipes
https://en.wikipedia.org/wiki/Montreal_Protocol
https://en.wikipedia.org/wiki/Onagawa_Nuclear_Power_Plant
https://en.wikipedia.org/wiki/Saint_Malo,_Louisiana
https://en.wikipedia.org/wiki/2008_Sichuan_earthquake
https://en.wikipedia.org/wiki/Mount_Merapi
https://en.wikipedia.org/wiki/January_2025_Southern_California_wildfires

Data sources
https://ourworldindata.org/greenhouse-gas-emissions
https://futureearth.org/2015/01/16/the-great-acceleration/
https://www.ncei.noaa.gov/access/monitoring/climate-at-a-glance/global/time-series/globe/tavg/land/12/9/1850-2024 Global temperatures since 1850
https://showyourstripes.info/c Warming stripes - University of Reading
https://www.slideshare.net/slideshow/great-acceleration-2015/43547922 Great Acceleration
https://coveringclimatenow.org/resources/ Climate resources for journalists

Maps
https://www.climate-charts.com/World-Climate-Maps.htmlhttps://earth.nullschool.net#top
/ winds and currents

https://earth.google.com/ altitude/depth shown in the bottom right corner
https://climatetrace.org/ Methane and other GHG maps

Sea level rise maps
https://www.floodmap.net/
https://coastal.climatecentral.org/
https://coast.noaa.gov/slr/#

Solutions
https://drawdown.org/

Boundaries
https://www.stockholmresilience.org/research/planetary-boundaries.html
https://www.kateraworth.com/doughnut/

Modelling tools
https://www.climateinteractive.org/en-roads/ Climate model

Courses/activities
https://climatefresk.org/world/
https://en.2tonnes.org/

Cartoons and comics
https://www.stuartmcmillen.com/comic/energy-slaves/
https://www.stuartmcmillen.com/comic/st-matthew-island/
https://climatechangeresources.org/resources/arts/cartoons/
https://climatesafety.info/bookmarks/cartoons-about-climate/
https://www.pinterest.com/mikaidt/climate-change-humour/
https://www.cartoonmovement.com/search?f%5B0%5D=keywords%3Aclimate

Other climate fiction
https://www.amazon.com/Kraken-Wakes-John-Wyndham/dp/0593450108
Climate fiction written before it was known to be an issue. Inspired
https://www.amazon.com/Ministry-Future-Kim-Stanley-Robinson/dp/0316300136
https://dragonfly.eco/ Database of Eco-Fiction
https://climate-fiction.org/ Climate Fiction Writers League

Climate non-fiction

References

https://www.amazon.com/Gaia-Planet-Management-Norman-Myers/dp/0385426267 shockingly prescient
https://www.withouthotair.com/
https://www.amazon.com/Last-Generation-Nature-Revenge-Climate/dp/1903919878
https://www.amazon.com/Knowledge-How-Rebuild-World-Scratch/dp/1847922279
https://www.amazon.com/Uninhabitable-Earth-Life-After-Warming/dp/0525576703

About the authors

Steve Willis is an engineer and innovator who works on industrial and environmental projects, and writes short climate action stories which explore potential positive outcomes to the climate crisis. Steve's background in heavy industry is combined with sharp observation, a vivid imagination, relentless persistence and a talent for lucid dreaming. He uses these unusual skills to continuously seek massive scale climate solutions, to identify climate start-up opportunities and to write stories which capture some of the essence of working on the climate crisis challenge.

Jan Lee is a Hong Kong-based digital native, who first published via Telnet in the 1990s. Following a decades-long career in corporate affairs and sustainability, Jan turned to writing and activism in retirement. Jan's science fiction stories have been published in various small presses and anthologies, and are collected in the book *Route One and Other Stories*. Jan's work has been nominated for a Pushcart Prize and recognised several times in the ' Writers of the Future' contest. Jan is Editor-in-Chief of *The Apostrophe*, the quarterly magazine of the Hong Kong Writers Circle.